CRAVING MOLLY

The Aces' Sons

By Nicole Jacquelyn

Craving Molly
Copyright © 2016 by Nicole Jacquelyn
Print Edition
All Rights Reserved

No part of this book may be reproduced or transmitted in any form or by any means, electronic or mechanical, including photocopying, recording, or by any information storage and retrieval system without the written permission of the author, except for the use of brief quotations in a book review.

This is a work of fiction. Names, characters, businesses, places, events, and incidents are either the products of the author's imagination or used in a fictitious manner. Any resemblance to actual persons, living or dead, or actual events is purely coincidental. The author acknowledges the trademarked status and trademark owners of various products referenced in this work of fiction, which have been used without permission. The publication/use of these trademarks is not authorized, associated with, or sponsored by the trademark owners.

Dedication

For the single mamas

and

the mamas of special needs children.

You're doing awesome . . . even when you think you aren't.

Don't forget to grant yourself a little grace.

Chapter 1

Molly

"He's looking at you."

"Shut up," I hissed, refusing to turn around.

I was uncomfortable as hell in a pair of tight jeans and a tank top that showed more of my boobs than had ever been available for public viewing—and that was saying something, considering I'd spent a year breastfeeding.

When my best friend since grade school had begged me to go out with her, even going so far as getting a babysitter lined up, I hadn't had the heart to tell her no. I'd known that my day-to-day wardrobe of scrubs wouldn't cut it in a bar setting, but I hadn't expected to be so . . . on display. Frankly, I just wanted to sit at the high table in the bar and nurse a few beers before going home and opening up my laptop to watch a couple hours of tipsy *Gilmore Girls*.

Unfortunately, Mel had different ideas. She'd been scoping out the guys in the bar all night, pointing out the ones she thought had big dicks and rating facial hair on a ten point scale. She was nuts. Outgoing to my introverted. The brunette to my blonde and the angles to my curves. Normally, we balanced each other out pretty well, but I was beginning to wish she was a little more like me and a little less . . . her.

"He's so hot. So hot. His facial hair is an eleven. Absolutely," Mel said seriously, looking over my shoulder. "I mean, he was hot in high school, but not that hot."

"Jesus, will you shut up?" I hissed again.

The back of my neck was burning. I didn't need her to tell me that Will Hawthorne was staring at me. I could freaking *feel* it.

I'd only seen him once since high school, even though we lived in the same town, but I knew he was hot. Jesus, he'd been drool-worthy when we were fourteen, and that kind of thing didn't just go away. Some guys just had *it*, whatever that *it* was. It didn't even matter what they looked like, they were just . . . attractive. They had that undeniable pull that made every woman take a second look. It was the way they held themselves, the way they moved, their confidence.

I think it was referred to as *swagger*—though I'd never intentionally say that stupid word out loud.

Will hit the jackpot and got both good looks *and* that magnetic pull. He was at least six feet tall and the lankiness I'd remembered from when we were kids had turned into very broad and muscular shoulders. He had his mom's dark hair and light brown eyes that I assumed must have come from his dad, though I'd never met the man. He also had a neatly trimmed beard that drew attention to his lips like a freaking flashing neon sign.

"Why the hell is he staring?" Mel murmured.

"Thanks," I scoffed, giving her a glare.

"No, I mean, you're hot, but . . ." she trailed off as she glanced over my shoulder again. "He's *really* not looking away."

"For God's sake," I finally snapped, turning slightly to look over my shoulder.

It took me a second to find him in the crowded bar. There were a ton of people between us and it looked like he'd come in with a group that he was sitting in the middle of, but the minute I found him, his eyes met mine. Holy shit.

He really was staring.

And then he was slapping some guy on the shoulder as he edged around him, not looking away from me as he started toward our table.

"Now look what you did," I snapped under my breath as I spun back around in my seat.

"He's coming over here," Mel said excitedly, her eyes widening.

I opened my mouth to say something back, but the words caught in my throat as a hand settled on the back of my stool.

"Molly," Will said, leaning in slightly so I could feel the breath of his words against the side of my forehead.

"Oh, hey, Will," I replied.

I wanted to pat myself on the back when my words came out all nonchalant, like I hadn't been talking about him for the past ten minutes.

"What's up, Melanie?" he greeted my best friend with a little chin lift, making her smile wide.

"Hi, Will!"

Oh, hell. She was totally getting off on this. We'd both known Will since we were kids. I'd started kindergarten with him in Mrs. Nelson's class, and she'd joined us in Mrs. Hallen's third grade class. We'd all gone to the same schools, shared a lot of the same classes and had graduated high school together, but to say we hadn't been on Will's radar would have been an understatement.

Mel and I hadn't been social outcasts, not at all. We'd had our little group of friends that we'd hung out with, and we'd done all the things that you were supposed to do—kissing boys and going to dances and bonfires and football games. But Will had been in a completely different social strata. We'd grown up parallel but never really intersecting after the fifth grade, so the fact that he'd remembered her?

Yeah, she'd be dining on the rush of that for weeks.

"How ya been?" Will asked me, his voice dropping as his face tilted toward me again.

If I just raised my head, we would have been practically kissing, but I didn't. Instead, I stared at my glass of beer, twisting it around with my fingers like a socially awkward freak.

"I'm good. Just working and stuff. You?" I asked my half-empty beer.

I think I might have blushed a little when he chuckled.

"Same," he said in amusement. "There a reason you're not looking at me?"

There was. There was a reason. Unless I knew someone really well, I had a hard time meeting a person's eyes when we were talking. I'd mostly figured out how to do it when I was working, since patients needed to know that I was paying attention to what they were saying, but outside that? Yeah, no dice. It flustered me, made it hard to follow the conversation.

But it wasn't like I could tell him that.

"Uh, no?" I mumbled, the inflection making it come out as a question as I met his light brown eyes.

Then, because I'd realized what I'd done, I started thinking of Stewie from *Family Guy* talking about one of Brian's girlfriends phrasing everything with an upward inflection, like she was asking a question every time she opened her mouth.

Will was saying something, but just like every other time I met someone's eyes as we had a conversation, I'd completely blanked out what he'd just said.

"Sorry, what?" I asked dumbly, looking back down at my beer.

"I asked if you wanted to come sit with us," he said with a teasing smile. "Damn, you're shit on my ego."

"Oh." I glanced at Mel, who had a dreamy expression on her face. "I don't think—"

"We'd love to!" Mel said quickly, cutting me off with a wide-eyed look in my direction as she slid off her bar stool.

Oh, crap.

I gripped my beer in one hand as I slid off the stool, stumbling a little when Will didn't move from his spot next to my chair and I ended up practically on top of him.

"You got a purse or somethin'?" he asked as his hand came to rest at the base of my spine.

"She never carries a purse," Mel replied helpfully, smiling at us like she'd just been invited to the cool kids' table. "She just keeps everything in her pockets."

"Musta been a tight fit," Will mumbled, pressing a little on my back so I'd start walking. "Not much room left in those jeans."

"Hey," I complained, looking up at him.

"That's a good thing, sugar. Believe me."

I tilted my head back down and caught sight of Mel raising her eyebrows up and down. Oh, God. She was going to embarrass the shit out of me. I knew she was.

"Everyone, this is Molly and Melanie," Will said with a smile as we reached the group he'd come in with. Then his arm wrapped a little further around my waist, one of his fingers sliding between the waistband of my jeans and the bottom of my tank top. "Molly and Melanie, that's my cousin Cam and his girl, Trix." He pointed to the couple then gestured to the men. "And these assholes are Rocky, Matt and Homer."

"Homer?" I asked under my breath.

"That's cause I always round the bases, darlin'," Homer said with a slimy smile, making me stiffen.

"Ignore him," Will ordered, glaring at the guy. "He's an idiot."

"Moose, you're gonna hurt my feelings," Homer joked, his face transforming so much as he chuckled that I realized he'd been testing me before.

I just didn't know what the hell the test was.

"You can call me Mel," my best friend chirped happily.

"Did he just call you Moose?" I asked as Will helped me into a seat.

I tried to keep my voice down, but it was so loud in the bar that whispering was completely out of the question.

"Nickname," Will replied, sitting down next to me as Mel found a place between a couple of the guys. I swear, that girl had never met a stranger.

"'Cause he gets shot and just keeps going," Matt said jokingly, making me freeze.

"What?" Mel asked in confusion as Will's cousin glared at the younger guy.

Will's hand slid up my back and rested at the base of my neck as he turned his eyes to Matt. "You're done."

"What?" Matt asked, throwing his hands up unsteadily, giving an indication of just how drunk he was. When he'd been sitting still, I hadn't really noticed, but now that he was moving, it was perfectly clear that the guy was plastered. "That's how you got the nickname."

"Get him the fuck outta here," Will ordered Homer, whose face had gone from jovial to livid in an instant.

I wasn't sure where to look. Rocky's face was impassive, Trix looked like she was about to throw up, Cam was scowling, and my poor best friend was watching everyone in confusion. Mel leaned toward Rocky as Homer muscled Matt to his feet and started frog-marching him across the bar.

"He's such a dipshit," Trix murmured angrily as Cam kissed the side of her head.

"Ignore him," Will told the table, his thumb starting to slide back and forth across the side of my neck. "Moll saw me at the hospital—she knows what's up."

"At the hospital?" Mel asked, looking at me accusingly.

"It was nothing," I ground out, making Will's hand squeeze my neck gently. Why was he still touching me? My muscles were so taut that I felt almost brittle.

"I call bullshit," she shot back.

"We're not talking about this here," I said, mortification setting in as the group around the table watched us argue.

"I was her patient," Will said quietly, looking at me with a small smile.

"For one night."

"Thank God."

"You were?" Mel said in surprise. "She didn't say *anything*."

"Of course I didn't say anything," I blurted, leaning away from Will's hand. "It's not my business to talk about the people I take care of."

"Oh, please," Mel said in astonishment. "You told me all about the guy that stapled his fingers together. And the lady that got the wine bottle stuck up her hoo-hah."

"I didn't tell you their *names*," I argued.

"Wait, a woman got a wine bottle stuck in her cunt?" Cam asked, chuckling as Trix elbowed him in the side. "I think we need to hear this story."

"Yeah, sorry," Trix said, her earlier look of devastation replaced by a small smirk. "I want to hear this, too."

"You can't stick things up there that have a, well . . . it suctioned, okay?" I could feel Will's amusement as I tried to explain the scenario. "Like . . ." I looked at the table and picked up my glass, pressing it against my mouth and chin and inhaling until I could hold it there with just the force of the suction. I dropped my hands to my lap, the glass still hanging from my face and shrugged my shoulders, making the entire table burst into laughter.

"Okay, we get it," Will said into my ear, gently pulling the glass from my face.

"How the hell did you get it un-suctioned?" Trix asked, leaning forward.

"The doctor drilled a small hole in the bottom," I mumbled, wiping my face off.

"Wait, is this someone we know?" Mel asked, eyes wide.

"No," I said automatically. "It doesn't matter!"

"So you work the emergency room?" Cam asked as Mel said something quietly to Rocky, making him chuckle.

"No." I shook my head. "Well, sometimes. I float around the hospital."

"She was one of my nurses when I was on the second floor," Will told them. "It was good to see a familiar face."

"I bet," Trix said softly, giving Will a small smile.

"Well, I still have no idea what the hell is going on, but I'm out of beer!" Mel announced, standing from her seat. "Anyone want one while I'm up?"

"I'll get 'em," Rocky intervened, rising beside her. "You can help me carry."

They took our orders and disappeared through the crowd, leaving me with Will, Cam and Trix.

"You don't seem old enough to be a nurse," Cam said once they were gone.

"I hear that a lot," I replied with a nod. "I'm actually not. I mean, I *am* a nurse. I just got my associate degree at the same time that I got my high school diploma, and I rushed through my bachelors."

"Holy crap," Trix said in surprise. "That must've been insane."

"It wasn't easy," I said with a laugh, growing more comfortable with the people around me. "But I have a daughter, so—" I paused in my explanation as I felt Will go still. "Yeah, uh, I had my daughter when I was younger, so I needed to get that shit sorted pretty quick."

"Aw, a daughter! We have twin boys. Holy terrors—both of them."

I laughed, ignoring the completely stiff man sitting next to me. "My girl's pretty easy. Busy—but sweet."

Trix opened her mouth to reply, but Will cut her off. "Mason's?" he asked gruffly.

"Yeah." I nodded, looking at him briefly before glancing away.

"Molly's boyfriend in high school was Mason Flanders," Will told Cam and Trix.

I braced.

Whenever people heard Mason's name, especially in Eugene, it always took them a moment to place it. But they always did. They knew who he was. The local kid who'd gotten onto the Oregon Ducks football team, only to drop dead of a heart attack during practice before he'd ever played a game. Fourteen years of playing football, fourteen years of running track and getting yearly physicals, and no one had ever found the heart defect until it had killed him.

I'd been five months pregnant.

Thankfully, he hadn't passed his broken heart onto our daughter. She had enough medical problems to deal with that were all her own.

"Oh, my God," Trix said quietly. "That sucks. I'm sorry."

"Thanks," I mumbled.

"Wait, that's the guy who—" Cam's words cut off. "Tough break, girl," he said softly.

"I had my dad and Mel, so we made it through," I replied with a tight smile.

"You'll always have me," Mel sang as she came up behind me, setting my fresh beer down on the table as she sloppily kissed the top of my head.

"And Mason's parents," Will said, grabbing a beer from Rocky. "They were always pretty cool, right?"

"Cunts," Mel replied, making the word come out as a cough.

I snorted, reaching for my beer. "Yeah, they're not around."

"That's crazy," Trix said, leaning against Cam as he wrapped an arm around her shoulder. "Especially if they lost their kid. My mom and dad would never let the boys out of their sight if something happened to me."

"Don't say shit like that," Cam muttered, glaring at her. "Nothin' happening to you. Ever."

"Yeah, yeah," Trix replied, rolling her eyes at me.

"It's all good—" My words cut off as Mel and Rocky started kissing. Right there at the table. Like they weren't in the middle of a crowded bar. I was pretty sure I saw Rocky's tongue.

Will laughed at the disgusted look on my face.

"You didn't mention you saw me, huh?" he said quietly, leaning down toward my ear so I could hear him.

"Of course not."

"Wasn't my best moment," he murmured, his voice tight.

I tilted my head up to look at him and swallowed hard. His face was closer than I'd realized.

"You'd had a hard day," I replied seriously, making his lips quirk.

"That's a fuckin' understatement, sugar," he whispered back.

"Yeah." I gave him a sad smile at the remembrance of that hellish day.

He'd come into the hospital, full of bullet holes and in and out of consciousness. When he was out, I'd heard that he was an ideal patient, in good physical shape and without any underlying health problems. While he was awake, though? He'd raised holy hell until they'd had to strap him down.

That's how I'd seen him. By the time he'd reached the floor I was on, he'd been stitched up and cleaned off, and was restrained like an animal.

"You don't wear glasses anymore," Will said abruptly, making me realize that we were still staring into each other's eyes like the main characters in a Lifetime movie.

"I do," I replied, looking back down at my beer. "I just have contacts in tonight. Less nerdy for a night on the town."

"I liked the glasses," he teased, just as Mel and Rocky climbed to their feet.

"We're out of here!" Mel announced as she grabbed her purse off the back of the chair. "You're good with Will, right?" she asked me, not waiting for an answer before saying, "Of course you are. Call me in the morning!"

She took off and I watched in horror as my ride walked away. She didn't even know that guy! He could be a serial killer. He could be into weird, kinky sex games. He could tie her up and make her his kitchen slave, which would never work since Mel sucked at cooking anything but ramen, and then he'd kill her for not doing her slave-job.

I shot to my feet, scrambling to stop her.

"He's a good guy," Will said, grabbing my forearm gently. "I mean, I doubt he'll marry her—but he's not gonna hurt her."

"What the fuck?" I snapped, my eyes wide. "She doesn't even *know* him!"

"Sugar, you don't have to know someone to leave the bar with them," Will laughed. "She's fine—I promise."

"But—"

"I'll text Rock and make sure he's on his best behavior."

"But—"

"You can text Mel, too."

"But she was my freaking ride!" I moaned.

I dropped back down into my seat as Will's smile grew wide. "I'll give you a ride home on my bike."

Oh, shitballs.

"I could grab a cab," I argued, still scowling.

"You don't want to ride with me?" Will's voice dropped, and for a second I thought he'd asked if I wanted to *ride him*.

"Uh, no, that's fine," I stuttered once I realized he wasn't trying to have sex with me. "Thanks."

"No problem." His arm went back around me, and for a moment, I almost wanted to lean in against his chest the way Trix was with Cam. They seemed so comfortable with each other.

I'd had that with Mason, the ease and comfort that came with being with a person for a long time. But Mason hadn't been into public displays of affection. I knew he was faithful, and his eyes never strayed, but I'd wondered sometimes if I'd embarrassed him. He was a football star, bound for great things, and I wasn't exactly the type of girl people had expected to see on his arm. We hadn't matched—not at all.

"We're gonna head out, too," Cam announced, kissing Trix's forehead. "Boys'll be home early in the mornin'."

"Alright," Will said with a nod, "Helpin' Dad out at the house this weekend—I'll see ya Monday, though."

"I think Gramps asked Leo to help with that retaining wall at the back of the house this weekend, too," Trix said as Cam helped her pull a leather jacket over her arms. "Are you helping with that?"

"Nah," Will shook his head. "Poet said he'd pay Tommy to help on Sunday, so I'm going to kick back and watch football."

"He's paying him?" Trix asked incredulously.

"That's what I said," Will chuckled. "If he is, I'm not helpin' for free."

"Yeah, right. You'll be there," Cam said, slapping Will on the shoulder. He turned to me. "Nice to meet you, Molly—"

"Duncan," I filled in. "You, too."

Trix smiled, but Cam's eyes narrowed. "Duncan?"

"Yeah." I grit my teeth. "And yes, my dad's the Club's attorney."

"And that's why she keeps her mouth shut," Cam muttered to himself with a small smile, his eyes still on me.

"You done?" Will asked.

Cam nodded and steered Trix away from the table.

"Is it really a big deal that my dad's—"

"Let's get outta here," Will said, cutting me off as he climbed to his feet.

"Maybe I want to stay."

"Do you?"

"Not really," I conceded, shrugging my shoulders.

"Then let's go."

He pulled me to my feet and grasped my hand firmly, pulling me through the crowded bar and out the front door. The air was cool outside and I wanted to bitch at Mel again for making me leave the house without a coat on. I was going to get hypothermia if I tried to ride on a motorcycle.

"Here, sugar," Will said, unbuckling a bag that hung on the side of his motorcycle. He pulled out a sweatshirt and raised it to his face to sniff it.

"It's not clean, but it doesn't stink," he said seriously, holding it out so I'd slip my arms into it.

I inhaled deeply as he pulled the huge sweatshirt over my head. It definitely didn't stink. It smelled like Will and a little bit like the inside of a garage. My heart pounded.

"You look cute as shit," Will said with a chuckle as he rolled the sweatshirt sleeves up.

"I *am* cute as shit," I said back, nodding my head.

I loved alcohol. Why didn't I drink more often? I should be going out once a week. It was fun.

"You realize that these helmets do very little to protect your dome, right?" I asked as he set a skull cap helmet on my head. "I mean, if you wreck this murdercycle, a helmet like this isn't going to help you."

"Murdercycle?" he asked, smiling as he buckled the helmet.

Wow, being out in the fresh air had made the little buzz I'd had going multiply by a thousand.

"It's a death trap," I told him seriously as he climbed on and helped me up behind him.

He turned his torso and looked down at me with a huge grin. "Might be a death trap, but it's fun as fuck."

Then he fired up the bike and pulled my arms tight around his waist.

I knew then that things were not going to end well. I liked his death trap a little too much.

Chapter 2

WILL

MOLLY DUNCAN.

I shook my head as she led me toward her little single-wide in the middle of a trailer park that looked like it was for old people. I was sure that my bike had woken a few of them up, but thankfully, no one had come outside to investigate. Especially since the moment I'd shut my bike off, the crazy girl had started shushing me, like my *voice* was going to wake the neighbors.

"Home sweet home," Molly announced as she pushed her way inside.

The place was clean. A bit shabby—but not run down. Her trailer was probably only about ten years old, and she had it all painted and decorated and shit. And there were toys all over the place.

"Do you want a drink?" Molly asked, fidgeting as I closed the door behind me. "I have soda and water. Or I have milk—but it's whole milk." She scrunched up her nose in disgust, and I wanted to laugh so fucking bad, but I could tell she was nervous and I didn't want to embarrass her.

But seriously? Did she just ask me if I wanted milk?

"I'm good," I said moving toward her. "I like your place."

"It's not much, but it's what we can afford. I didn't want to be in debt, so I made sure that we made a life within our means—shit." She dropped her chin to her chest and squeezed her eyes shut. "I should've just said 'thank you,' huh?"

"That woulda worked, yeah."

"Okay, thank you."

I watched her as her gaze shot around the room and her hands fidgeted, her fingers coming up to her lips before dropping back down again. After she'd done it a couple times, she finally looked up and met my eyes.

"I make you nervous?" I asked. I knew I did, but I also wanted to hear her say it.

She was like a bunny—

Jesus.

What the hell was wrong with me? A *bunny*?

Straight out? Molly was the type of woman that every guy wanted to settle down with, and no guy touched otherwise. It wasn't necessarily because she was innocent—she wasn't. She'd had a kid already. But you *knew* just by looking at her that if you hooked up with her, your days of random pussy were over.

She was sexy as hell—round ass, slender waist, nice big tits—but it was clear that she didn't get around.

She wasn't out fucking randoms.

She wasn't a barfly.

The woman was a single parent and had a good job.

She was old lady material.

Wife material.

Fuck.

I should have never walked up to her at the bar.

"It's just weird, you know?" Molly said, throwing her arms out to her sides. "I've known you forever, so I feel like I *know* you. But I don't, really. We were friends in grade school—everyone's friends in grade school! But you could be a total douche now."

"Are you asking if I'm a douche?"

"No!" she blurted, eyes wide. "I'm just saying I feel like I know you, but I really don't."

"I'm the same guy you grew up with," I murmured, taking another step closer. Fuck, she was cute. I wanted to bite her, make her whimper for me to stop and then beg me to start again.

"Do you want to watch a movie? Let's watch a movie!" she suggested out of nowhere, spinning around and racing toward the nice-as-shit entertainment set up she had going.

"Nice TV," I said in surprise. How the hell had I missed the massive flat screen mounted on her living room wall?

"Thanks," she chirped, grabbing a couple remotes and flopping down onto the couch. "I'm an only child, so my dad goes a little overboard on birthday gifts."

"That right?" I asked, moving toward the couch.

"I know, I know. So why do I live in a trailer, right?" she asked with a small smile. "He'd totally support us—no question. But I want to do it on my own. I have a good job, so there's no reason for him to be paying my bills."

Complete Old Lady material.

I was so fucked.

"You like being a nurse?" I asked as I sat down beside her. I wanted to wrap my arm around her, but I was pretty sure she'd bolt off the couch with some excuse to leave the room.

"I love it," she answered. "I like helping people, and the human body is freaking fascinating and gross." She laughed. "Really gross. But that's what's cool about it."

"Did you—"

"How's your mom?" she asked at the same time.

"My mom?" There went the half-chub I'd been sporting since I'd seen her in the bar earlier.

"Yeah—I loved her when we were kids," Molly said, leaning her head back against the couch and rolling it toward me. "She always brought the best snacks and when I'd stand next to her, she'd run her hand down the back of my head like she was smoothing my hair down."

"Oh, yeah?"

"Yeah." She sighed, giving me a sleepy smile as she lifted the remote in her hand toward me. "You pick."

She was going to fall asleep. We knew it, but instead of getting up to leave and letting her go to bed, I took the remote from her hand and turned on the TV.

"How about *300*?" Molly asked as I scrolled through the cable listings.

"Really?"

"I'll probably be asleep before anything actually happens," she said, quietly laughing.

"You want me to go?" I looked down at where she'd curled herself into a ball on the couch.

"Not really."

"Alright." I reached down and pulled at the laces of my boots, breathing a sigh of relief when I pulled them off and my socks weren't stained and didn't smell like ass. "Come here," I murmured, pulling Molly against my side.

I was in the fucking Twilight Zone.

I tried to remember the last time I'd spent time with a chick when I hadn't been getting into her pants—but I didn't have even one memory. From the time I was fourteen years old and I'd realized how soft women's bodies were, I'd had one end game. Getting off.

There wasn't a chance in hell of that happening with Molly as she sleepily leaned into me.

I hadn't even kissed her.

"Oh, I forgot about the uniforms in this movie," Molly murmured with a low hum. "Look at those muscles."

I froze, glancing down at her as her eyes widened.

Then I covered her face with my hand. "Aren't you falling asleep?" I grumbled. "Better shut those eyes."

Less than fifteen minutes later, her body was like a noodle, and her head was sliding farther and farther down my chest with each breath she took. There was no way she was comfortable like that, but she slept right through it.

Screw it.

"Will?" Molly asked as I lifted her up so I could stretch out on the couch next to her.

"Still here," I said quietly, kissing the top of her head.

"Oh, good."

Then she was out again—even as I moved her limp arms and legs around so she was lying against the back of the couch and covering me like a blanket.

I was such a pussy. If any of the boys had seen me then, they would have given me shit about it for the rest of my life.

I reached out and nabbed the remote—shutting off the TV so the house was quiet and dark. Then I just lay there, wide awake as Molly drooled on my chest.

She was a drooler. Why wasn't that shit bugging me?

I'd known little Molly Duncan for as long as I could remember. When we were kids, she'd been this tiny little thing that always had lopsided pigtails and wore shit that sparkled. Always with the sparkles.

As we'd gotten older, she'd just sort of faded into the background of our schools. It's not like I hadn't known when she was around, I'd just never cared. She wasn't a girl that put out. All the boys had known that by just looking at her. And even though you heard shit about locker room boasting and bets being made about getting into girls' pants, she'd never been the topic of much conversation. She was just *there*—answering questions in class and giggling with her friends just like every other high school girl.

She'd become a bit more visible when Mason Flanders transferred to our school sophomore year and started dating her, but their relationship meant that she was an even less likely lay, so I'd continued to ignore her.

Hell, I probably never would have looked at her again if I hadn't seen her at the hospital. Even in a bar, my eyes would have slid right past her.

I closed my eyes and sighed, putting my hand on Molly's back as she shifted against me.

I'd been out of my mind when she'd walked into my hospital room that night. Between the drugs and what had gone on that day, I'd been fucking rabid. A family barbeque had turned into a shoot-out with some guys that I'd used to buy steroids from, and in the end, four of my family members were dead and my mom had been shot in the chest. Looking back, I wasn't surprised that the nurses had strapped me down. I'd needed it. But at the time, it had felt like a prison. I'd been in the same hospital as my mother, but no one would tell me where she was or how she was. I hadn't even known if she was alive or not.

"Let me the fuck outta here," I yelled, pulling hard at the straps on my wrists. The metal groaned as the restraints shifted, and I found myself wishing that I hadn't stopped taking the fucking steroids. I needed to find out what the fuck was happening.

"Will!" a voice shouted. "Stop."

I looked toward the door where a couple of orderlies were standing, but I couldn't see shit beyond their wide chests. Jesus, those fuckers were fat. I could take them.

I clenched my teeth and pulled at my arms again, my chest burning so bad that for a second, I thought for sure I was going to pass out.

"Will, quit!" the voice said again, closer.

I opened my eyes to see a familiar face staring down at me. I knew those blue eyes that were almost hidden behind a pair of glasses. I knew that dark blonde hair.

"Molly," I ground out. "Untie me."

"I can't."

"Bullshit!"

"I really can't," she said softly.

The tenderness in her expression fucking gutted me and I slammed my eyes closed again as my stomach clenched on a sob.

"Just let me up," I said hoarsely, opening my eyes.

"You have to calm down," she said back. Then I felt her fingers in my hair. "They won't untie you until you can keep your shit together."

"I'm good," I promised. "I'm good."

"I know," she sighed, her fingers still running through my hair. "But I can't undo the restraints."

"Let me the fuck up, you cunt!" I yelled back, my patience with her gone. I ripped at the restraints again as she jumped in surprise, her hand jerking away from my head. "I'll fucking kill you!"

Molly Duncan's eyes went wide as I shouted, then shut as she shook her head.

"Your mother would kick your ass for talking to me like that, William Hawthorne!" she yelled back, startling me. "Now, shut the fuck up and I'll go see how she's doing!"

My mouth snapped shut. She was going to help me, thank fuck. I had to know. I had to know how my mom was. I knew Tommy was fine. And Rose was good, too. Mick was—no. I couldn't think about that. I needed to know about my mom.

"Thank you," I said around the lump in my throat.

"Of course," she said, her voice soft again as she reached out to give my forearm a squeeze before leaving the room.

She'd come back a while later and let me know that my mom had made it through surgery. She'd also brought my little brother Tommy with her, and as he stood by the side of the bed, she'd unbuckled the restraints. I guess she'd known that I wouldn't lose my shit with my baby brother there, looking like he was going to fall over. He'd been wearing a borrowed set of scrubs and he'd still had Mick's dried blood on his neck and parts of his arms.

She'd never even said a word when she'd come to check on me later and found Tommy next to me in my hospital bed, holding my hand. She'd just gone about her business, taking my blood pressure and shit like there wasn't a teenage boy lying there, crying in his sleep.

Jesus, maybe being around her wasn't my best idea. Just seeing her face brought back a host of shit that I never wanted to think about again. I'd never been able to forget the sight of my baby brothers going down, the younger shielding the older, but at least I usually had a handle on that shit. I didn't think about it. I pressed forward. If I let myself think about the events that led up to the worst day of my entire goddamn life, I lost focus. I took stupid fucking risks, lost control.

My mother couldn't handle losing another one of her children. She wouldn't survive it.

Molly mumbled something, and when I glanced down at her, she was smacking her lips and raising her eyebrows. I knew right then that I was already in. It didn't matter that she was going to fuck everything up.

I fell asleep at some point, with my feet hanging off the end of the couch and my head resting on one of the arms.

Chapter 3
Molly

My first thought when I woke up the next morning was that my mouth tasted like absolute ass.

My second thought was the realization that I was lying on top of Will, and had been doing so all night.

"Mornin'," he rasped, as I groaned against his pec.

It was a nice pec. Firm. Defined, but not too large. I hated when guys had bigger tits than I did.

"I can't believe you stayed," I told his sternum as I tilted my head down as far as I could. My breath was probably rank.

"No shit. My neck is fuckin' killin' me. Should've taken you to bed," he grumbled.

I laughed lightly as I moved my left arm, flexing my hand as it tingled. We were wrapped so far around each other on my couch, I wasn't sure how I could even get up without elbowing or kneeing him somewhere vital. I probably should have cared that I'd just spent the night with Will—even if it had been platonic—but I didn't. I'd had fun, the kind of fun that I'd almost forgotten in the past few years.

I reached to grab the back of the couch and used one arm to hoist my upper body up, then realized that one of my legs was wedged in between Will's hip and the back of my couch. I yanked at my leg, but all it accomplished was jerking my hips against Will's, making him groan. Oh, he was hard. Very hard.

"You do that again, and—"

As he spoke, I yanked at my leg again, and all of a sudden I was upright, bracing one hand on Will's chest as he sat straight up, jerking my hips forward and making my leg slide free, our lower halves slamming together.

My breath caught, both because he'd startled me, and because his face was really close to mine and no way in hell was I introducing him to the monster that had died in my mouth.

"Oh, shit," Will grumbled, searching my face. "You're even pretty in last night's makeup."

He leaned in to kiss me, and I jerked my head to the side. I was *not* kissing him. Did he have no olfactory receptors?

"Fine," he breathed, one of his hands leaving my hip to tangle in my hair. He jerked gently and my head tipped back.

Then his mouth was at my throat. *Sucking.*

Holy crap, he was good at that.

I let go of the back of the couch and gripped his head, his smooth black hair sliding through my fingers.

"Should get a fuckin' medal," he murmured against my neck as the hand not currently holding my head slid around my hip and gripped my ass hard. "Won't even let me kiss you after I kept my cock in my jeans all fuckin' night."

I laughed a little and he froze.

"Kept your cock in your jeans?" I murmured into his ear. "Who says *cock*?"

"You givin' me shit?" he asked, biting down gently.

"If you don't know, I'm not doing it right."

"I'll show you doin' it right," he growled, making me shriek as he flipped us over.

I laughed as he growled and nipped at my neck, his fingers digging into my sides.

"Stop!" I ordered, my stomach starting to ache as I laughed.

"The hell are you doin' to me?" he asked against my skin, kissing my neck lightly as his hands went still.

"What do you mean?" I ran my hand over the back of his head as his entire body relaxed into mine.

Just as he was starting to push himself up, someone started knocking on my door and then we heard a key turning the deadbolt.

"Shit!" I hissed, pushing at Will's shoulders as I scrambled out from under him. "Get up!"

I was standing in the middle of the living room and Will had barely sat up when my dad walked through the door carrying my little princess.

She was clapping her hands, eyes on me, as my dad froze.

"What the hell are you doing here?" my dad snapped, making the baby jerk in surprise.

"Dad!" I scolded, moving toward him. He handed me the baby as I reached for her, but his eyes never left Will's.

"This is Will Haw—"

"I know who he is. What's he doing in your house?" he cut me off, his glare moving to me.

"None of your goddamn business," I hissed back.

"Duncan," Will finally said, lifting his chin a bit in greeting. "How's it hangin'?"

"Good grief," I murmured under my breath as my dad's shoulders tightened. Will was purposely trying to piss him off, and it was working.

"This is why I took my granddaughter last night? So you could bring an Ace home?" Dad's voice was full of derision, and it was so vile that I felt a little face press into my neck as small fingers pinched at the skin of my arm.

"Watch your fuckin' mouth," Will ordered, stepping forward.

I lifted my hand in his direction, making him stop.

"Get out of my house," I ordered quietly, my voice shaking.

"Are you kidding me?" Dad huffed, looking at me like I had two heads.

"You're the one who's being an asshole," I replied. "You're the one who gets to leave."

"I'm not keeping her again so you can go out screwing bikers," my dad warned as he stepped backward.

I didn't bother to reply as he slammed out of the trailer. He was being a jerk, and in a couple of hours he'd realize it and apologize. There had only been a few times in my life that my dad had spoken to me in that tone of voice, and each time he'd felt like shit afterward.

"Hey," I murmured. "You want to meet my friend Will?"

I looked up to see Will watching me intently. He'd moved closer without me realizing it, and was only a foot away when our eyes met.

I was embarrassed, but I hid it as I gave him a sheepish smile.

"Rebel," I said as my daughter's face came away from my neck. "This is my friend Will. Will, this is Rebel."

As Reb turned to face Will fully, his face didn't change expression at all. He didn't show even the smallest hint of surprise, so I knew that he was guarding his reaction.

Rebel's hand went toward her forehead then slowly moved away, as she shyly signed *hello*.

"That's hello," I told Will proudly, swallowing the lump in my throat.

"Hello, Rebel," he said sweetly, bending a little at the waist so he could meet her eyes. He glanced up at me. "Can she hear?"

"Yeah. Yes," I said, clearing my throat. "She hears fine—she's just not verbal yet."

Rebel's hand reached up to scratch at the side of her head above her ear, knocking her little purple glasses askew.

"No, baby," I reminded her. "You have to keep those on so you can see."

She huffed and glared at me, making Will smile. Then she kicked her legs in the universal sign for *let me down right this second.*

I set her on her feet and watched as she toddled toward her room.

"You didn't say anything," Will said, pulling my attention back to him. "With you all night and you didn't say a goddamn word."

"Why would I?" I asked seriously, looking at him in confusion.

"Are you shitting me?"

"You knew I had a daughter."

"I didn't know you had a—"

"Be very careful what you say right now," I warned, my voice vibrating with anger.

Will's head jerked back in surprise before he scowled at me, taking a step forward. "I was gonna say a *special needs child,*" he said, shaking his head. "Jesus Christ."

"Why is that your business?"

"Oh, I don't know!" Will's voice rose before his words cut off and he clenched his jaw. "So you didn't fuckin' blindside me. Was this a motherfuckin' test?"

"Oh, my God," I blurted, throwing up my hands. "You've got a very high opinion of yourself."

I crossed my arms over my chest as he silently stared at me.

"No, it wasn't a test. You came home with me from a *bar*. I didn't even think you'd ever meet her!"

"Oh, yeah? You take a lot of men home from the bar? Make 'em watch TV and sleep on your couch then kick them out before your kid gets home?"

"This is ridiculous," I mumbled as Rebel came rushing back down the hallway, carrying a stuffed giraffe my dad bought her at the San Diego Zoo the year before. "I didn't talk about Rebel at all last night. It's not like I was freaking hiding her."

I bent down to fix Rebel's glasses as she reached my side. She must have run into the bedroom and took them off to scratch at where they rubbed against the sides of her head. My little sneak. Too bad for her, she'd put them back on upside down. "Don't take off your glasses, Reb," I told her for the eighteen millionth time. "You need them to see."

She held up her giraffe and smiled sunnily. "Yeah, I see your giraffe, kiddo. Don't take off your glasses."

I turned back to Will. "My daughter has Down syndrome. That's her truth. It's not something I hide. It's not something I use to test people. It's just her life. Our life."

Will gave me a terse nod, then crouched down. "It was nice to meet you, Rebel."

Reb smiled brightly and held out her giraffe, pulling it quickly back to her chest when Will looked like he was going to take it. Her expression morphed into the non-verbal equivalent of *I'm just showing you, dude. Hands to yourself.*

"Cool giraffe," Will said softly, dropping his hands. "Is that your favorite?"

Rebel gave a short nod, watching him with shy eyes.

"I like alligators. Do you like alligators?"

She tilted her head to the side. I wasn't sure if we'd ever talked about alligators.

They watched each other for a long moment before Rebel turned away without warning, running back down the hall in her weird, little person gait.

"I'll see you around," Will said tonelessly as he stood back up.

I was frozen as he stepped into his boots and left the house without tying the laces.

Like he couldn't leave fast enough.

The door closed behind him and I heard his bike start up just as

Rebel came meandering back down the hallway, carrying a duck, a bunny and two bears in her arms.

I wondered if she thought one of them was an alligator.

"Auntie Mel is here!" my best friend announced a few hours later as she came through my front door. "And I brought Rebel a taco!"

"She's not supposed to be eating that crap!" I called back as I rinsed out our soup dishes and glanced at Reb, who was sitting in her high chair clapping her hands merrily.

"Hey—no junk food is your deal, not mine," Mel argued, setting a paper-wrapped soft taco on Reb's messy tray. "I also brought c-a-n-d-y."

"At least she's in her high chair and not on my couch this time," I mumbled, turning away as Reb reached inside the paper and pulled out some shredded lettuce with her fingers.

"Exactly," Mel countered, moving over to my side and leaning against the cupboard. "I got it with no cheese—since you're not doing dairy anymore."

"I've got a half-gallon of milk in the fridge if you want it," I said quietly, glancing over my shoulder. "I'm going to have to throw it out."

"Is cutting out dairy actually helping?" she asked, laughing as Reb started pulling apart her tortilla.

"Not yet, but this is the last step before I have to cut out gluten. You know what a pain in the ass that'll be? Pray that cutting dairy works."

Mel nodded.

Reb was healthy. She didn't have the heart problems that a lot of people with Down syndrome dealt with, and we were lucky that we'd caught her eyesight problems early. But she had eczema on her torso and thighs that just wouldn't go away, no matter what we tried. It was scaly and rough and it *itched*, and trying to stop an almost two year old from scratching when something itched was practically impossible. Rebel would scratch at her skin until it bled, leaving her open to infection.

Doctors were finding that sometimes eczema was a symptom of a food allergy, so we'd been going down a list, cutting things out for a while to see if it helped. Milk was the current item on the list.

"So what happened last night after I left?" Mel asked, grabbing a rag and wiping down the counter.

"Oh, you mean after you abandoned me?"

"Come on, you were fine with Will."

"Yeah, I was. He brought me home and stayed the night."

"What!" Mel yelled, her head whipping toward me.

"We didn't do anything," I grumbled. "We watched a movie and fell asleep."

"Good grief," Mel grumbled. "You had that hot guy here all night and you didn't bang him?"

"No, I didn't *bang* him," I hissed, glancing over at Reb. "We were on our way to . . . something this morning, but then my dad showed up with Rebel."

"What did Will do?"

"He was cool." I finished rinsing the dishes and dried my hands. "But he took off right after. How was your night?"

"Rocky is nuts in bed," Mel said, waggling her eyebrows up and down. "I think I had like five orgasms."

"Nuh uh," I argued.

"Oh, yeah. Dude knows *exactly* what he's doing. I'm lucky I can walk."

"Are you going to see him again?" I asked, watching as her lips quirked up in a small smile.

"Probably not," she answered, shaking her head. "We didn't even exchange phone numbers."

"What? Seriously?" I went to Rebel, who was no longer eating, but smearing her taco into the soup left at the edges of her tray.

"It's fine," she assured me. "We both knew what it was going in—I've got no complaints."

"You're nuts. I couldn't do that."

"Obviously, since Will was here all night and you didn't do anything. Did *you* exchange numbers?"

"No," I replied, realizing it as soon as she mentioned it. We hadn't exchanged numbers or even mentioned seeing each other again. I lifted Reb from her seat and carried her toward the bathroom. "Come on, she needs a bath."

I set Reb in the tub, stripped her down and turned on the water as Mel came to stand in the doorway.

"He seemed really into you," she said, fiddling with the lotions and creams on the countertop.

"I don't know," I replied, shaking my head. "We're a lot to take on, you know? It's not just me."

"If that's his issue, he's a douchecanoe."

"You can't really blame him. We're twenty-one. Most people our age don't have any kids."

"But a lot of them do," Mel argued, coming in to sit on the closed toilet seat.

"It's fine," I said, reaching out to gently take Reb's glasses off. She was disoriented for a minute until she figured out why her world was so blurry once again.

"Well, it was fun while it lasted, right?" Mel asked, leaning down to brace her elbows on her knees and her chin on her hands.

"Yeah, it was." We made eye contact and giggled. Even though Will had been a complete asshole before he'd left, it *had* been fun while it lasted. "Will smells really good," I said quietly. "And I rode on his murdercycle."

"Fun, right? It was a good thing that the guys were there last night, 'cause I wouldn't have been able to drive. Rocky drove us home on his bike and then took me to my car this morning."

"We should do it again," I said with a smirk.

"Yeah?"

"But probably not until like . . . next month. My dad was pissed that Will was here, so he's not going to babysit for a long ass time."

"Your dad has a stick up his ass."

"He just worries."

"He worries that he has a giant stick up his ass."

I snorted just as Reb squealed, smacking her hands into the rising tub water, soaking me and Mel.

"You're crazy!" I sang to Reb, making her laugh and slap the water again.

I let her play for a while as Mel and I chatted about anything and everything. That was the beauty of being best friends with someone. You could segue from the awful security guard at your job to a discussion on mall cops to the movie *Mall Cop* and somehow end up discussing Jennifer Lawrence's open letter about getting paid less than her male counterparts, with no breaks in between.

We continued to talk as I emptied the tub and climbed inside with Reb, shutting the curtain so I could turn on the shower and bathe us both. Mel held out a towel and wrapped it around Rebel as I handed her out so I could wash my hair, and she followed me into my room as I grabbed some clean clothes for us out of a laundry basket at the end of my bed.

"What do you want to do today?" she asked as she wrangled Rebel into a diaper. "I need to get some Christmas shopping done."

"It's only October."

"I like to be done before everyone else so I don't have to deal with idiots taking up all the parking spaces close to the stores."

"You want to go to the mall, Reb?" I asked, pulling a shirt over my wet hair. She gave me a short nod and climbed to her feet, her hands rubbing distractedly at the eczema on her little belly.

"Okay, first, let's grease you up!" I called, catching her as she tried to run out of the room.

I pulled the thick cream the doctor had given us off the top of my dresser and sat down on the bed, pinning a squirming Reb between my thighs. "Should we blow on it?" I asked her as I squeezed some of the cream into my palm. She hated when the lotion was cold, so we'd started blowing warm air over it before I rubbed it in. I wasn't sure if it actually warmed it up, but she believed it did, so it was worth the few extra seconds it took.

Reb leaned close to my hand, and I felt her warm, wet breath waft over the skin of my palm.

"You're not supposed to eat it!" Mel exclaimed, making Reb giggle.

I rubbed my palms together swiftly then started slathering the cream all over Rebel's torso, grabbing some more cream when I was done and smoothing it down her arms and legs, too. She didn't have eczema on her arms at the moment, but that didn't mean that it wouldn't show up at some point if I didn't keep her lubed up.

"Okay, let Auntie Mel get you dressed and we'll go," I ordered, setting Reb on her feet. "I need to take out these contacts before they're permanently glued to my eyes."

"You slept with them in?" Mel asked in surprise as she quickly pulled a t-shirt with snaps at the crotch over Reb's head. She was probably getting a little old for those types of shirts, but they still fit her and the snaps kept the shirt down so Rebel couldn't scratch the eczema on her stomach when I wasn't looking.

"I fell asleep pretty quick last night," I mumbled, making Mel laugh. "Give me five minutes."

When we got to the mall, Mel immediately pulled us into a store and started browsing through the racks as Rebel leaned over the side of her stroller, reaching for a display of necklaces that were the perfect height for little fingers.

I didn't know why the hell they put the sparkly shit down so low.

"I thought we were Christmas shopping," I complained as I tried to steer Rebel away from anything that would catch her attention.

"We are—for me. I deserve Christmas presents, too," Mel said seriously, holding up a shirt for my approval.

"That's ugly as shit," I said flatly, making her put it back.

"You're bitchy when you don't get laid," she replied.

"So I've pretty much been a bitch for the past two years?"

"Yes."

I laughed. "You're an asshole."

"Yes, but I'm your asshole, darling," Mel sang, pulling a dress from the wall and dancing with it from side to side.

"Molly?" a woman's voice called somewhere behind me.

"Oh, hey. Trix, right?" Mel asked as my eyes widened.

"Yeah—we met at the bar last night."

"I remember," Mel snorted.

"Oh, hey," I greeted, turning around to see Trix, an older woman and two younger girls.

"Farrah, this is Molly and Melanie. They went to school with Will, and we saw them at the bar last night."

"What's up, girls?" Farrah said with a smirk, making me like her instantly. She was wearing a baggy pair of jeans and a flowing top, her hair in loose braids down her chest. She should have looked ridiculous, but for some reason, it seemed to fit her. "This is my daughter Lily and my niece Rose."

"I'm Will's little sister," Rose piped up. The two little girls looked a lot alike, but Lily's head was tilted down, like she was shy or something.

"I remember when your mom was pregnant with you," I said, smiling. Rose looked so much like Mrs. Hawthorne, it was uncanny.

"Really?"

"Yep. She was huge."

Rose and Lily laughed, and that's when Lily's head popped up.

She was blind. Her eyes were beautiful, dark brown with sooty lashes and I couldn't find anything wrong with them, but they were vacant.

I glanced at Farrah and Trix to see them watching me intently.

"You must look like your dad, Lily," I told her with a smile. "You don't look anything like your mom."

"I know!" she laughed, her voice like a little fairy's. "Mom says I got my dad's pretty skin before he started covering it with tattoos. He's Mexican."

"Your skin's pretty glorious," Mel piped in. "Yours, too, Rose. Me and Mel can't keep a tan."

"It's all in the moisturizing," Farrah informed us, wrapping her arms around the little girls' shoulders. "Remember that, ladies. Drink water and moisturize."

"She always does this," Lily told me conspiratorially. "She used to be a beautician, so she thinks she knows all the secrets."

"Once a beautician, always a beautician," Farrah said loftily. "We're like the Marines."

"Jesus," Trix mumbled, laughing under her breath.

Rebel chose that moment to start flailing her arms and legs. Her stroller was pointed toward Mel, so she'd pretty much been hidden and wasn't happy that we were ignoring her.

"Oh, no," Mel crooned as she leaned down. "You weren't the center of attention for five minutes, whatever shall you do?"

"I like that one," Farrah said quietly to Trix.

"She went home with Rock last night."

"Good, maybe she'll be the one to pull his head out of his ass."

I tried to pretend like I didn't hear them, but they weren't exactly trying to mask their conversation.

"Come here, baby," I said as Mel lifted Reb out of her seat. As soon as she was in my arms, I turned back toward the group.

"This is my daughter, Rebel," I announced, fixing Reb's glasses so they weren't crooked on her face. "Can you say hi, Reb?"

Reb signed *hello*, and looked at the group with a huge smile.

"She doesn't talk yet," I said, glancing at Lily, "So she's waving."

"How the heck are you going to talk to her?" Rose asked Lily, whose mouth twisted up in a grimace.

"You can talk to her," I said quickly. "She can hear just fine, she's just not talking yet."

I looked up at Trix and Farrah, and both women were smiling cheerfully at Rebel as she batted her eyelashes at the little girls.

"Hi, Rebel," Lily said softly, her eyes pointed over my shoulder. "I'm Lily. How old is she?"

"She's almost two."

"Don't babies start talking when they're like one? Curtis and Draco are only one and they never shut up. Neither does Charlie."

Mel snorted behind me as Farrah huffed.

"Draco and Curtis are my boys, and Charlotte is Farrah's." Trix informed us. "They babble."

"They say a lot of words, too," Rose pointed out.

"Well," I said as I glanced over at Mel, who gave me a small smile. "Rebel has Down syndrome. Do you know what that is?"

"A couple of the kids at my school have that," Lily said, nodding her head.

"Yeah, so it's just a little harder for Reb to master stuff than it is for other kids. She'll get it eventually, though."

"Oh. Okay."

"Lily, I think she wants you to hold her," Rose said, leaning around her aunt to talk to her cousin. "She's got her arms out."

Rose was right. Rebel was leaning forward, reaching for Lily.

"Oh, um," I said, glancing helplessly at Farrah.

"It's okay. She holds Charlie and the boys all the time—she knows what she's doing."

Lily took a tentative step forward and lifted her arms.

I didn't want to be an asshole. I really didn't. But Rebel was sort of a live wire. You never really knew how she would behave and I was really afraid that Lily would drop her.

I took a deep breath and handed Rebel to Lily, who immediately propped Rebel on her hip with one hand under her tush and the other solidly around her back.

"You like Lily, huh?" Farrah asked Rebel, leaning down to look into her eyes. "I like her, too."

Rebel smiled and lay her head down on Lily's thin shoulder.

Lily beamed. "She totally loves me," she announced.

"She's like the baby whisperer," Trix told me, watching Lily. "Sometimes she's the only one who can calm the boys down for a nap."

"Okay, girls, we need to get cracking," Farrah announced. "Brenna's present isn't going to buy itself."

"Do you want to walk with us?" Lily asked, her expression pleading as Rebel's fingers sifted through the hair hanging over her shoulder.

"I think—"

"Sure. I'm not liking anything in here." Mel chirped, cutting me off.

"Okay, I guess we will," I said through my teeth.

"Give Rebel back to her mama, Lilybug," Farrah said softly.

"I'll hold your hand, okay?" Lily told Reb as I took her away and strapped her back into her stroller.

We left the crowded store and headed out into the main part of the mall, and as soon as there was a little room to move, Rose led Lily to the side of the stroller so she could hold Rebel's hand as we walked.

My panic must have shown on my face because Farrah sidled up to me immediately. "As long as you don't plan on starting or stopping fast and you're not into running little girls over with your stroller, she'll be fine," she told me, nodding toward Lily. "Rose leads Lily around like she's an extension of her body. They know what they're doing."

"I hope Rebel has a friend like that," I said quietly, watching the girls as they giggled at my baby's antics.

"Well, they're cousins," Farrah pointed out with a laugh. "I married my best friend's little brother, so they've been connected since birth. I'm not sure if Rebel will ever have what Rose and Lily have—most people don't. But I'm sure she'll have a best friend."

"Does Lily go to a school for the blind?" I asked, immediately feeling like I'd overstepped. "Ugh, ignore me."

Farrah laughed. "No, she goes to regular school, and has a tutor three afternoons a week. We couldn't separate the girls after Lily lost her sight."

I wanted to ask a million questions. They were right on the tip of my tongue, but somehow I kept my mouth shut. Farrah was the first mom I'd talked to that had a special needs child—and even though the girls were totally different, I wanted to know how she did it. I wanted to know the secrets. Sometimes I felt so alone.

After half an hour of visiting with our new friends, Mel and I said goodbye and walked toward the other end of the mall, where we'd parked the car.

"What the hell was that?" I hissed once we'd gotten far enough away to not be overheard.

"Gathering intel," Mel replied, bumping her hip against mine.

"What intel? You talked about makeup and asked if Trix worked out!"

"Did you see that woman's ass? She had ass for days!"

"You're so annoying!"

"Hey, they invited us. I just thought it would be cool to find out a little more about Will."

"We didn't find out anything new about Will."

"Sure we did—about his family, at least."

"I probably won't even see him again," I muttered, grabbing Rebel's coat from the storage space under the stroller. I stopped at the door and shifted around to face her, my eyes going wide. "Oh, shit."

"What?" Mel asked, moving forward. "Oh. Shit is right."

Reb had poop soaking through the little leggings she was wearing.

"This is because of that fucking taco!" I bitched as Rebel watched me with wide eyes. "Does your tummy hurt, baby?"

I lifted her out of the stroller and wrinkled my nose.

"I'm sorry," Mel said softly. "Do you have clothes for her?"

"No, I didn't even think to bring any," I mumbled, pulling Reb to my chest. "Let's just get her to the car. We'll turn up the heat and I'll change her in the backseat and leave her in a diaper for the ride home."

The next fifteen minutes were a disgusting mix of groaning and laughter as I wrestled with Reb in the back of my car. When I finally had her cleaned up, my car stunk, but she was happy as a clam. I buckled her into her seat and crossed my fingers that she wouldn't have another accident on the ride home—car seats were much harder to clean than babies.

"Okay, no more tacos," Mel said in amusement as I backed out of our parking space.

"Ya think?"

"Yeah, yeah. You know, you never explained why you hadn't said anything about seeing Will," she said, turning to face me. "What was that about?"

"Do you remember when that shooting was all over the news last year—some guys came in and shot up a family barbeque?"

"Yeah." I could see realization dawning on her face.

"Yeah—that was Will's family."

"Holy crap," she whispered.

"From what I heard later, his youngest brother died. His mom was in the hospital for a while, and there were a few other people who died, too."

"That's nuts. Why would someone shoot them?"

"Live by the sword, die by the sword," I murmured, immediately feeling like shit for saying it. "They're part of the Aces Motorcycle Club and I'm guessing it had something to do with that."

"But Will's brothers are way younger than us."

"Yeah, I know."

We were silent for a minute as we got out onto the road.

Then both of us gasped as two police cars quickly followed by another three flew past us, their lights and sirens blaring.

"Holy shit!" Mel exclaimed as I pulled quickly to the side of the road. "They were hauling ass!"

"Where'd they go?" I asked, turning in my seat to try and catch a glimpse of the cars.

"They pulled into the mall."

"I wonder what happened?"

"Robbery?"

"That was a lot of cop cars for a robbery."

Chapter 4
Will

"You should be careful," my dad warned me as we carried my mom's old patio table toward the shed in their back yard. "Fucking around with the suit's daughter."

"Who told you?" I grunted, almost tripping over a rock in the yard before I righted myself.

"Who do you think?"

"Cam's such a fuckin' busybody."

"Yeah, he is," my dad chuckled.

"It was nothin'," I said as we set the table inside the shed. We were getting ready for winter, putting all the summer shit inside so it didn't get ruined. The rain and snow wouldn't really be an issue with the patio furniture, but after two years in a row of the wind knocking the table over and shattering the glass top, we'd started putting it all away.

"You like her, it's not nothin'," Dad pointed out as we headed back for the chairs.

"She's got a kid."

"So?"

"So she's got other shit goin' on."

"She single?"

"Yeah, but—"

"Asa!" my mom called from the back door. "Come in here!" Her voice wobbled, and my dad took off at a run.

I followed him inside and found my mom sitting on the couch

watching the news.

"Sugar, I told you to stop—"

"It came over the radio," Mom interrupted him. "That's why I turned on the TV."

My mom wasn't fragile—far from it. But since the day my brother died, she'd had nightmares that kept her awake at least three nights a week. Sometimes Dad had to remind her to eat, and sometimes I wondered what she would have done if she didn't have three other kids to worry about.

My parents had come to an agreement a couple months after Mick died. Mom would start going back to the shrink she'd seen when I was a kid, and she'd try her best to stay away from things that would trigger her nightmares—like the news.

"Rosie was just there." Mom's voice came out strangled. "She just got home twenty minutes ago."

"Right, baby, so she's fine. You don't need to watch this shit."

My dad reached for the remote, but Mom slapped his hand away, making him huff in annoyance.

I sat on the arm of the couch and listened to the anchor announce a special report. Apparently, there had been a shooting—my gut rolled at that—at a local mall. The suspect was dead, but they had no idea why it had happened or how many other people were hurt.

Dad finally snatched the remote out of Mom's hand and shut off the TV. Before she could bitch him out, he was cupping her face in his hands and murmuring something to her that I didn't catch. That was my cue to leave.

I went back into the kitchen and grabbed a bottle of water out of the fridge as I shrugged off the flannel I was wearing. It was too hot in the house to be wearing that shit inside.

"Hi, brother," Rose greeted as she shuffled sideways into the kitchen, shaking her hands out to the side.

"What're you doin'?"

"Making an entrance," she announced, twirling around.

"You're a nut."

"I saw your girlfriend today," she sang, pushing by me to get a juice box out of the fridge.

"What're you talkin' about?"

"Molly," she answered with a sneaky smile. "Her baby's really cute and she wears *glasses*. She looks like a little old professor."

My entire body locked up.

"Where'd you see her?" I asked, already knowing the answer.

"At the mall. Her and her friend Melanie were—where are you going?"

"I'll help you out tomorrow, Dad!" I yelled as I grabbed my flannel off the countertop and walked quickly out of the house.

I felt like I was going to throw up.

It wasn't happening again.

No fucking way.

I hopped on my bike and swallowed down the bile in the back of my throat as I made my way to Molly's trailer park.

Her car was parked out front, but that didn't mean shit. She could've ridden with Melanie to the mall.

I was off my bike and pounding on her front door within less than a minute, and when it opened and I saw that she was perfectly fine, I thought for a second that I was going to throw up anyway.

"Will? Are you okay?"

Her eyes went wide when I pushed into her house, but I didn't care. I needed to get my hands on her.

I grabbed her hip as she shuffled backward, and used my other hand to close the door behind me. "Where's the baby?"

"Afternoon nap—"

That's all I needed to know.

I slammed my mouth down on hers in what had to be the worst first kiss in the world ever. My teeth knocked into hers and I tasted blood in my mouth—I'm not sure whose it was. But I didn't care. I didn't fucking care if she beat me to shit, I needed to feel her.

The adrenaline that had beat at me on the ride over needed a fucking outlet. My hands were shaking as I cupped the back of her head, and hers were soothing as she reached up to smooth one across my cheek.

"What's wrong?" she asked against my mouth.

She asked what was wrong—but she hadn't told me no.

Green light.

I pressed her against the wall and reached down to grip the backs of her thighs, lifting her so I could fit between them.

She moaned and I groaned as the kiss finally found a rhythm. A fucking wet and messy rhythm.

Jesus. She tasted like apple. I ground my hips against hers and she whimpered into my mouth, one of her hands going into my hair. Pinning her against the wall with my hips, I let go of her legs so I could run my hands over her shoulders, down her arms and up her sides as I reassured myself that she was okay.

She was okay.

She was okay.

"Fuck," I ground out as I ripped my mouth from hers. "Fuck!"

"Will?" Her legs tightened around my waist as her hand slid out of my hair.

"*Motherfucking hell.*"

"What is *wrong*?" Molly demanded, her hands going to the sides of my face to force me to look at her. "What happened?"

"You see the news?" I asked, meeting her eyes.

"No. I've been giving Reb a bath and then putting her down for a nap. Why?"

"Turn on the news," I said flatly, stepping back so that her legs slid down my thighs and she was standing on her own two feet again.

She looked at me in confusion, then grabbed my hand, pulling me with her to the couch.

"What station?" she asked as we sat down.

"Any of 'em."

"Oh, no," she breathed, her hand reaching out to squeeze my thigh as she tuned in to the local station. "We were just there."

"I know," I replied grimly. "Rose said she saw you."

"And you thought—" she trailed off as her eyes focused to me. "We're fine."

"See that now."

"We saw the cop cars as we drove away," she said, muting the TV as she turned to me. "We weren't there."

"You saw the fuckin' cop cars?" I growled, my heart starting to pound again.

"Yeah, but we were already leaving. We—"

An inarticulate noise came out of my throat as I grabbed the back of her neck.

"You know how long it takes for a cop to respond to a 911 call?" I asked roughly. "You were there."

"I'm fine."

"Jesus Christ."

"Will," she whispered, crawling on top of me.

The minute her ass hit my thighs, I lost my shit. She was trying to comfort me or something, but all I could feel was the weight of her pussy on my cock.

I was on my feet and dropping her to the couch before she could protest, my hands going straight to the snap of her jeans.

"Will?"

"You sayin' no?" I asked, jerking the jeans and panties down her thighs.

"I'm not saying no," she whispered, her eyes wide.

I ripped the jeans off the rest of the way and stared. Ah, shit. She didn't dye her hair and the freckles that covered her shoulders and cheeks also ran all the way up her thighs.

"Shirt," I ordered, jerking mine over my head.

"I've got stretch marks," she said nervously, her hands hesitating at the bottom of her sweatshirt.

"I don't give a fuck." I grabbed a condom and tossed my wallet to the floor, trying to focus as I shucked off my jeans. "Shirt, Molly."

I was naked and suited up by the time she finally started pulling the sweatshirt off, but I didn't have patience for her slow movements. I yanked her off the couch and tore the shirt over her head, my hands automatically going to the clasp of her bra.

"Um," she murmured nervously as I got my first sight of her tits.

They looked heavy. Thick.

I fell to the couch, pulling her on top of me so I could bury my face between them.

Jesus, she had no angles. Every single piece of her was rounded and soft.

I lifted one of her tits and weighed it in my hand. Yeah. I was going to dream about them for months.

"Will?" she asked as I stuck two fingers in my mouth, getting them nice and wet.

"Gorgeous," I ground out as my hand slid between us.

"You don't have to say that." Her breath hitched as my wet fingers found her clit.

"Gorgeous," I said again, sliding those same fingers inside her. "Shit, you didn't need this did you?" I asked, jerking my hand up. "Already wet."

She groaned and dropped her head to my shoulder.

I pulled out of her and grabbed my cock, pressing it down until the tip was riding right inside her.

"Drop," I ordered, my hand on her tit falling to her hip.

Her breath was coming out in heavy pants against my neck.

"Drop," I ordered again, slapping her hip lightly.

Then she did, and I was pretty sure my head was going to explode.

"Oh, *fuck*!" I ground out as she took me in halfway. "That's right," I mumbled, pulling my hand from between us to grip her thigh. "Keep going. You're so fucking sexy. Keep going, Moll."

I knew I was rambling, but I couldn't seem to stop the words falling out of my mouth as she rocked, taking a little more in each time.

Her head came away from my neck and her eyes were wet as they met mine.

"You good?" I asked as she pressed down again.

"It feels so good," she mumbled, her words ending on a feminine grunt.

Jesus. Moans were good, screaming was better, but when a woman grunted like that? It was hotter than anything else. It meant she was working for it.

When her ass finally hit my balls, she let out this high-pitched noise from the back of her throat and I was afraid for a second that I was going to embarrass myself.

"Don't stop," I ordered as she froze. "Ride me."

My hands were sliding all over her. I couldn't touch enough. I fucking loved it that she was on top—it meant that my hands were free to pinch and pull and grip.

She didn't lift up the way I expected her to. Instead, she did this hip roll that had me just barely sliding out of her before pressing inside again. It wasn't what I needed, but by the way her breath hitched, it must have been exactly what she needed.

"Look at you," I said softly, pulling the ponytail out of her hair so it fell in waves over her back and tits. "Fuckin' goddess."

That's exactly what she looked like. Some sort of fertility goddess, with her little pouch of a belly, heavy tits and round thighs. Hell, I'd been sleeping with the wrong types of women.

I pinched her nipples between my fingertips as she rocked, and when I didn't get the reaction I wanted, I pressed harder, then harder, until finally, she jerked, tipping her head back as she moaned.

She was perfect.

Her hand came off my shoulder and slid down her belly until it was wedged between us. "I need just a little more," she gasped, as if in explanation.

"No," I murmured, shaking my head as I gave her nipples another hard pinch. "You keep your hands on me," I said, leaning forward to kiss her. "My hands on you."

I pulled her hand from between us and pulled it around my back before wrapping my hand around the top of her thigh so my thumb could reach her little red clit peeking out from where we were connected.

She moaned into my mouth as I began to press, and her hips moved faster.

It wasn't just ego that had me wanting to get her off without her help. I was all for a woman doing her part. But I'd noticed that women tended to ease up once they started to come—like they couldn't focus on what they were doing anymore. If I was the one driving it, I could make the orgasm last a fuck of a lot longer.

I wanted Molly to lose her mind.

"Look at you," I said quietly as her forehead rested against mine. "Look how white your skin is against mine, so fuckin' pretty."

"Jesus, Will," she replied, panting. "I'm so close."

"Keep going," I ordered, licking her lips. "Your clit is so fuckin' swollen and hard."

"Are you going to keep giving me a play by play?" she teased, her breath hitching as I pinched her nipple hard and lifted her entire breast with it.

"You like it when I give you a play by play," I growled. "My thighs are fuckin' dripping with you."

I twisted her nipple and let her tit fall, and she came hard, her pussy clamping down on my cock almost to the point of pain.

She moaned loud and long, her head falling forward until her hair was almost completely covering her face.

Then it was finally my turn.

I slid forward off the couch onto my knees and used one arm to shove her coffee table out of the way so I could lay her on the floor. I stayed up on my knees and held her hips high so I could pull back and shove back in hard.

"I'm going to come again," she said in surprise, her back arching as she reached down to dig her nails into my thighs. "Please, oh, *fuck*."

I must have been hitting just the right spot because she was suddenly flooding my dick, making everything even wetter.

Her tits bounced with every thrust, her nipples red from my fingers.

I came when her pussy clamped down on me the second time, making my vision go black at the edges.

I dropped back onto my heels as I caught my breath and tried to force my stiff fingers from the tight grip I had on her hips. I could feel sweat dripping down my back, and the hair at the sides of my face was wet.

"You're absurdly good at that," Molly said after a moment, reaching up to cover her tits with her hands.

I was still inside her and she was already feeling self-conscious. Ridiculous.

"So are you," I said, falling forward on my hands so I was bracing myself above her.

What was left of my anxiety disappeared when she grinned at me.

"You're so handsome," she said softly.

I scoffed and pulled back, grimacing as I slid out of her.

"Oh, no, did the condom break?" she asked worriedly as she glanced down.

I reached down to take it off with a snap, shaking my head. "Nope, sugar, that's all you," I answered with a grin.

I reached down to my hip and swiped my hand across the wet there, smoothing it over my lower stomach as she gaped at me. Then I gave my half-mast cock a tug.

"You're nasty," she whispered.

"And you love it," I replied, laughing.

"Oh, my God," she groaned, covering her face with her hands. "I totally do."

"Come on," I said, still chuckling as I stood up and pulled her with me. "We need a shower."

"I need to disinfect that couch," she grumbled as I tugged her past it. "And we need to be quiet so we don't wake the baby."

I found my wallet on the floor and snatched it up—just in case—then let her lead me through her bedroom and into the master bath. She turned on the shower as I stared at her ass, wondering if she'd let me have her again.

"Come on," she said quietly as she stepped inside the huge tub. The thing was so big, I bet she could practically swim in it when it was filled.

"I can't believe there was a shooting at the mall," she said quietly as I pulled her against my chest underneath the spray of water. "That's nuts."

"Don't go there anymore," I ordered, leaning over to get a bar of soap from the ledge of the tub.

"I have to go to the mall," she said with a small laugh. "We don't go there very often, but we can't just not go ever."

"Shop somewhere else."

"You worry too much."

"You ever seen someone die from a gunshot wound?" I snapped, realizing how stupid the question was after I'd said it.

"Yeah, actually I have," she said quietly, stepping back.

"Then you know." I lathered up my hands and ran them over her chest, down her belly and between her thighs. "You have to be careful."

"I am careful," she argued stubbornly as I put her back under the spray and soaped myself up. "I'm always careful—but I can't become a recluse."

As she brushed off my worry like I was being an idiot, the full effect of what I'd done getting involved with her hit me.

"Do what you want," I said in irritation, moving around her so I could rinse myself off. She watched as I made sure all the soap was gone then stepped out of the shower. I grabbed a towel hanging from the rack and sniffed it before drying myself off.

"Are you mad?" Molly asked as she followed me out of the shower.

"Nope."

I walked out of the bathroom and headed for my clothes. I was stupid for going over there. A lot of shit had happened since the shooting that had killed my little brother. Life went on, and it wasn't exactly like I was living a squeaky-clean one. I'd been around guns—hell, I'd been shot at. The Aces were constantly having to police our boundaries and keep contacts and clients from fucking with us. The shit we shipped meant that we were always on guard.

But just the thought of a shooting involving women and kids made me fucking crazy. My reaction wasn't normal, I knew that. But if it was up to me? All the old ladies and kids of the club would live inside the club gates, like a fucking commune.

Luckily, most of the old ladies had a keen sense of self-preservation.

They didn't take chances and the phrase 'better safe than sorry' was pretty much their way of life. They'd all seen firsthand what happened if you let your guard down.

So why had I thought that I could get with a woman who didn't have the sense to stay the fuck away from a shooting? Why had I thought I should get with anyone at all? I wanted another person to worry about like I wanted the fucking clap.

I pulled on my jeans and buttoned up the fly just as Molly came down the hallway in a towel.

"I don't understand why you're mad," she said, coming to a stop at the end of the couch, just as I nabbed my shirt off the floor.

"Not mad, Molly." No, I wasn't mad—I just wanted to get the fuck out of there. Showing up had been a bad idea.

"I thought we were having fun," she said in confusion, taking a step forward. "I thought—"

"It was fun," I cut her off, pulling on my socks and boots.

"Then why are you leaving?"

"I got shit to do and your kid's gonna be up soon, right?" The words weren't too bad, but the way I'd said them made Molly step back again, her arms crossing protectively over her chest.

"Right," Molly replied, her chin lifting.

I pulled my flannel up my arms and stuffed my wallet in my pocket before walking toward her. I leaned down to kiss her, but my lips hit her cheek as she turned her face away.

"I'll call you," I said, moving past her toward the front door.

"Sure you will," I heard her whisper behind me as I pulled the front door open and escaped through it.

I was such a fucking idiot.

Chapter 5

MOLLY

"Oh, come on," Mel whined, flopping down across my bed. "I want to go out."

"Then go out!" I snapped, shoving clean clothes into my dresser. "I'm not stopping you."

"I don't want to go by myself."

"Too bad."

I dodged her grasping fingers as I rounded the bed, picking up Rebel and setting her into the laundry basket I was carrying into her room. She barely acknowledged me as she played with a little board book that had a different textured animal on each page.

"You're being a baby!" Mel called as she followed me into Reb's room. "He probably won't even be there."

"Aren't we going so you can try and see Rocky again?"

It had been three weeks since Will had left my house like his ass was on fire, and I hadn't heard a word from him, not that he had my number or anything. We hadn't exactly exchanged them when I was riding him on my damn couch. But Will knew where I lived and where I worked. If he'd wanted to see me, he would've. Clearly, he didn't want to.

"I just want to go out!" Mel sang. "And my sister said she'd watch you-know-who, so why are you telling me no?"

"Because I don't want to go."

"Sure you do. You love hanging out with me and you love beer."

"I don't want to get dressed and wear makeup. I just want to hang out in yoga pants and eat my weight in ice cream. I'm fucking exhausted."

"Please?"

"Melanie," I warned.

"Please? Please? Please?" Each time she said the word, she changed her tone of voice. I knew from experience that she'd just keep going if I didn't stop her.

"Fine," I grumbled. "But I'm not getting all gussied up."

"Totally cool," Mel said quickly, lifting her hands in a placating gesture. "Wear whatever you want."

I huffed as Rebel began to laugh at something in her book.

"You want to hang out with Heather tonight?" I asked Rebel, lifting her out of the basket.

"I'm just going to go call the sisterbeast while you're still telling me yes," Mel said, skipping out of the room.

"You realize your Auntie Mel is annoying, right?" I asked Reb as she watched me with wide eyes. "I mean, she's fun sometimes, but man does she drive me nuts."

Rebel reached up to put her hand on my cheek.

"Can you say *Mama*?" I asked softly as Reb tilted her head to the side. "I know you can. I heard you saying it in your room the other day. You want to try? *Ma-ma*."

She quickly shook her head.

"Yes. Say *Ma-ma*."

Another head shake.

"*Ma-ma. Ma-ma. Ma-ma*." I said over and over, my voice growing growly and making Reb burst into a fit of giggles.

"You're so stubborn," I exclaimed loudly, kissing her on the forehead.

"We're set for tonight!" Mel called from the doorway.

★ ★ ★

A FEW HOURS later, Mel's seventeen-year-old sister was pushing through the doorway, her bright purple mohawk sticking up at least six inches from her scalp.

"You changed the color," I said with a smile, walking over to pull her into a tight hug. I loved Heather. She looked so much like Mel, but where Mel always dressed super trendy, Heather made sure she stuck out in a crowd. Hence the purple mohawk that had been red the last time I'd seen it.

"Yeah, the roots were out of control," she said, hugging me back. "Now, where's my baby?"

"Sisterbeast!" Mel called as she came out of the bathroom.

"Gerta," Heather replied, calling Mel by the middle name she hated.

"We shouldn't be very late," I started, stuffing my phone into my pocket.

"Yes, we will," Mel cut in. "Very late."

"No worries." Heather shrugged. "I've got no place to be."

Just then, Rebel came out of her room, waddling down the hallway with a huge smile on her face.

"Reb!" Heather called excitedly, dropping to her knees. "You've got hair just like mine!"

Rebel giggled as she threw herself at Heather with all the force of her twenty-pound body. I'd used some of the colored hair goop that Heather bought her for her first birthday to spike up the top of her hair, so she looked like a little blue dinosaur.

"Just make sure you wash it out before she goes to bed, okay?" I said as they giggled together on the floor. "That stuff stains everything."

"No prob, mama," Heather said, flicking her hand at me in a shooing motion. "Get outta here."

"Fine," I grumbled, leaning over to kiss Rebel on the cheek. "Thanks, sisterbeast."

I followed Mel to the car and climbed in her passenger seat, immediately turning to her once I had my seatbelt on.

"Do not leave me in the bar again," I warned. "You can drop me off at home if Rocky decides to rock your world again."

"Look at you with the puns," Mel replied happily.

"I'm serious, Melanie."

"Yeah, yeah. Let's just see how it goes."

I huffed and fell back against the seat. I really didn't want to go out, and I was still irritated that she'd talked me into it. I hadn't actually left the house in yoga pants, though I'd considered it. Instead, I'd pulled on a pair of loose jeans and a t-shirt I'd gotten at the Down Syndrome Buddy Walk a couple years before. I was PMSing, I had a zit on my forehead, and I'd refused to put any makeup on in a lame attempt of protest.

As we pulled up to the same bar we'd gone to three weeks earlier, I wished I'd used at least a little foundation to cover the zit.

The place wasn't as packed as it had been before, but there was still a pretty big crowd of people playing pool and sitting at the tables around the room. After a quick look around, I deflated a little when I realized Will wasn't there.

Good. I didn't want to see him anyway.

"Come on," Mel said, grabbing my hand. "I'll grab our drinks, you grab that table in the back."

I made my way across the bar, wishing I'd gussied up a *little* as I passed a bunch of women who were obviously looking for a hook-up. Their hair and makeup were flawless and almost every one of them were wearing dresses.

I looked like a hobo in comparison.

Oh, well. I lifted my chin a little as I pulled out my phone and placed it on the table as I sat down. Hopefully, Mel would have a drink or two and we could leave. I glanced down at my shoes and felt my face heat as I pulled my feet under my chair. The checkered Vans I was wearing were at least ten years old, and I'd worn them out forgetting that Mel had filled in some of the white checks with Sharpie so it looked like I had a digital dick and balls on the toes of my shoes.

"Beer for you and beer for me," Mel announced as she sat down across from me. "See, isn't this fun?"

"We could've drank beer at my house," I replied flatly.

"Oh, come on. You're not going to be like this all night, are you?" she complained. "Bottoms up—once you have a couple drinks in you, you won't be in such a pissy mood."

"I'm not in a pissy mood," I bitched. I was in a completely pissy mood.

"How's work been going?" Mel asked, ignoring me. "And have you and your dad made up yet?"

"It's fine, and yes. He never stays mad for very long, and then he feels like shit about it."

"He should have," Mel grumbled. "It's not like you're some skank. He overreacted big time."

"I think he was just surprised," I said, taking a large sip of my beer. I'd only drank about half by then, but I could already feel the tension in my shoulders fading away. "He was used to Mase, ya know? He'd be completely freaked out if I started seeing someone now."

"Well, what does he think? That you'll just be single forever? That's ridiculous."

"I can't really see me dating anyone." I shook my head. "I like being by myself too much."

"Yeah, right. You just haven't found the right guy yet," Mel replied, making me wince. "Or maybe you have."

"Don't go there."

"What?" she asked innocently. "I'm just saying, you weren't all 'I'm going to be a lonely old spinster' after that night with Will."

"Yeah, and look how that turned out."

"You got smokin' hot sex the next day? Poor baby."

"Until he ran out of my house!"

"Maybe he had shit to do."

"I haven't talked to him in weeks, Mel. Drop it."

"Well," she said softly, glancing over my shoulder. "I have a feeling you'll talk to him pretty soon."

"I'm going to fucking kill you," I hissed, my entire body freezing in place.

"No, you won't. You'll be too busy—oh, hey, Rocky."

I sighed in disbelief as the handsome guy from that first night rounded our table and leaned down to kiss Mel lightly on the lips.

"I didn't know you'd be here already," he said quietly, smiling.

"We got here before the rush," Mel said with a shrug of her shoulders.

"You wanna come sit with us?" he asked, glancing at me before quickly looking back to Mel.

"No," I replied curtly.

I hated that I could feel Will watching me. I hated that I'd worn old baggy clothes to prove that I didn't care, and now I just felt stupid. And I hated even more that underneath the baggy clothes, I was wearing one of my only matching bra and panty sets—just in case.

"Molly," Mel scolded, looking at me in disbelief.

"Go ahead," I told her like a pouting five year old. "I'm going to stay here, though."

Rocky chuckled, glancing back over his shoulder at the group he'd come in with. If Mel left me to sit with him, I was going to walk my happy ass home.

"It's all good, girl," Rocky said to me, pulling out a chair. "I'll sit here."

"She's in a mood," Mel said tightly, glaring at me over her beer.

"Oh, fuck off," I murmured, picking up my phone like there was something super important I needed to check.

"Seriously," Mel continued. "She's not usually like this."

"I'm right here," I snapped, not looking up from my phone.

"I'm guessing my boy pissed her off," Rocky said, leaning back in his chair.

"He didn't piss me off," I mumbled.

"He didn't call, he didn't write . . ." Mel said dramatically, batting her eyelashes.

"Will you shut the hell up?"

Rocky laughed again, and I seriously considered throwing my phone at Melanie's head.

"Are we sitting over here?" another voice piped in, and I turned to see Homer sauntering over toward us. "Table's a little small."

"Looks like it," Rocky answered. He stood up from his seat and pulled Mel with him, sitting back down in her chair and pulling Mel onto his lap. "There—we've got more room."

I clenched my jaw as Homer took Rocky's seat, leaving the chair right next to me vacant.

"How you been?" Homer asked Melanie, like they were old friends.

My eyes narrowed.

"Good. Just working a shit ton."

My body tensed as a big hand grasped the chair beside me and pulled it out, and seconds later, Will dropped into the seat. I wanted to freaking scream.

Melanie had obviously been hanging out with these guys and she hadn't said a word. She'd made it seem like she was just hoping that she'd run into Rocky, but she must have known they'd be at the bar that night.

"Molly," Will greeted, leaning toward me.

I refused to look up from my phone. Instagram was hopping and I needed to check out everyone's photos. It was imperative I didn't miss a single one.

"Hey, Will," I greeted my phone.

"You pissed?"

"Why would I be pissed?" I asked, looking up. He was staring down at me, his entire torso turned in my direction, and he'd leaned an elbow on the table in an attempt to close us off from the others.

"Uh—"

"You're in my space," I told him flatly.

"You liked me in your spa—"

"Unless you want me to embarrass you in front of your friends, you'll back up," I warned, narrowing my eyes.

Instead of doing what I'd ordered, Will just smiled. "Not easily embarrassed," he murmured, lowering his face close to mine.

"I'm not into pegging, Will," I replied loudly. "Stop asking me to put things in your ass."

Will's head jerked back in surprise and his jaw dropped.

"Jesus Christ," Homer mumbled in disgust across the table.

"I'm out," I announced, pushing my way past Will's broad shoulders. "Anyone want another? No? Good."

My face burned as I stomped across the bar. I thought I'd embarrassed Will, but I'd completely embarrassed myself, too. Talk about cutting off my nose to spite my face.

I'd just reached the bar when all of a sudden, a large hand was gripping my arm tight and pulling me away.

"Knock it off." I jerked my arm back, but Will didn't let go, and soon he was dragging me away from the crowd and into the short hallway that led to the bathrooms.

"The fuck was that?" he asked, crowding me until I'd backed into the women's restroom.

"I told you to get out of my space!"

"Not gonna happen."

"Get away from me," I snapped, pushing at his chest.

"What the fuck is wrong with you?" He stepped back and closed the door behind him, turning the lock with a quiet snick.

"Maybe I'm just not interested," I said finally in exasperation.

"You're interested."

"Not anymore."

"Bullshit."

"Why the hell are you being such a dick?" I threw my hands in the air. "We fucked, big deal. I'm not your fucking girlfriend."

Oh, good move, Molly. Pretend like he's the one freaking out because you guys never made any promises. Turn it around. Deflect!

"That's what this is about?" he asked in disbelief. "Got your panties in a twist 'cause I didn't call you?"

"Oh, fuck off. I didn't even notice," I replied, crossing my arms over my chest.

"You noticed."

"Nope."

"Sugar, I was outta town," he said, taking a step forward. "Don't have your number."

"I don't care."

"Come on, Moll." He took another step closer. "Don't be like that."

"I'm not being like anything. We done here?"

Instead of answering, he moved even closer, blocking me in with his hands braced at my hips on the sink.

"You didn't miss me?" he asked, leaning over to press a gentle kiss on the space where my neck and shoulder met. "Not even a little?"

"No," I replied. However, I didn't move away as his lips ran up my neck.

"I missed you," he said, his lips brushing against my earlobe.

"I doubt you even thought of me."

"Hell, yeah, I did. Every time I jacked off, I thought about your cunt squeezing my dick. You think about me when you got yourself off?"

"Nope," I lied, swallowing hard as one of his hands slid under the side of my t-shirt.

"You still mad?"

"Yes."

"You wanna have an angry fuck?"

"You're such an asshole," I murmured as his hand slid to my belly.

"That's not an answer." He dropped to his knees in front of me and grabbed my hips, holding me in place.

I dropped my arms as he began to slip my t-shirt up my belly, then braced them behind me as I felt his lips against the skin there.

"You're so damn soft," he said quietly, his short beard scratching across my skin.

"Hey, I need to use the bathroom!" someone called from outside the locked door, following up with a series of knocks.

"Use the men's," Will yelled back, not taking his lips from my skin.

I heard them huff, then nothing, as Will continued to run his lips and tongue across my skin, moving higher and higher with each pass until my t-shirt was bunched above my breasts. Goose bumps covered my arms as Will gently bit the skin under my right breast.

"You wear this for me?" Will asked, staring at my bra as he got to his feet.

"No," I lied again. "I didn't even know you were going to be here."

His nostrils flared as his eyes finally met mine.

"That right?" he asked angrily.

I opened my mouth to reply, but snapped it shut again.

Why the hell was he pissed? He was the one who hadn't called! He'd taken off after getting off. Hit it and quit it. He didn't get to be pissed.

"I figured, I might as well be prepared for anything," I said with a shrug after a moment of tense silence.

"Good thing you came prepared," Will whispered, leaning down until his lips were just barely brushing mine. "So did I."

He reached down and pulled a condom out of his pocket, slamming it down on the sink.

My eyes widened as his meaning sunk in. "Fuck off!" I yelled, my voice trembling. It was one thing for me to insinuate I was looking for a hook-up, it was something completely different if he was. *I'd* been lying about it!

I pushed off the sink to storm past him, but before I could move, he'd spun me around and pinned my hips to the sink.

"Calm down," he growled, trying to catch the elbows that I was swinging back at him.

"You calm down," I screeched.

"Molly," he said again, his voice growing deeper. "Knock it the fuck off."

I threw my head backward in an effort to hit him.

"I brought the goddamn condoms for you, you crazy bitch," he hissed as he dodged me.

I froze, giddy that he'd come looking for me and pissed as hell that he'd called me a bitch.

"You did not," I argued quietly, meeting his eyes in the mirror for the first time.

"Mel told Rock she was bringin' you tonight. Why you think I'm here?"

"You were here before."

"That's 'cause Trix likes it here, and she barely gets outta the house, so we let her pick."

I didn't know what to say. I couldn't quite believe what he was saying, even though I really wanted to.

"I came for you," he said seriously, still holding my gaze in the mirror. He reached down and cupped between my thighs, jerking his hand up. "I came for this."

His words were both appalling and a bit of a turn on.

"Molly?" Mel yelled through the door. "You okay?"

"Tell her you're fine," Will said quietly.

"I can hear you, asshole!" Mel yelled. "Open the fucking door!"

I pressed back against Will, and he let me push away from the sink so I could let my best friend in.

"I came to find you and heard you yelling," Mel said flatly, glaring over my shoulder at Will.

"Told you she was fine, babe," Rocky said, reaching out to grab Mel's arm. "Leave 'em to it."

"Fuck off, Rocky," Mel replied, dodging him so she could grab my hand. "We're leaving."

"Bitch, you—"

"Call me bitch again," Mel hissed, turning toward him. "See what happens."

Will took advantage of the distraction, wrapping an arm around my waist from behind. "Don't leave," he whispered into my ear, fisting my t-shirt in his hand.

I shook my head. I knew if I stayed, I'd end up in bed with him, and the next day I'd feel like shit when he took off again. I didn't want to be the booty-call. I didn't want to become a party girl, going out to bars just on the chance he'd show up and give me attention. That wasn't me. That wasn't my life.

"Come with me to my parents' house for dinner tomorrow," Will said quietly while Mel and Rocky continued to argue. "I'll pick you and

Rebel up."

I opened my mouth to decline, but I didn't.

Because I really wanted to go with him. I wanted him to introduce me to his family. I wanted some type of normal relationship, and he was giving me a glimpse of that.

"What time?" I asked, relaxing a little against his chest.

"Five." I felt his lips against the side of my head.

"Let's go," Mel ordered, jerking my hand.

I didn't look behind me as she tugged me across the bar, but I felt Will's eyes on me until we walked out the door.

CHAPTER 6

WILL

I WAS NERVOUS. Shit, I hadn't been so nervous over a chick since Britney Miller taught me how to get a girl off during my sophomore year of high school.

Yeah, I started having sex at fourteen, but hadn't known what I was doing until two years later. Needless to say, those first two years I'd been lucky to get laid, but after that? They'd started begging for it.

I was in my mom's SUV on my way to Molly's to pick her and her kid up, and I was sweating so bad, I was pretty sure there were wet spots on the pits of my shirt. My parents would like Molly—I knew they would. And they were pretty fucking cool. It's not like they'd grill her or some shit like that.

But I was taking her home with me. To meet my family. And I'd only fucked her that one time.

I was making a commitment to a girl I'd only fucked once, one who had no fucking clue how to protect herself and didn't even realize she needed to.

I alternately wished she'd wise up and realize I'd lied to her the night before when I'd said I was out of town and hoped she'd never find out. I hadn't gone anywhere but the garage and my apartment, drinking myself to sleep so I wouldn't go over to her place again. Seeing her—bringing her into my life—was a fucking idiotic decision, but when Rock had mentioned meeting Mel at the bar, I'd given up on trying to stay away.

I wiped my hand over my face as I turned into Molly's trailer park.

When I pulled up in front of her place, I flexed my hands on the steering wheel before parking. My entire body was strung tight as a fucking wire.

I was just opening up my door when Molly came out of the house. She had a bag over her shoulder and the baby on her hip. Her head was tilted down like she was talking to Rebel, but she hadn't noticed me. After locking the door behind her, she started down the stairs off the porch, but froze on the last step as she finally saw me standing there.

"Oh," she mumbled, looking past me at my mom's car. "I didn't think you were coming."

"What?" God, she was pretty. She had her hair braided away from her face, and she was wearing a dress that hit right at her knees and was covered in flowers.

"I thought you'd changed your mind," she said softly, smiling a little as she shrugged her shoulders.

"What? Why?" I glanced at Rebel, who was pulling at her little purple glasses, and stepped forward just as she'd pulled them off her face. "No, no, baby girl," I reminded her softly. "You need those to see." I set them back on her nose, making sure the little arms were set above her ears.

"It's almost six o'clock, Will," Molly said, looking at me like she wasn't sure if she wanted to cry or smile. "You said you'd be here an hour ago."

My eyes widened. "Shit!" I reached out and pulled the bag off her shoulder, feeling like an asshole. "I musta had the time wrong last night, sugar. Come on, dinner's ready when we get there."

I turned and walked back toward the SUV, setting her bag inside.

"Uh, Will?" Molly called, laughter in her voice. "We need to move Reb's car seat over."

"Right," I muttered, rubbing the back of my neck. I was fucking this up. I walked back toward Molly's car and yanked open the back seat, only to realize that I had no fucking clue how to get the car seat out. The seat belt was lying there, obviously not in use, but the damn car seat wouldn't budge.

"Hey, William," Molly said right behind me.

"What?" I snapped, automatically apologizing.

"Here, take Reb," Molly ordered, pushing me out of the way before setting the little girl in my arms.

I froze as I pulled the baby to my chest, then exhaled loudly as Molly climbed halfway in the car, messing with the seat. Her dress had risen up a few inches in the back, and the loose fabric molded to her ass as she twisted and turned, trying to free Rebel's seat. My mouth began to water until I was brought back to the present by small fingers sifting through my beard.

"Hey, princess," I said softly as Rebel continued to pet my beard. "Whatcha doin?"

Rebel didn't answer, her brown eyes focused on her fingers and my face.

"Got it!" Molly announced as she pulled the seat from the car.

I carried the heavy seat over to my mom's rig and set it up for Molly so she could buckle it in again.

Goddamn, that view.

I almost forgot that I had Rebel sitting on my forearm when Molly contorted to fit her knee into the car seat as she tightened the little straps connecting it to the seat of the car.

"You have to put your weight on it to get it tight enough," Molly told me, her voice a little muffled.

"That's what she said," I replied automatically, wincing when she laughed and hit her head on the roof of the car.

A couple minutes later, we were headed to my mom and dad's while Rebel kicked her legs noisily in the back seat.

"We probably should've just taken my car," Molly said with a huff as she tried to straighten up her hair. "It's a pain in the ass to transfer that seat."

"We'll get one for this rig," I answered without thinking, making Molly freeze.

"I don't mind moving it—"

"I didn't mean—" We both spoke at the same time, but neither of us finished our sentences, leaving us in an awkward quiet.

"Thanks for inviting me," Molly finally said, reaching over to squeeze my arm where it rested on the middle console. "I haven't seen your mom in years."

"She's lookin' forward to it," I replied, clearing my throat.

I slid my arm off the console and wrapped my hand around her bare thigh, and just like that—my nerves were gone.

"Oh, my God," Molly said suddenly. "So last night, I put some blue hair putty shit in Reb's hair—"

"Why?"

"Because Mel's little sister was coming over and she has this long, purple mohawk—"

"Didn't know Mel had a sister."

"Would you let me finish?" Molly asked, laughing. "So last night I put it in, and I asked Mel's little sitter to wash it out before bed. But they accidentally fell asleep on the floor in the living room, and I didn't have the heart to wake Reb for a bath."

"Sweet mama," I said quietly, making her smile.

"So I gave her a bath when she woke up this morning—but her hair was still tinted blue!" Molly snickered again. "I had to wash her hair *again* to get the stuff out and she got blue crap all over her favorite blanket, which she was completely pissed about."

"Why didn't you just leave it?" I asked as I pulled into my parents' driveway.

"I couldn't bring her to your parents' house with blue hair," Molly said seriously, reaching to unbuckle her seatbelt.

"Moll," I called as she fidgeted with her dress. "Molly, look here."

She turned her head toward me, but she didn't meet my eyes.

"Look at me."

"What?" she asked, finally making eye contact.

"My parents wouldn't think twice if you brought your kid dressed in a monkey costume. They don't give a shit about stuff like that."

"Okay."

"Now, quit fidgetin'."

"I'm not."

"You are. Quit it."

"You don't get to say anything, you're not meeting my dad for the first time."

"Sugar, I know your dad."

"Exactly!"

"And you know my mom."

"When I was a kid," she said, drawing out the last word in annoyance.

Damn, she was cute. I grabbed her braid in my fist and pulled her lips to mine, sliding my tongue into her mouth as she opened it to protest. That was all it took for her body to relax, her shoulders dropping as her hand found the front of my shirt.

"Now, come on," I ordered, giving her one last kiss, because fuck, she tasted good. "Dinner's waitin' on us."

"I can't believe we were just making out in your mom's car," she grumbled as she hopped out of the car and moved toward Rebel's door.

"Five years ago, you wouldn't have cared," I teased, grabbing her bag as she unbuckled the baby.

"Five years ago, I wouldn't have been kissing you at all," she shot back, pulling Rebel to her chest.

I scowled at the thought of her with Mason.

"Well, you're mine now," I said roughly, setting my hand at the base of her spine to steer her up the walkway.

"I didn't agree to that." Her voice was light, but there was thread of warning in it that I ignored.

Because I'm a fucking idiot.

"You will," I promised as I used the hand holding her bag to open up the screen door, then held the heavy wood one so she could step inside.

"Sounds like Mom's in the kitchen," I said, walking toward the noise as Molly froze in the entryway.

"Should I take off my shoes?" she asked, glancing down at the lace-up boots she was wearing.

"Hell, no." I laughed, then realized that she was really fucking nervous. Not just slightly nervous, but ready to fucking bolt.

I walked back toward her, and caught her chin in my hand as she looked everywhere but at me.

"Just dinner, baby," I said softly, making her eyes finally meet mine. "Not a job interview."

"I'm not really good meeting new people," she whispered in embarrassment, her eyes drifting from mine again.

Jesus. I'd never in my life seen her act the way she was then, and I'd grown up with her. She'd always been quiet, but this level of shyness was way beyond what I remembered. Rebel laid her head down on her mom's shoulder, like she could sense something was wrong.

"They're gonna dig you," I promised, lifting both my hands to the sides of her face so she couldn't look away from me again. "And stop lookin' away from me when you're talkin' to me."

"I can't help it," she muttered in frustration.

"Next time you do it, I'm gonna reach out and pinch your nipple," I warned, making her eyes go wide. "Don't care where we are or what we're doin'."

"I don't do it on purpose!" she hissed.

"Bet you'll be more conscious of it now," I replied with a grin.

"Asshole," she whispered.

"Hey, when'd you get here?" My dad said from somewhere behind me, making Molly's body tense.

I ignored him and leaned forward, kissing Molly hard. I didn't slide my tongue in, figuring that would freak her out, but the kiss was still open-mouthed and wet. I felt Rebel's fingers in my beard near my ear, but I didn't stop kissing her mother until Molly had relaxed against me.

"William Butler Hawthorne," my mom called out just as I was pulling away. "I'd like to see Molly, too, you know."

I smiled and turned, grabbing Molly's hand as I towed her toward my mom.

"Jesus, you got pretty!" Mom said happily as she pulled Molly in for a hug. "I knew you would be with that long blonde hair."

"And I actually brush it now," Molly replied jokingly.

"You were so cute with those lopsided pigtails. I could've picked you out of a crowd—from the back."

Molly laughed quietly, but stepped back against me as my dad came closer, draping his arm over my mom's shoulders.

"Molly, this is my husband, Asa," Mom introduced them.

"Call me Grease," Dad said gruffly, lifting his hand to shake Molly's. Then he looked down to Rebel and smiled. "She's a sweetheart."

"This is Rebel," Molly said, leaning even harder against me. "Can you say hi, Reb?"

Rebel shook her head once, making me chuckle.

"That's alright," Dad said softly. "Get to know each other first, yeah?"

As he was talking to Rebel, I heard someone on the stairs and turned to see Lily and Rose sliding down the carpeted stairway on their asses.

"Hey, Rebel!" Rose called out as she stood up, unconsciously dropping her arm down to guide Lily toward us.

"Hey, girls," Molly called out. "Look, Rebel. Your friends are here."

Reb's head popped up and she started kicking her legs in excitement, pushing at Molly's chest with both hands.

"You can't get down yet, boo," Molly told her firmly, shifting Rebel in her arms.

"Dinner's on the table, should we head that way?" Mom asked, diverting Rebel's attention.

"Come on, baby," I said softly in Molly's ear as I pushed her forward to follow my parents toward the kitchen. "That wasn't so bad, right?"

"Your dad's huge," she whispered back over her shoulder.

"I'm not real small."

"But you're not scary."

"Depends on who you ask," I mumbled as we reached the kitchen.

Tommy was already sitting in his seat, doing something on his phone. Dad was forcing Mom to sit down while he grabbed drinks out of the fridge, and the little girls were messing with Lily's place settings—probably so she'd know exactly where everything was.

"Where'd this come from?" I asked Mom as I pulled out a seat for Molly next to a gray and blue high chair. I was glad as fuck that my mom had thought of it, because it hadn't even crossed my mind.

"Trix let me borrow it for tonight," Mom said happily.

"Thank you," Molly said, setting Rebel in the chair. "And thank Trix for me."

"I will."

"Molly, this is my brother, Tommy."

"Whoa—I remember when you were a baby," Molly said as she sat down in her chair. "It's good to see you again."

"Yep," Tommy replied dismissively.

I wanted to rip the little fucker's head off.

"Thomas Asa Hawthorne," my mom growled, snatching Tom's phone out of his hand.

"What's goin' on?" my dad asked as he came back from across the room.

"Your son just got grounded off his phone for the rest of the night," Mom said, taking her glass of water from Dad.

"Are you fuckin' kiddin' me?" Tommy blurted, eyes wide.

Dad reached down quickly, grabbing Tommy by the scruff of the neck. "You think you're big enough to take me on?" he asked menacingly, not even bothering to set the sodas in his other hand down.

"No," Tommy rasped, swallowing hard.

"Then I better never hear you talkin' to my wife like that again."

The little girls were still talking quietly to each other, but Rebel was completely motionless, staring at my dad with wide eyes. I glanced toward Molly and found her staring at her lap, where her fingers twisted nervously.

"It's all good, sugar," I said softly, reaching over to rub her back.

"I don't—" she looked over to me, but just as quickly looked at Rebel, who was kicking the footrest of the high chair hard while her entire body arched against the tray at her belly.

"Rebel," Molly called soothingly, shooting to her feet. "What's wrong?" She pulled Rebel out of the seat and the baby wrapped her arms around Molly's neck like a vice.

"I'm so sorry," Molly said sheepishly, glancing around the table. She tried to put Rebel back in her seat, but it wasn't happening, so she finally just sat back down next to me with Rebel on her lap.

She sat there trying to soothe Rebel as the rest of the table started dishing up their plates and Dad finished handing out drinks.

"Where you want it, Lily?" he asked quietly, waiting for Lily to point at an empty place on the table. "Alright. Straw's by your left elbow."

He handed me a couple of sodas, then finally sat down himself.

"You want mashed potatoes?" I asked Molly as they got to me.

"A little, please," she whispered back. "Do you know if your mom puts milk in them?"

"Uh." I looked down at the potatoes. How the fuck was I supposed to know? "Hey, Ma? You put milk in these?"

"What?"

"In the potatoes."

"Yeah—it's Gram's recipe."

Molly was glaring at me when I looked back down at her. Was I not supposed to ask?

"No potatoes for us, then," she said so quietly I almost couldn't hear her.

She took some steamed carrots and roast, thanking me for each one.

Jesus, the table was practically silent as we all dug in. The little girls giggled every once in a while, but none of the adults said a word as we ate. It was awkward as fuck, and I started sweating again.

"Reb, you want some carrots?" Molly asked, lifting a tiny piece of steamed carrot to Rebel's mouth. She opened it like a little baby bird and snatched up the carrot quickly, making me chuckle.

Molly kept feeding her tiny bites, and was still feeding her by the time I'd completely cleared my plate. I fucking loved my mom's pot roast. It was my favorite—probably the reason she'd made it.

"Baby, you gotta eat, too," I reminded Molly as she put another piece of meat in Reb's mouth.

"I'll just eat when she's done," Molly replied with a smile.

"Food's gonna be cold."

"It's okay, I'm used to it."

She was smiling about it—but it bugged the hell out of me.

"Here, I'll take her," I said, reaching for the baby.

I stuck my hands in her armpits and lifted.

"I don't know if she'll go to you," Molly warned as I pulled Rebel onto my lap.

"She's fine," I replied as Reb reached up and patted my beard. "Now eat."

"Reb still has to eat," Molly argued, lifting another bite to Rebel's mouth.

"I'll feed her. You eat." I took the fork off my plate and speared a carrot that Molly had already cut up, waiting for Rebel to finish chewing before I gave her another bite.

"See? Eat," I ordered.

"Will says you're a nurse, Molly?" my dad said, interrupting our conversation.

Molly's entire body tensed. "Yes, at the hospital."

"You like it?"

She nodded. "Yes, I do."

"Eat, baby," I reminded her softly, just as she was setting her fork down. She picked it back up, glancing at me then back to my dad.

"What kind of nursing do you do?" my mom asked. "I always thought it would be cool to work in the maternity ward."

"Labor and Delivery *is* fun," Molly answered, relaxing slightly. "I work all over the hospital, but I don't get up there very often."

"You were Will's—" Tommy started to say.

"Not discussing that tonight," my dad interrupted with a pointed glance at Rose and Lily.

"Molly's best friend is seein' Rocky," I told my parents, changing the subject. "You remember Melanie Connor, Mom?"

"Aw. Yeah, I do! She was full of piss and vinegar—reminded me of Farrah," Mom said with a smile.

"Good—maybe he'll finally divorce that woman," my dad said

casually, cutting into his pot roast.

"What?" Molly asked, glancing at me as she sat up straighter in her chair.

"Christ, Dad," I mumbled, shaking my head as I put another carrot in Rebel's mouth.

"What? Ain't a secret. Kid's been married since he was old enough to fuckin' shave."

"Rocky's married?" Molly hissed at me.

"Not our business," I warned.

"The hell it's not!"

"Molly—that's between them."

"She doesn't even know!"

"You sure about that?" I asked, making Molly's mouth snap shut.

She turned her head away and stiffly began to eat. My mom pulled her into conversation and they discussed all sorts of shit, but the entire time we sat there, Molly refused to look at me. It was blatant, and had Tommy watching me in amusement as I tried to get her attention.

"I'm going to go get the dessert," my mom announced after a while, hopping out of her chair. It only took her a second to grab the cake pan off the counter, and then she was back, cutting up my favorite pineapple upside down cake. Shit, she'd made my fucking birthday dinner—down to the cake. All we needed were some candles.

"Do you make that from scratch?" Molly asked my mom, a tentative smile on her face.

"Yep—this is my Gram's recipe, too," Mom answered proudly.

"Cool," Molly said with another smile. "I'm just going to go clean Rebel up. You guys eat without us."

"You don't want cake?" my dad asked, like Molly was insulting my mom.

"Um." Molly's face grew a little red as she glanced at me. "Rebel can't have milk."

"Will, why didn't you say something?" my mom scolded, snatching the cake back off the table.

Fuck. I felt like such an asshole, as Molly sat there red-faced. She was embarrassed and had tried not to make a big deal out of it, but my parents wouldn't let shit go.

"I didn't know," I said uncomfortably.

"That's okay, Will," Molly said softly.

"She allergic or something?" my dad asked, because he couldn't just fucking drop it.

"No, she has a skin condition—"

"Contagious?" Dad cut in.

"Jesus Christ," I spit out, getting to my feet. "Does it goddamn matter?"

Rebel jerked as I got to my feet, but wrapped her arms around my neck as soon as she got her bearings.

"Will," Molly called, embarrassed. "It's fine."

I looked down at her hand on my hip, then met her eyes. I was making it fucking worse.

"She has eczema," Molly told my dad, her fingers curling into my belt loop as I stayed on my feet. "It's not contagious. And she's not allergic to milk, but once I stopped giving it to her, the eczema stopped flaring up as much."

"She can't have any?" my mom asked. "Not even when it's cooked in? Or cheese?"

"I haven't tried." Molly shook her head. "It's been so nice not having her scratching at her skin until it bleeds that I haven't wanted to chance it."

"I can understand that," Mom said, nodding. "My son Mick was allergic to strawberries, of all things. We didn't even keep strawberry soda in the house." She chuckled.

"I'm gonna take her in to the living room," I said, leaning down to kiss Molly's forehead. "You have some cake."

"You don't have to do that," she argued, trying to stand up until I pressed my hand down on her shoulder.

"She's gonna send half a'that cake home with me."

"Why do you get half?"

"It's my favorite," I answered, leaning down to kiss her again. "And I'm *her* favorite."

I turned and carried Rebel out of the room as my brother and sister argued over who was my mother's favorite. I needed a few minutes to get my shit together after that clusterfuck.

Chapter 7

MOLLY

"Hey, Will," I called softly as he drove us home from his parents house that night. "Could you not leave me next time?"

The car jerked a little to the left at my words and Will quickly straightened it out before glancing over at me. "Leave you?"

"Yeah," I met his eyes then looked away, setting my hand down on his where it was resting on my thigh. "Just—you know—when you left me at the table."

"Rebel couldn't have the cake, right?"

"No, I know," I said in frustration. I hated feeling needy, because I wasn't. But after he'd left me alone with his family, I'd been unbearably uncomfortable. I didn't know them, and his dad was an asshole.

Mrs. Hawthorne had talked almost non-stop as she cut up the cake and served it, wrapping a huge slice of it for Will to take home, but the rest of the table had been noticeably silent. I'd barely taken two bites when it had become too much and I'd escaped to go find Will and Rebel.

I'd found them on the floor of the living room. Will had been flat on his back with his arms crossed behind his head, while Rebel had straddled his chest, poking at his face. He'd huffed every time she moved, like she was knocking the wind out of him, and she'd been giggling like he was the funniest thing she'd ever seen.

"I was just really uncomfortable," I said, lowering my voice to almost a whisper.

"That was only family," Will said incredulously. "What're you gonna do when it's an entire clubhouse full of people?"

"Not go," I replied half-jokingly. The other half of me was not joking in the least. I didn't want anything to do with his motorcycle club. I didn't know what they were into, but I knew it wasn't good. It was hard for me to imagine Will there.

"Sorry you were uncomfortable," Will replied gruffly. "Thought you'd found your footing before I left."

My skin prickled at his tone.

"Your dad threatened your brother before he'd even sat down at the table," I snapped.

"Tommy's a prick—you think it's okay for him to talk to my mother like that?" Will snapped as he turned down my street.

"Of course not!"

"So what's got your panties in a twist?"

"He threatened to beat up his teenage son!"

"No, he didn't."

"I heard him."

"You heard what you wanted to hear, Molly," Will said flatly, turning off the car and throwing his door open.

My nostrils flared as he shut the door behind him, cutting off our conversation. Oh, hell no. I threw open my door and scrambled out of the car.

"You think it's okay for him to treat his kids like that?" I asked incredulously as I rounded the hood. "Seriously?"

"You got any brothers?" Will asked, turning to face me as I reached him.

"You know I don't."

"Then you got no fuckin' idea what you're talking about."

"That's bullshit!"

"What's bullshit is you goin' over to my parents' house so full of yourself that you fuckin' pick them apart before we even sit down to dinner."

"I didn't do that!"

"Right," Will scoffed, reaching up to scratch at his beard as he shook his head.

"Your dad is *scary*, Will."

"Scary?" he asked through clenched teeth. "Yeah, okay."

"He is."

"Agreed."

"Then why the hell are you mad at me?"

"Because you're makin' him out to be this goddamn monster when you don't know what the hell you're talkin' about and it's irritating as fuck!"

"He threat—"

"Yeah, I heard you the fuckin' first time," Will said, cutting me off. "You don't know them. You don't know shit. You've never seen Tommy lose his shit—and I hope like fuck you never do. That kid is angry, Molly. He goes off the fuckin' rails."

"So get him some help!" I blurted. Will's explanations were fucking ridiculous. I didn't understand why he wasn't seeing what I was seeing. Were they all so dysfunctional that this shit was normal?

"You think they haven't tried?" Will asked, taking a step toward me. "You think they haven't done everything they can? My dad would die for Tommy—for any of his kids. But Tommy's practically an adult and he doesn't want to talk to some shrink—"

"I'm sure calling them shrinks is really fucking helpful."

"—but he knows that my dad won't let him lose it. All it took tonight was a couple of words, and Tommy knew what the fuck he'd done. He knocked that shit off, and you obviously didn't notice him apologizing to my mom two seconds later."

I stared at him in confusion. How the hell did we even get to that point of the conversation?

"Boys are different than girls, Molly," Will said, trying to get his temper under control. "Especially teenage boys that have testosterone makin' them nuts. Tommy is ten times worse because he's dealin' with PTSD and fuck knows what else."

"I was uncomfortable when you left me with people I didn't know," I replied stiffly, trying to bring the conversation back to its original intent.

"You have boys with me," Will said softly, still not letting it go, "I'm not gonna let them talk to you with disrespect. Not ever."

"That won't happen," I mumbled as Will pressed me up against the driver's door.

"What?" His big hand wrapped around the front of my jaw and tilted my face up until we were eye to eye.

"Why are we fighting?" I asked, searching his face.

"Sugar, you were ignorin' shit tonight."

"No, I wasn't."

"Yeah, Moll, you were. So set on seein' shit one way—you didn't even notice the rest of it."

"Not true," I whispered as he leaned down closer to me.

"You see him making sure my ma sat down? Gettin' up to get the drinks so she'd get off her feet?" He waited until I nodded before continuing. "Made sure Lil had everything she needed where she could reach it. Called your baby a sweetheart. That's my dad, babe. He's scary, yeah. But he's a softy when it comes to family."

"He freaks me out," I muttered as Will brushed his lips against my cheek.

"You think I'm any different?" he asked against my jaw.

"I know you are."

"No, you don't. You see me when I'm with you," he replied with a chuckle, sucking at the skin of my throat.

I slid my hand to the back of his neck, swallowing hard as I tangled my fingers in the hair there and pulled his head back.

"What don't I see?" I asked as he inhaled sharply through his nose.

"That I'm just as scary," he growled, jerking his head forward and biting playfully at my neck.

My body relaxed in increments as I giggled, and before he was done, I was wrapped around him and pinned against the side of the car.

"We better get sleepin' beauty inside," Will finally said, biting my earlobe.

"Okay," I said as he set me on my feet. "Are you coming in?"

He looked at me like I was nuts.

Rebel had fallen asleep as soon as I'd buckled her into her seat, and she stayed that way through the entire ride home, being carried into the house, and as I changed her diaper before putting her into her crib. I pulled her blanket up to her shoulder and leaned heavily against the side of her crib as I watched her sleep.

Will was waiting for me somewhere in the house, but I needed a few minutes to myself. I needed to breathe.

I really liked Will. He made me feel good, happy. But he also made me feel crazy. When I was with him, I no longer recognized my quiet life. The one I'd been living since Rebel was born and everything had changed.

I liked my job. I liked watching cartoons with Reb, and playing with her little molding clay set, and waking up late on my days off and then spending the entire day in my pajamas because we didn't have anywhere to be. I liked it quiet, and with Will life was anything but.

It felt like we fought all the time about stupid shit. We didn't agree on anything, and both of us got angry with the other at the slightest thing.

What was I doing?

"She still sleeping?" the man I'd been thinking about said softly from the door of Rebel's room.

"Yeah, I just wanted a minute," I answered, still looking at Rebel and softly rubbing her back.

"Take your time, beautiful," he said, tapping the doorframe softly. "I'll wait."

He walked away and I sighed, only waiting a minute before following him out and shutting Rebel's door quietly behind me.

"What're you doing?" I asked when I found him in the kitchen, bent over the counter with his back to me.

He jerked in surprise, then lifted a hand to brush it across his mouth as he turned to face me.

"Thought you'd be a minute," he said, chuckling in embarrassment.

My stomach clenched as he brushed at his mouth some more. I walked slowly into the kitchen and looked behind him, my heart thundering for a reason I couldn't pinpoint.

"Cake?" I asked in surprise as I caught sight of the unwrapped tinfoil.

"It's my favorite and I didn't get any," he said quickly, turning his body toward the counter. "I'll make sure it's all gone before she wakes up."

God, why couldn't he make any sense? Sometimes I looked at him, and he seemed like a stranger—intimidating and unbreakable. Then he'd turn to me and quickly try to explain why he was eating cake—like a little boy who'd just gotten caught.

"Can I have a bite?" I asked, wrapping my arms around his waist.

"Well," he hesitated.

"Are you serious?"

"No," he said, his lips quirking. "But pineapple upside down cake is serious business," he whispered. "You have to pay attention."

"Why's that?"

"'Cause you have to have the right ratio of cake to pineapple," he said, using a fork to cut through the cake that he'd already put a huge dent in. "You have to have some pineapple in every bite."

"What happens if you don't?" I asked with a smile as he lifted a bite to my mouth.

"Then the entire cake is ruined." His voice went husky as I pulled the cake off the fork with my teeth.

"Yum, that's really good," I mumbled, covering my mouth with my hand.

"She makes chocolate and cherry upside down cake, too. That one can be your favorite," Will informed me as he scooped a bite much larger than he'd given me into his mouth.

"Maybe pineapple is my favorite," I argued as he fed me another bite.

"Can't be."

"Why?"

"'Cause it's my favorite."

"So?"

"So if it's your favorite, I'll have to share." He stuffed another large bite in his mouth. "That's not gonna work for me," he mumbled around the bite.

I mock glared, then before he could stop me, leaned down and licked the top of his cake, smiling in triumph as his jaw dropped.

"Sugar," he scolded, shaking his head. "I've had my tongue all over you—you think your spit bothers me?"

Then he proceeded to put the rest of the cake in his mouth, his cheeks filling as he struggled to chew it. He turned and put his fork in the sink, then rolled up the rest of the foil and tossed it in the garbage.

"You're still going to pay for that," he warned, his glare completely ruined by the crumbs stuck in his beard.

"You've got a little something," I gestured to my own face, trying to hold back a laugh.

"You want some?" he asked, smiling widely as he lunged for me, laughing as I tried to run. "Come on, you wanted more, right? I was savin' some for you!"

I gasped and giggled as he chased me into the living room, tackling me onto the couch. Squirming, I tried to throw him off me, but Will was built like a tank. He was solid muscle, and muscle was *heavy*.

"Ew!" I screeched as he pinned me down, straddling my waist as he leaned down until his beard was rubbing against my mouth and chin. "It's gone! It's gone!" I laughed until my stomach hurt, but he continued to rub his beard all over my face.

"You gonna lick my cake again?" he asked, breathless.

I screwed my mouth up to the side as his brows furrowed. "Is that a euphemism?" I asked seriously.

Will threw his head back and laughed loudly, shaking the entire couch.

"Moll, you can lick that cake whenever you want," he said, leaning back to reach down and grip the erection trapped behind his jeans. "You want some now?"

I burst out laughing as he grinned, falling back over me. "I got some cake for you," he mumbled, pressing his lips to mine. "Fuck, I dig you, woman."

His tongue slid into my mouth, and all laughter left us as I reached up to grip the back of his head. He was still braced up on his knees, our bodies barely touching, but I felt that kiss everywhere.

"Come on," he ordered, pulling away from my mouth. He climbed off the couch and pulled me with him, grabbing my ass as he ushered me down the hallway to my room. By the time we got through my bedroom doorway, there was no space between us. Will's hands had travelled both north and south, with one hand gripping my breast and the other up the front of my skirt.

"Will," I moaned as his fingers pressed against the front of my underwear.

"Hands on the wall," he said roughly.

The hand on my breast fell away and I arched in response, my ass pressing against his thighs. Our height difference was really fucking annoying sometimes. I felt his hand brush my lower back as I braced my hands against the wall, then his fingers were at the back of my neck, sliding the zipper of my dress down.

"You looked gorgeous today," he said quietly as his lips landed against the skin between my shoulder blades. "All dressed up."

"Hurry," I replied, reaching down between my legs to press his hand harder against me.

He chuckled against my back, then jerked his hand from between my legs, making me huff in frustration. I opened my mouth to complain, but closed it again when my dress was pushed off my shoulders. I lowered my arms and let it slide to the floor, and when Will unclipped my bra, I let that fall, too. I dropped a hand to push at my panties, but he slapped it away and pulled those off himself.

Putting my hand back on the wall, I looked over my shoulder to find Will pulling his shirt over his head. His jeans were already undone, his dick out and covered in a condom.

"Been thinkin' all night about throwin' that dress up and fucking you," he explained, kicking off his boots and jeans. "But when it came down to it, I wanted to see all that pretty pale skin."

"I'm not that pale," I argued, dropping my head forward as he stepped in close.

"You are compared to me," he said, pushing my braid over my shoulder so he could kiss the back of my neck.

He dropped to his knees and I froze, then awkwardly shuffled my feet wider as he pressed against my inner thighs with his hands. It was a weird position, his face almost pressed against my ass. I didn't consider myself a prude, but I'd never had—*oh, holy hell.*

He grabbed one hip and used the other hand to press against my lower back until I was arched, my ass high in the air.

Then his mouth descended and my mind went blank. I didn't care how I was positioned, how I looked, what noises I might be making. The only thing I cared about was the mouth between my legs, licking and sucking at my skin.

I came like that, my legs shaking so badly that Will kept a hold of me as he stood back up.

He spun me around and kissed me hard, his hands on each side of my jaw like he was afraid I'd turn my head away.

I stumbled as he pulled me away from the wall, but he didn't go far. He fell to the edge of my bed, and tore his mouth from mine, our harsh breathing the only sound in the room.

Groaning, Will planted his face between my breasts, his hands lifting them as he took one and then the other into his mouth, sucking hard then biting my nipples.

My hands were frantic, running over every part of him I could reach. They slid over his shoulders and biceps, down the groove of his spine and back up the thick muscles on either side. His skin was smooth except for random scars I found with my fingertips.

"Turn around," he ordered, twisting my hips until his face was once again pressing against my back.

He pulled me down, pausing for only a second to situate my legs on either side of his before I felt him, pressing insistently until he slid inside me. My skin broke out in goose bumps and I shivered as he pushed harder, my body stretching until my ass was pressed tightly against his groin.

Bracing my hands on his knees, I let my head drop forward as I sucked in a lungful of air. Sex wasn't supposed to be that good. It wasn't supposed to be so addictive that you were willing to do anything to get it—but that's what it felt like then. I couldn't imagine him anywhere else but inside me, and I couldn't imagine a day when I'd ever turn him away.

I rolled my hips, my thighs burning.

"Not this time," Will rasped, his hands leaving my waist to slide down my hips and over my thighs. "Fuckin' bounce, Molly."

One finger hit my clit, circling softly as I followed his instructions and raised my body, dropping back down hard. I did it again and again, and each time, his dick slid over a spot that had my eyes watering. The pressure was insane, almost too much, but I couldn't stop—even when my legs felt like they were going to give out.

My hair grew damp with sweat as Will murmured filthy things in my ear, urging me to keep going, telling me how good I felt.

My legs were on fire and I was ready to scream in frustration, when suddenly Will was pushing my body up and twisting us toward the bed. I landed face down on the mattress with my feet still braced on the floor, and without pausing, Will snapped his hips forward.

"Oh, shit," I groaned, using one hand to brace myself against the bed as I reached out with the other to grab his thigh. It was slick with sweat, the muscles there bunching as he thrust.

I was so close to orgasm, I was holding my breath. Within a minute, I was gasping and holding back a scream as it washed over me. I felt it from my scalp to my toes, and for a few seconds, it was almost painful.

"Jesus Christ," Will groaned in pleasure as he continued to thrust. "You fuckin' soaked me."

He pulled out abruptly, and I could hear him snap off the condom as he dropped to his knees and pressed his tongue to my overly sensitive flesh. The quiet sounds of his fist sliding over his dick filled the room as I mewed quietly against my comforter, too exhausted to even try to move as his tongue swept over me softly.

He came with a curse against my skin and I grinned.

He sounded as wrecked as I felt.

"I just came all over my hand," he grumbled, making me giggle deliriously. "Be right back."

I crawled up the bed as soon as he'd left the room and flopped down against my pillow, my eyelids heavy.

What was I doing?

Could I really ignore the problems that were staring me in the face? I liked Will, but sometimes his comments made me wonder if I even really knew him. His dad was . . . ugh. I really didn't like that guy. Sure, he'd been sweet to his wife, but that didn't really mean anything, did it? There was still something about him that set me on edge, something just below the surface that I couldn't quite pinpoint.

I knew he was part of the Aces and Eights Motorcycle Club, and that he worked at their garage as a mechanic, just like Will. But what else did he do? Did he drag Will into their illegal stuff? My stomach rolled at the thought.

"Here, sugar," Will said softly as he came back into my room. "Let me clean you up."

He sat on the edge of the bed and parted my legs, using a warm washcloth to wipe gently at my thighs and pussy. Then he was gone again, taking the washcloth back into the bathroom.

Will turned off the light and cracked open my bedroom door as he came back in the room, then crawled into bed beside me.

"Okay?" he asked, pulling me into his side.

"Okay," I whispered back as he kissed my forehead.

All doubts left me as he tucked the comforter around my bare shoulder, making sure none of the cool air could seep in around it.

Chapter 8

WILL

"I FUCK UP your luck with that girl?" my dad asked a week after Molly, Rebel and I'd had dinner at his house.

"Her name's Molly," I mumbled, following him in to the room behind the bar where the club held meetings. I wasn't sure what was happening, but they'd woken me up at the ass crack of dawn and forced me out of Molly's bed on her day off, so I wasn't real excited about it.

Rebel had been waking Molly up like four times a night for the past week—for no reason. Her little ass would just wake up, bang on the side of her crib with her feet, and then fall back asleep after Molly sang to her. It was cute the first night, but after that, Molly had started looking more and more worn down every day. She was falling asleep most nights as soon as Reb did, and was barely able to get up for work the next morning.

"She didn't seem to like me much," Dad said with a chuckle.

"She's fine," I replied dismissively, grabbing my chair and settling in.

"You still seeing the suit's daughter?" our president, Dragon, asked as he came in the room behind us. "Not gonna end well."

"Not gonna end at all," I shot back.

"We'll see."

I ground my teeth together and dug my fingers into my eye sockets. My eyes were fucking burning. I'd been spending my nights with Molly, which meant I'd been waking up every time she did—and it was catching up to me. It was probably time I slept in my own bed so I could get a solid night's sleep, but even the thought of it made me feel like an asshole. It wasn't like Reb would stay asleep if I wasn't there. I'd be sleeping good while Molly was still waking up all night—that didn't work for me.

As soon as everyone had found their places at the table, Dragon sat back in his chair and glanced around the room.

"Russians have been making some noise," he announced, making the rest of us sit up straighter in our chairs. "Nothin' definitive yet."

"This about Rocky?"

"Of-fuckin'-course it is."

"Jesus Christ."

"Only good Russian is a dead one."

Dragon raised his hand and the table grew silent.

"The suit's been talkin' with the DA in Boise, and they're pretty sure that they can cut Rock a deal if he rolls on the Russians."

"Oh, fuck no," Cam said from across the table. "We don't rat."

"He's not gonna talk, not about club business," Dragon replied, leaning forward. "But Rock's married to one of their daughters . . ."

About six months before, Rocky had gone to a meet with some Russians who were interested in creating a partnership with the Aces—our contacts for a cut of their sales. At first, we'd thought it was bullshit, so we'd sent in Rock, who already knew the assholes, to get the lay of the land.

It wasn't real clear what had gone down, but Rock had ended up surrounded by DEA and FBI. They'd been watching the Russians for a while and had been under the impression that they'd finally hit pay dirt when an Ace rolled up.

Thankfully, Rock had had a reason for being there. One of the guys they'd sent to meet him was his wife's cousin. Didn't matter if he hadn't seen the bitch in over a year—the excuse still worked.

It all went to shit, though, when they searched Rock's bike and found a good amount of weed and the parts to an unregistered AK. The crazy fucker could build the thing in less than a minute, so he always carted it around.

Brothers went down all the fucking time for different shit. We got caught up for parole violations, possession, gun charges—you name it, they picked us up for it. And most times, we kept our mouths shut and did the time.

But Rocky had been picked up in Idaho, where he was from. Where he'd grown up. And in Idaho, the skinheads had it out for Rock because of some shit that had gone down when he was locked up the first time. He'd had the backing of the Russians that time—but that was gone since he'd aligned himself with us. We had no connections in the Idaho state pen, no way to protect him from the fuckers. If Rock went in, he wasn't coming out.

"So, what?" I asked, meeting Dragon's eyes. "What's he gotta give them?"

"Just names," Dragon answered.

"The fuck?" Cam asked.

"People at his wedding." Dragon smiled. "That's all they want."

A knock at the door had us all turning that way, then Rocky was poking his head in.

"Come on in, Rock," my dad called out. "Talkin' about you, anyway."

Rocky slid in the door and closed it behind him, leaning against the wall since he didn't rank a seat at the table. I wondered how long that would last. Rocky was a good guy, I'd trust him at my back any day.

"You had to fuckin' marry a Russian," old Samson called from down the table, shaking his head as Rocky smirked.

"First girl to let me fuck her ass," Rocky called out. "Thought it was love."

The table roared with laughter.

"You good with givin' 'em names?" Dragon asked, cutting through the laughter.

"It's that or I'm a dead man," Rock replied quietly.

"You know why they want to know who was at your wedding?"

"Got a good idea."

Dragon stared at him for a minute, then nodded his head once. "Start walkin' down memory lane, Rock. You've got some time to get that shit sent over—but not a lot of it. Don't talk to anyone but Duncan—he's your contact. Anyone from the DEA tries to chat you up, walk the fuck away."

"Will do," Rocky murmured, lifting his chin at the men around the table before turning toward the door and letting himself out.

"Not gonna end well," my dad said after the door had closed.

"We'll make it end well," Dragon answered, something passing between him and my dad as they made eye contact.

"Now that that shit's over, I wanna know about Moose's new woman," Cam joked, lightening the mood at the table.

"Shut the fuck up." I flipped him off as he grinned.

"She's cute—timid as a rabbit, though," my dad said with a smile, relaxing into his chair.

"Not up for discussion," I ground out.

"If she lets you fuck her ass, that doesn't mean it's love," Samson called, making the boys chuckle.

"No way in hell is my boy getting that," my dad choked out, laughing his ass off. "That girl is sweet as sugar."

The muscles in my arms and back locked as I tried to calm my shit. They were just messing with me. They always fucking messed with me. If I let on that it bothered me, it would make them worse.

"I don't know, man," Cam said, laughing. "Homer said she seemed up for anything—"

"Enough," I roared, flying out of my seat. My skin felt too tight for my body. I wanted to hop over the table and beat the words out of Cam's mouth.

"Calm down, son," my dad growled.

"You let some fuck talk about Mom like that?" I asked, knowing the answer.

"Just givin' you shit, Moose," Dragon said calmly, looking bored with the whole thing.

His words made me even angrier. I fucking hated when they acted like I was a kid. Like I overreacted to shit. Yeah, I'd fucked up before, screwing around with steroids that made me fucking crazy. Everyone knew it. But that didn't mean that I wasn't a brother just like the rest of them. I'd paid my dues for my fuckups. I pulled my goddamn weight. I took the fall when I had to, did the runs no one wanted, and I was a fucking genius of a mechanic.

"We done?" I asked, refusing to sit back down.

Dragon stared at me for a full minute, probably to remind me who the fuck was in charge, then lifted his hand and slammed the gavel down.

I was out the door before anyone else had even risen from the table.

"Moose, man, wait up," Cam called behind me as I stormed completely out of the clubhouse. "We were just givin' you shit."

They were. I knew that. It still made my skin crawl.

"Fuck man, we've fucked with you worse than that before."

"If someone said that shit about Trix, you'd lose it," I pointed out, coming to a stop.

"Different and you know it," Cam mumbled.

"Not really."

"You that far gone?"

"Pretty much." I gripped the back of my neck in frustration.

Things were fine with Molly. Good. But the woman had fucking blinders on, and I knew the moment they came off, I was going to be in a whole heap of shit. After she'd freaked out about my dad, I was dreading the day I that had to pull her farther in to the life. And it would happen. At some point, we'd be at that place where she needed to know shit, and the minute she did, she was going to bail and I wouldn't be able to protect her.

I knew it, yet that didn't keep me from stopping by her house every fucking night.

"Make the announcement, then," Cam said, getting my attention again. "Bring her around."

"Won't work," I replied, shaking my head.

"Boys'll lay off, man. You know they will."

"Molly's fuckin' clueless," I informed him, watching his face drop in shock. "Her dad must've fuckin' sheltered her from shit, because she's got no fuckin' clue."

"Duncan's kid? Seriously?"

"She's afraid of my dad. Thinks I'm different."

Cam laughed incredulously. "You need to work that shit out."

"I know that."

"Cut her loose," Cam said seriously. "Will, she's that fuckin' clueless, she could cause major fuckin' problems."

"Fuck that." I walked toward my bike and pulled my helmet off the gas tank.

"Women like that," Cam called out, shaking his head. "They don't keep their mouths shut."

"I'm not tellin' her shit."

"Doesn't matter," Cam said in frustration as I climbed on my bike. "She'll know shit anyway."

I didn't reply as I fired up my bike. Molly didn't know anything. Most old ladies didn't know much, but Molly knew close to nothing. She saw my cut, knew I was an Ace, but that was the extent of it. She didn't want to hear about the club, had no interest in going anywhere near it.

I pulled out of the gates and headed for Molly's place without conscious thought. I'd barely been home since we started hanging out again. I mostly just stopped by to grab clean clothes and make sure no one had broken in. It wasn't in the best part of town, but the neighbors were pretty cool. They stayed out of my business as long as I stayed out of theirs.

Shit, I wasn't sure what the fuck to do about Molly. I wanted her badly, and there was something about her that just kept me coming back for more. She wasn't someone I'd normally go for, wasn't classically beautiful or built. She didn't show off her body.

But fuck, when I got her naked, it was like every holiday rolled into one, and when we were fully dressed and just hanging out, she made me laugh. She was so goddamn sweet. She took good care of her kid and never lost her patience, at least with Rebel. Even when we were arguing, I wanted her.

I knocked on her front door and waited less than a minute for her to unlock it and let me in.

"I thought you had to work," she said in embarrassment, smoothing back her messy hair as I went inside.

She was wearing an ugly set of flannel pajamas that had reindeer all over them, and a pair of thick, fuzzy socks. Rebel came waddling over as I began to smile, and I laughed a little. The baby was in nothing but a t-shirt and a diaper, but she had a pair of Molly's socks pulled all the way up her thighs and a stocking cap pulled down almost covering her eyes.

"Did I interrupt?" I asked, looking back at Molly as Reb came closer and raised her arms so I would pick her up.

"It's a lazy day," Molly answered, crossing her arms over her chest before laughing and dropping them back down. "God, you *had* to show up today, didn't you?"

"Didn't want to miss the lazy day." I leaned down, still smiling, and kissed her.

"You didn't know it was lazy day," Molly replied against my mouth.

"What do you do on lazy day?" I asked as I pulled back.

"We watch TV," Molly answered, turning to walk farther into the living room. "And we cuddle up in the blankets and lay around."

"Reb lays around?"

"Well, she doesn't really appreciate lazy day," she said seriously. "But she plays in here and lets me be lazy."

I looked around the room and scoffed. The comforter and a pillow from Molly's bed were bunched up on the couch, a mug of something was on the corner of the coffee table, and toys were spread out all over the room. There was Play-Doh on the table, stuffed animals lined up in front of the TV, the pieces of some sort of board game tucked into the windowsill. Shit was everywhere.

"You made a mess," I told Reb, fixing her crooked glasses. She nodded in reply, her little face serious.

"It's okay," Molly said, climbing back into her nest of blankets on the couch. "It's lazy day—I'll clean it all up later."

See? That shit right there. It fucking got to me. She didn't give a shit that her kid was tearing apart the house. As long as she was having fun and wasn't getting hurt, Molly was totally relaxed.

"Let's clean up a bit, yeah?" I said softly to Rebel, setting her down on the floor and getting down on my knees so we were at the same level.

"Can you help me put the Play-Doh back in the containers?" I asked, reaching for the clay. "Where's the blue container?"

"You don't have to do that," Molly said, pushing her blankets off her lap.

"Lay back down, sugar," I ordered, making her scrunch her nose at me. "We got this—no, that's orange, baby girl."

I helped Rebel find the blue container and we cleaned up most of the mess on the table. That shit was irritating as fuck, because the minute you stuck two colors together, there was no separating it again. Most of Rebel's Play-Doh was a mix of colors that we ended up just stuffing into any container we found.

I threw Reb's stuffed animals into a laundry basket, then wiped down the table and put the Play-Doh on top of Molly's fridge. I didn't want to deal with that shit again. When I went back into the living room, Rebel was curled up on Molly's lap, and the only part of her visible was her little face.

"Room for me?" I asked as Molly put some kids movie on the TV.

"Come on in," she said with a grin, lifting one side of the blankets.

I shrugged off my cut, laying it over a chair, then kicked off my boots before sitting down next to her. Rebel's little knee dug into my groin as she crawled into my lap, and I huffed out a laugh at the scowl on Molly's face.

"Women can't resist me," I told her, laughing harder when she elbowed me in the side.

We sat there quietly for a few minutes watching the opening credits of the cartoon, but before anything exciting happened on the TV, Rebel was sliding sideways off my lap. She'd fallen asleep sitting straight up. I caught her before she went far, and scooped her up in my arm like a newborn, her little feet dangling as I pulled her glasses off and set them on the table. When I turned to check if Molly had seen that Reb was asleep, I found her the same way, her head resting on the back of the couch.

The lack of sleep was catching up to both of them.

I carried Rebel into her room and lay her gently in her bed, pulling her blanket up around her shoulders. I didn't want her to be cold since she wasn't wearing any pants, but I didn't see any other blankets in her room, so I grabbed a clean towel off the top of her dresser and laid that on top of her blanket.

When I was sure she wasn't going to wake up, I left the room, feeling pretty fucking proud of myself that I'd put the baby down for a nap. Well, I guessed she was technically a toddler, right? Didn't matter. She still seemed like a baby to me. Normally, Molly dealt with anything to do with Rebel. She did all the diapers and getting her things to eat, and getting out of bed at night when Reb woke up.

It made sense. She was Rebel's mom, and I was just a guy that was hanging around. But it still made me feel like an asshole when we both woke up at night and only Molly got out of bed to get Rebel back to sleep. The kid wasn't mine—but it felt wrong to not help out.

"Where's Reb?" Molly asked blearily as I sat back down next to her on the couch.

"She fell asleep," I replied as I pulled her against my side. "I put her in the crib."

"Okay," she mumbled against my ribs. "I'm so fucking tired."

Her breathing slowed as her body leaned more heavily into mine. God, she was cute as hell. Her hair was a rat's nest, and she hadn't even tried to straighten it up while I was helping Rebel clean up her mess. She'd just left it that way, like she couldn't be bothered to fix it. I pulled her body up and stretched out, situating Molly between me and the back of the couch. I pulled off her glasses and leaning over as far as I could without waking her up, I dropped them on the coffee table and snagged the remote to turn the volume up a little so I could finish watching the movie.

At some point, I must have fallen asleep, because I woke up later to Molly scrambling off the couch and Rebel yelling in her room.

"I thought she didn't—" the rest of my words were muffled under Molly's hand as her eyes filled up with tears.

"Just let me listen," she whispered, going completely still with her hand covering my mouth.

"Mama!" Rebel yelled loudly. "Mama!"

It wasn't the babble that we usually heard, and she wasn't just talking to herself. Rebel was actually calling for Molly by name.

Molly's lips trembled and she gave a little laugh, lifting her hand off my face.

"I waited a long time for that," she said softly. Then she practically skipped down the hallway to Rebel's room.

I sat up and scrubbed my hands down my face. She *had* waited a long time. Rebel was almost two, she was walking and getting into shit on a daily basis, but she hadn't said her first word until five minutes earlier. It was a big deal.

My chest felt tight as I rolled up Molly's comforter and set it on top of her pillow. I'd heard the baby girl's first word. And she hadn't been messing around, either—you could tell by her tone that she was pissed. She'd probably been in there awake for a while, but we hadn't heard her pounding on the side of the crib because the baby monitor was in Molly's room across the house. I grinned.

I wanted to tell someone. I wanted to tell everyone.

"Look who's awake," Molly said brightly as she carried Rebel into the room wrapped in the towel I'd tucked her in with. "And she's got a new blankie."

"She didn't seem warm enough," I mumbled, coughing a little. "I wasn't sure where the extra blankets were."

"So you used a towel?" Molly teased, reaching down to get Reb's glasses off the table.

"Worked, didn't it?" I smiled smugly when Reb reached for me, almost falling from Molly's arms before I caught her.

"Who's that, Rebel?" I asked, pointing to Molly as Reb leaned her head against my chest.

"Mama." She said it like she'd always been saying it, like it wasn't a new thing she'd picked up. Like Molly wasn't watching her in wonder.

"What's my name?" I asked.

Nothing.

Molly laughed. "Nice try."

"Can't fault a man for trying," I joked.

I rubbed Rebel's back as she sat quietly in my lap. She felt good there, her little body completely relaxed against mine. Her hair was curly and matted in the back where she'd rubbed it against her sheets, and she was still wearing Molly's socks pulled up past her knees. She barely weighed anything.

Molly grabbed her pillow and comforter and carried them into her bedroom. Between the nap and Rebel's first word, she was practically dancing.

"Are you hungry?" she asked as she came back in the room.

"How about I take you out?"

"Out?"

"A restaurant? You know, where they cook your food and clean up after you," I replied as Rebel sat up and started climbing off my lap.

"I have to get dressed," Molly hedged.

"You should probably at least put a bra on."

"I didn't think you noticed."

"Sugar, I always notice your tits."

"You're going to have to be more careful," Molly admonished, her eyes widening. "She's saying words now."

The look on her face was pure happiness. I don't think she would have cared if tits *was* the next word Reb picked up, as long as she was talking.

"I'll watch my mouth."

"No, you won't," Molly replied dryly.

"No," I agreed. "I won't."

Reb chose that moment to smack the coffee table hard with a plastic boat she'd found on the floor.

"I'll get her dressed," I said nonchalantly, getting to my feet.

I was testing the waters. Molly didn't seem to have any issue with me being around Rebel—holding her and helping her eat sometimes. But we were new—we weren't yet in a place where I helped out. I wanted to be.

Fuck, after the last few minutes, I wanted all of it.

"Are you sure?" Molly asked nervously, glancing down at Rebel.

"Sure." I leaned down and kissed her softly. "Go get dressed."

"It's cold outside, so make sure she's in pants and a sweater," she said quickly. "And her socks are in the top drawer. The long socks—all the short ones are cute, but they fall down her heel and it drives her crazy."

"No problem," I replied with a nod.

"And the far right side of her closet has all of the clothes that are too big still, so don't use those."

"Okay."

"And she needs a t-shirt under the sweater—one of the ones that snap shut at the bottom. That way her little belly doesn't get cold. And—"

"Moll," I cut in, physically turning her toward her bedroom. "I got it. I fuck up and you can change her, yeah?"

"Okay." She nodded then raced for her room, probably so she could try and finish getting ready before I was done getting Rebel ready.

"You want to go get some lunch?" I asked Rebel, picking her up off the floor.

She signed *eat*, nodding like a little bobble-head.

"Okay, lets get you some pants, then." I carried her into her bedroom and set her down on the floor. "You can't go out when you don't have clothes on," I told her as I grabbed some *long* socks out of her dresser. "Remember that when you get older. Not only would you be cold, but I'm never letting you out of the house without pants—so don't even try it."

Reb watched me with a smile as I grabbed some little purple pants and a sweater that matched out of her dresser.

"Some day, your feet are going to fit in these socks," I informed her as I sat her down and pulled Molly's socks off her legs. "Then we'll have to find you some super long ones so you can pull them way up your legs. Bet you could use mine when the time comes, I've got pretty big feet."

I took off her glasses and set them aside before pulling off the little shirt she was wearing and putting a little white one right back on, snapping it in place. I didn't want her to get cold. Shit, maybe I needed to talk to Molly about turning her furnace up.

"You need a Harley shirt," I informed Rebel as I pulled her little pants up and over her diaper. "Or a sweatshirt, since it's getting cold out. You want me to get you one?"

She smiled, her eyes unfocused without her glasses.

"Okay, sweater on," I said as I pulled the little penguin sweater over her head. "There, now we can put your specs back on. How's that? Should we go show Mama how good we did?"

"Mama," Rebel said loudly.

"I'm right here," Molly said from the doorway, fully dressed in some jeans and a sweater that just barely hung off one shoulder.

I wondered if she'd been watching me the whole time.

"How'd I do, coach?" I asked, getting up off the floor as Reb climbed to her feet and hurried toward Molly.

"You did good," Molly murmured, giving me a soft smile as she bent over to pick up Rebel. "Rebel, my love, we need to do something with that hair."

Rebel scrunched up her shoulders and shook her head slowly, making me laugh. Every time her head moved, little flyaway curls that were sticking up from the top of her head weaved back and forth.

"Quick ponytail," Molly said seriously, nodding her head.

They left me standing in the middle of Rebel's room with a smile on my face.

Chapter 9

MOLLY

"I THINK I need to take her to the doctor," I told Will groggily a few weeks after Reb started calling me *Mama*. I stumbled out of bed for the second time that night. "This can't be normal."

"Mama!" Reb yelled, the sound blaring through the baby monitor in my room. "Mama!"

"I can't believe she's awake again," Will rasped, sitting up as he rubbed at the scraggly beard on his face. He hadn't trimmed it in a while, and he was beginning to look like a doomsday prepper, complete with bloodshot eyes and a perpetual scowl on his face. We'd been spending every night together for weeks, and we both usually woke up the next morning feeling like crap because we'd barely gotten any sleep.

I glanced at the clock as I stumbled out of the room, noticing that it had been only an hour since I'd gotten Rebel to sleep the last time she'd woken up. I couldn't decide if her sleeping habits were getting worse, or if it just seemed like they were because I was so freaking tired.

"Why are you awake again?" I whispered to Rebel as I walked into her room to find her standing up in her crib. "It's time to be asleep, boo."

"Mama," she replied, her tired eyes brightening as I reached for her and lifted her into my arms. Her head immediately went to my shoulder as I cuddled her against my chest. She was exhausted, and I couldn't understand why she was having such a hard time sleeping.

"Want me to sing the bedtime song?" I asked softly. She nodded her head against the side of my neck, so I started singing "Ten in the Bed," closing my eyes as I swayed from side to side. When I finished the song, her body was relaxed against mine, but when I went to lay her back down, her little fists gripped the t-shirt that I'd worn to bed.

"Come on, baby," I murmured, sighing. "You have to go back to sleep."

I was almost in tears as I started the song again. I was so exhausted.

About halfway through the second verse of the song, I turned my head to see Will quietly walking into the room.

"Come on, sugar," he said, wrapping his arms around us from behind. "Just bring her to bed with us."

I had a rule that Rebel had to sleep in her own bed—I didn't want her to get into a routine where she wouldn't sleep in her crib—but at that moment, I was so tired that anything that would let me sleep sounded like a good idea. I let Will guide me back to my room, and I climbed into my bed still holding Rebel to my chest. As soon as I lay down, her little head popped up to see what was going on.

"Time to sleep, baby girl," Will said firmly as he lay down on the other side of the bed. He reached out as I rolled to the side and started rubbing Rebel's back as I laid her on the bed between us.

"Do you think this will work?" I whispered as Rebel pulled her knees up to press against my belly.

"Willin' to try anything at this point," Will murmured back.

I gave him a small smile and closed my eyes, falling asleep to the quiet sound of the callouses on Will's hand scraping against Rebel's pajama shirt and her warm breath against my chest.

Three hours later, we were awake again.

"Might as well get up for the day," Will mumbled as he sat up and slid hid his feet to the floor. "You don't work today?"

"No, I'm off," I said, as Rebel popped up and started bouncing on the mattress.

"Got an hour before I gotta head out." Will grabbed Rebel under the armpits and swung her up off the bed. "Go back to sleep for a bit." He stood up from the bed as Rebel wrapped one arm around his neck and grabbed a fist full of his beard with her other hand.

"She needs her diaper changed and breakfast, and you need to get ready," I replied, shaking my head as I moved to get up.

"Sleep, sugar," Will ordered, putting a hand to my chest and shoving me gently back down. He leaned over with Rebel clinging to him like a monkey and kissed my lips lightly. "I'll take care of Reb, and I'll take a shower at the clubhouse."

He stood back up and strode out of the room, saying something quietly to Rebel. I heard his footsteps fade down the hallway as I closed my eyes again, but before I could fall asleep, his voice came over the baby monitor that we'd never turned off the night before.

"You sleepy, princess? Yeah, me, too." I smiled as I heard the drawers in Rebel's dresser open and close. "We're gonna get you dressed since your mama keeps the house so damn cold. Sound good?"

It really wasn't that cold.

Will's voice grew faint, like he'd moved away from the monitor, so I reached out of the blankets and turned the volume up a little.

"I gotta work on an old Mustang today, which should be pretty nice. Beats working on a 1994 Mazda, you know? Those cars are shit. Don't know if you'll ever be able to drive, baby, but if you do? I'll get you a good car. Something that's built like a tank, cause if you're anything like your mama, you'll be running into shit left and right."

"Mama," Rebel replied.

I backed into something once. One time. And it hadn't even been anything important—it was a stupid curb that shouldn't have been there.

"I can teach you all sorts of shit about cars. You gotta know how to check your oil and change your tires just in case I'm not around to help ya with that. Don't wanna get stuck out on the road somewhere with a flat."

Will was quiet for a few moments.

"It's alright if you can't drive, though," he said quietly. "I'll still teach you about cars. Maybe when you're older, I can take you out to the garage and you can help me with shit. Show you how to change the oil and stuff so you can help your mama out."

"Mama," Rebel said again.

"Yeah, princess, your mama's sleepin'. You've been keepin' her up all night. What's that about, huh?" Rebel giggled the way she always did when Will was tickling her ribs. "Nah, don't pull at your ears, baby. You're gonna hurt yourself."

He kept talking for a little while longer, but eventually they left Rebel's room and I fell back asleep to the low sounds of Will making Rebel breakfast in the kitchen.

★ ★ ★

"I'M NOT SURE what's going on," I told Rebel's doctor later that day. Thankfully, the doctor's office knew Reb and all of her medical history, so when I'd said that she wasn't sleeping well, they'd gotten us an appointment right away. You really couldn't overlook anything when dealing with a child with Down syndrome, because all of their habits and medical issues wove together into a bigger picture that we had to keep an eye on. I couldn't just say something was a phase and would get better, because there was always a chance that there was an underlying issue that I wasn't seeing, especially since Rebel couldn't tell me what was wrong yet.

"How often is she waking up at night?" Doctor Mendez asked, smiling at Rebel as she let her blow warm air on the end of her stethoscope.

"Some nights it's only like three times, but other nights it's been six or seven."

"Whoa, so you're really not getting any restful sleep," the doctor replied.

"Couldn't you tell?" I joked, waving my arm in front of me to call attention to my sweatpants and greasy hair.

She laughed. "Well, sometimes, kids Rebel's age just have wonky sleep patterns. But we'll check her out and see if we can figure out what's happening."

She listened to Rebel's heart and lungs, then pushed on her little belly, making my baby laugh and squirm. When she pulled out the little thing to check her ears, Rebel froze, then scrambled back onto my lap.

"Mama," she said frantically, her little fingers digging into my skin.

"She's talking? That's great!" the doctor said, keeping her voice cheerful as she moved closer.

"Just one word," I replied, rubbing Rebel's back. "But it's the best one."

"Who knows, it might be the word that opens the floodgates," she said, leaning down to steady Rebel's head as she looked in her ear.

"You think?" I asked, tightening my arms as Reb began to squirm.

"I've seen it happen," Doctor Mendez said with a nod. "All done with that ear, Rebel, can I check the other one, please?"

We wrestled with Rebel until her head was turned far enough for the doctor to get a good look in the other ear, and my stomach rolled as Rebel whimpered against my chest. I hated when I had to make her do stuff that obviously scared her. It seemed like a trend with us, since she had to go to the doctor more often than most kids and they always seemed to have to poke and prod at her.

"Okay, all done, Rebel." Doctor Mendez leaned back on her little rolling stool and met my eyes. "She's got ear infections in both ears, which is probably why she didn't want me to touch them."

"Oh, crap. Again?"

"They're not too bad this time, but I want to take a look at her tonsils, too, before you go." She glanced down at Rebel and gave me a wry smile. "We'll give her a couple minutes before I bug her again."

We left the doctors office a half an hour later with a prescription for antibiotics and the news that Rebel needed tubes put in her ears. We'd been dealing with ear infections her entire life, and I knew that the tubes were the next line of defense against them, but that didn't calm my panic. They were going to have to use general anesthesia for the procedure, and people with Down syndrome were notoriously sensitive to anesthesia.

I tried not to think about all the things that could go wrong, but it didn't work. I was freaking out.

I'd dealt with Rebel's medical issues her entire life, and honestly, we were lucky. She'd never had to have invasive surgery or even an IV before, and I knew that there were a ton of kids in the world that went through those things on a daily basis for their entire lives. I was a nurse. I'd seen them.

However, those children weren't *my* children.

I needed someone to tell me it was all going to be okay. I needed my dad.

I put Rebel in the car and got into my seat, calling my dad before I'd even put the key in the ignition.

"Hello?"

"Hey, Dad. Want to have dinner tonight?" My voice wobbled a little.

"What's wrong?" he barked, and I could hear him shuffling something in the background.

"Nothing. We're fine."

"Something's wrong," Dad argued.

I glanced in my rear view mirror at Rebel, whose head was already listing to the side as she fought to stay awake. "Reb needs tubes in her ears," I said quietly.

"We knew this was coming, right?" he said gently. "Just a matter of when."

"Yeah, but the anesthesia—"

"Come on over to the house," he said, cutting me off. "I'll head home now and meet you there."

"We can just come over later," I said, dropping my head back against the seat.

"Nah, come now. I'm done for the day anyway."

I laughed a little as he hung up the phone before I could argue further. He'd been pulling that move for as long as I could talk. If he was done with a conversation or didn't want me to argue with him, he just hung up the phone or changed the subject so he didn't have to hear it.

★ ★ ★

"Your grandpa isn't a jungle gym," I told Rebel after dinner that night as she stood on my dad's thighs, trying to get a knee up on his shoulder so she could climb all over him.

"She's fine," Dad said with a laugh, smoothly setting Rebel back on the floor so she could climb her way back up again. "So what's the news with the tubes?"

I pulled my legs up so I was curled into his recliner, and sighed. "The doctor wants to do them next Thursday, as long as the antibiotics have cleared up the infection. So I'll take her into the office on Wednesday to check them, then to the hospital on Thursday morning."

"What did she say about putting Reb under?"

"That the anesthesiologist knows what he's doing and she'd trust him with her kids."

"Ok, then. What's got you worried?"

"Everything. Reb's going to hate the IV. She won't understand what's happening and I'm afraid she's going to be scared. I'm worried that she'll have a bad reaction to the medicine they give her. I'm worried that she'll wake up and I won't be there. I'm worried about everything."

"It's okay to be worried, kid," Dad said, setting Rebel on the floor again as she tried to get her knee on his shoulder. "There'd be something wrong with you if you weren't. But you can't let it make you crazy. You're not making Reb get a tattoo or pierce her ears, you're making her get tubes in her ears so those ear infections don't mess with her hearing. You have to do it. There isn't a choice here."

"That doesn't make it easier."

"Nah, it doesn't. But necessary, yes."

Dad growled at Rebel and tossed her into the air, the muscles in his tattooed forearms flexing as he caught her. I took a deep breath as I watched them, calm settling over me like a warm blanket. I knew the feeling was temporary, but I still let myself relax into the chair.

My mind had been racing all afternoon with possible reasons I could ask the doctor to hold off on the surgery, and I think that may have been fueling my panic. Trying to find just one excuse to back out had made everything worse, but listening to my dad as he mentioned that the surgery wasn't a choice had lifted that burden from my shoulders. He was right. Rebel needed the surgery. No matter how I felt about it or how scared I was, putting tubes in her ears would stop the pain of the ear infections she'd been getting for as long as I could remember.

My phone rang on the arm of the chair and I snatched it up as soon as I saw Will's name on the display.

"Hello?" I answered.

"Hey, sugar. Where are you? I'm at the house and you're not," Will said.

"Oh, shit. Sorry, I forgot to tell you we were having dinner at my dad's."

"No worries," he said easily. "Doctor figure out what's going on with the baby girl?"

"Yeah," I glanced up and found my dad watching me from across the room. "She's got ear infections in both ears."

"Ah, shit. Poor thing. They give you meds for it?"

"Yeah—hey, can I call you back?" I said uncomfortably as my dad continued to stare.

"Sure. Let me know when you're headed home and I'll meet you here."

"Okay." I hung up the phone, pulling my dad's move without a thought.

I set my phone carefully on the arm of the chair before meeting my dad's eyes.

"Who was that?" he asked, sitting Reb next to him on the couch.

"Will," I answered, lifting my chin.

"Thought you were done with that."

"We've been seeing each other for a while," I replied as his eyes tightened in anger.

"Thought I told you to stay away from the Aces."

"I thought I told you that I'm an adult and I can see anyone I want."

"You're bringing Rebel into that life?" he asked glancing at her. "You think that's what Mason would want?"

"Mason's dead," I replied flatly. "And you didn't like him much when he was alive, so I'm not sure why you'd bring him up."

"Yeah, you've obviously never given a shit what I say."

"Will's good to me," I said softly, getting to my feet. "He's sweet to Rebel and he acts like I'm the best thing he's ever seen."

"He's neck deep in Aces shit," Dad replied in frustration, climbing to his feet, as well. "He's a fucking criminal. He's been arrested half a dozen times."

"I don't see that!" I said, my voice rising. "He's not like that with me."

"He's like that all the goddamn time, Molly Ann! You can't just shut that shit off. That's his life."

"You don't know what you're talking about," I ground out, moving toward Rebel's bag at the end of the couch. "And I'm not arguing with you about it."

"Those people will pull you into the gutter with them, is that what you want?" Dad asked as I picked Rebel up.

"You tell me, Dad," I mumbled, meeting his eyes. "You've been working for them for twenty years, what's it like in the gutter?"

He didn't move. Not a single muscle. But I think that was the closest my dad ever came to hitting me. He was furious beyond anything I'd ever seen.

I turned and walked away before things got any worse.

"I'll be here when it's over," Dad called as I reached the front door. "When he fucks you over or gets you into something that scares you, I'll be right here."

I slammed the door behind me when I left.

★ ★ ★

"Hey," I mumbled that night as I opened the door for Will. "Sorry about earlier."

"No problem. Reb sleepin'?" He wrapped an arm around my shoulders and shut the door behind him as he backed me farther into the house.

"Yeah. I gave her some pain medicine for her ears, so hopefully she'll stay asleep longer tonight." I rubbed my forehead with the tips of my fingers, sighing. "I know she gets ear infections. I feel like the worst mother ever for not realizing that she had another one."

"How would you know?" he asked, shrugging out of his leather vest and tossing it over the back of the couch. "Not like she coulda told you."

"Yeah, but the pulling on her ears thing, and the not sleeping, and the foul mood should've given me an idea," I replied ruefully as he unlaced and pulled off his boots.

"Well, you know now, right?"

"Yeah." I smiled as he stood back up and moved toward me. The minute he reached me, his hands went around my back and he was gripping my ass, lifting me until my legs wrapped around his waist.

"She'll take her meds and be good as new. Good thing, too. I'm used to not gettin' much sleep, sugar, but I was startin' to feel like a zombie."

"I'm sorry," I said quietly as he reached over to make sure the door was locked, then turned and started walking toward my bedroom. "You don't have to stay here every night." I rubbed my lips along the edge of his ear, and felt a small sense of satisfaction when I felt him suck in a quick breath. He loved it when I put my lips on his ears and neck, those were his sweet spots.

"You kickin' me out?" he asked with a chuckle as he walked us through my bedroom doorway.

"No." I leaned back and looked into his eyes, wrapping my arms completely around his neck. "But you don't have to stay if you don't want to."

"Wouldn't be here if I didn't want to be," he replied softly, leaning forward to kiss me gently. "What's wrong?"

My face contorted and I dropped my head as I felt the tears I'd been fighting all night flood my eyes. All it took was one softly worded question and I wanted to sob like a baby.

"Molly?" Will asked again, one of his arms rising to wrap tightly around my back. "What the hell?"

"Sorry," I choked out, trying to get my shit together. "Sorry."

"Quit apologizing and tell me what the fuck is wrong." He dropped onto the bed and ran his fingers through my hair.

"They have to put tubes in her ears," I finally replied when I knew my voice wouldn't break.

"That's what's got you all upset? Shit, sugar. Both my brothers had that done when they were kids. Not a big deal."

"It's different for kids with Down syndrome," I argued, raising my head from his shoulder. My voice grew panicked and the words tumbled out of my mouth quickly. "They have issues with anesthesia and Rebel's never had to have anything invasive done. We don't know if she has allergies or if she's extra sensitive or—"

"Baby, stop," Will ordered, his hand tightening in my hair. "It's gonna be fine. Her doctor wouldn't do it if he thought it was gonna go bad, right?"

"Her doctor is a woman," I replied stupidly.

"Alright, *she* wouldn't do it if she thought it was gonna go bad," Will said patiently.

"But what if she's scared?" I asked, my voice catching. "I don't want her to be scared."

"Moll," Will whispered tenderly, pulling my head down to run his lips over mine. "It's gonna be fine, baby. I promise. She won't be scared, she'll be out. They're not gonna do anything when she's awake."

I nodded even as I started to bawl. I didn't want to go through with it. Maybe I was being ridiculous, but I was still scared out of my mind.

"Jesus," Will mumbled, moving us so that we were lying down on the bed. "You're fuckin' exhausted and it's makin' everything bigger than it is."

"So many things could go wrong," I whimpered as he pulled me tighter against his chest. "What if—"

"Enough," he ordered gruffly, pulling the blankets over us. "You're not playin' the *what if* game tonight. You need some fuckin' sleep. You still wanna play that game with me tomorrow, I'll be all ears."

I cried against his chest as he shushed me, but I couldn't seem to get it under control. Realistically, I knew that the surgery would probably go off without a hitch. Will was right, it was a simple procedure. However, that truth did nothing to stem my panic.

"Stop," Will ordered gently as he ran his hands up and down my back. "Stop it, Molly."

I inhaled deeply and let the breath shudder back out, letting his gruff words soothe me. If anyone else had spoken to me in that tone, I would have told them to go fuck themselves. It was ridiculous that he kept telling me to stop crying. However, as he spoke, his arms held me tight against him, and I could hear his heart thundering in his chest as he tried to get me to calm down. He was as wound up as I was.

My breath finally evened out after a few more minutes, leaving only occasional hiccups that shook my whole body. My swollen eyes grew heavy and I shut them as Will's hand lifted to push my hair back from my face. A few moments later, when I was almost asleep, I felt Will pull away from me. I didn't say a word as he tucked the blanket up over my shoulder, but I cringed as he climbed out of bed. I didn't blame him for leaving.

I opened my eyes and glanced up to see Will looking down at me as he unbuckled his belt. He shucked his jeans and socks off then reached up to pull his t-shirt and flannel over his head.

"I know you're awake," he said quietly as he pulled the blankets back again to crawl in next to me.

"I thought you were leaving," I rasped, my words muffled by my pillow.

"'Course not."

My lips tipped up in a small smile at his easy reply. Of course he wasn't leaving.

I let him pull me against his chest and fell asleep almost instantly.

Chapter 10

WILL

"Hey, Moose!" a voice called, followed by someone thumping against the side of the car I was under. I cursed as I dodged dirt and other nasty shit that they'd knocked loose with their thumping.

"What?" I growled out, sliding out from underneath the car. My face and neck felt gritty with the shit that had been sprinkling down on me from inside the engine all damn day.

"Dragon wants to talk to you," Woody said, smirking at me.

"Fine." I got to my feet and tried brushing off my jump suit. Little flecks of dirt flew through the air, but it wasn't making much of a difference.

"That shit's nasty," Woody said, backing up a step.

"Get used to it, you'll be under here before too long."

"No fucking way," he said with a laugh. "I'm getting the fuck out of here."

"Oh, yeah?" I asked, only half listening. The kid was a punk, but he was funny as hell. He hung around the club quite a bit when he wasn't in school because his dad had been a member before he died of old age. Doc was old as shit when I was a kid, so I had no idea how he'd managed to knock some chick up, but we had living proof in Woody and the goofy-as-fuck smile he wore around that looked exactly like his dad's.

"I'm gonna go to college," he said as we walked out of the garage bay. It was getting cold as fuck outside, but we kept the doors open anyway. There was too much shit in the air to keep them closed when we were working, we'd fucking suffocate.

"Good for you—know what you're going to do?"

"Doctor, maybe," he mumbled, wrapping his arms around his chest.

"Got the grades for that?"

"Nah, I'll probably have to join the military or something first. But I gotta get the fuck outta here."

I slammed to a stop at his tone. "You got problems?"

"Bitches, man," he said with a derisive laugh, trying hard as hell to sound older than he was.

"You talkin' about Cece? You know she's my cousin, right?"

"She's—" his mouth snapped shut and he shook his head. "Leo wants to fuckin' kill me and Cecilia doesn't know what the fuck she wants."

"Still?" I asked in surprise. They'd had some sort of weird teenage love triangle going on for over a year.

"She says she loves me," he said quietly, looking anywhere but at my face. "But she won't stay away from him."

"You guys don't know what the fuck you're doin' at your age," I said incredulously. "Fuckin' cut bait, man."

"You're not that much older," he spat, straightening his shoulders in offense.

"Yeah, and I still don't know what the fuck I'm doin,'" I said with a derisive laugh, ignoring his scowl as I stripped my jumpsuit off, leaving it on the ground outside the door as I walked into the warm clubhouse.

"You lookin' for me?" I asked as Dragon as I sat down next to him at the bar.

"You want some coffee?" his wife, Brenna, asked as she cleaned the countertop. I didn't know why she was doing it. There were plenty of other people to clean up messes around the club that were far lower in the hierarchy than the president's old lady.

"Please," I answered with a nod.

"You're covered in . . ." her words trailed off as she waved her hand in front of her face.

"Yeah, I'll be back at it in a minute, didn't see the use in cleanin' off now," I grumbled, making her laugh as she poured me a cup of coffee.

"Okay, I'll leave you to it," she said as she set the mug in front of me. She paused for a moment when Dragon reached out, and I looked away as he used her hair to slowly pull her forward and kiss her goodbye.

"You can look back now," Dragon said in amusement after Brenna had left the room.

"Just givin' you some privacy."

"Don't need privacy to kiss my woman," he said, taking a drink of his coffee. "How's the suit's daughter workin' out?"

"Her name's Molly," I ground out. Swear to Christ, they never said her name, even though I'd been with her for almost two months.

"Molly, then," he conceded with a nod.

"Good."

"You gonna bring her around?"

"I'll get around to it," I mumbled, scratching at the shit in my beard.

"So it's just temporary, then." He nodded like he understood.

"No, it's not." I stopped scratching at my beard and took a drink of my coffee. "Just haven't had time to bring her around."

"Yeah, you've been flyin' out of here like somethin's chasin' ya every night. What's goin' on with that?"

"Is there a problem?" I asked seriously, turning to face him. "Didn't know it was a requirement to spend all my time here."

"See," Dragon said darkly, setting his mug down. "That's what concerns me. Couple months ago, you were happy as hell to hang out with your brothers, but lately you wanna be anywhere but here. If there's a problem, need to know about it."

"There's no problem," I snapped, getting to my feet.

"Sit your ass down," Dragon growled, glaring until I followed the order. "You got a woman that's pullin' you from the club, that's somethin' that needs to be fuckin' dealt with."

"I do my part," I ground out. "I do everything you fuckin' ask."

"I don't need some fuckin' mindless soldier following orders," he barked, reaching out to cuff the side of my head. "My boys are fuckin' loyal, they work for the club because they goddamn love it and they get what they put in. So where the fuck has your head been?"

"It's here."

"Nah, kid. It's not."

I grit my teeth against the urge to tell him to fuck off. I pitched in more than anyone. I never bitched about the shit that no one else wanted to do and I got stuck with. Rocky had been fucking Mel for as long as I'd been with Molly, but he hadn't brought her to the club, either. Was he sitting next to me getting bitched out? Of course not.

It all came back to the bullshit I'd pulled back when I was juicing. I'd never get out from under that fucking umbrella. I'd taken steroids for less than six months, and in that time I'd fucked up so bad that I was pretty sure no one in the club was going to trust me again.

And the worst part? I didn't blame them.

They'd forgiven me, sure as shit, but they'd never forget. None of us would ever forget.

The guilt of that kept me up at night. It burned in my belly when everything was quiet and I had time to think, especially now that I was with Molly. Her presence seemed to drag all of the old shit up. I wasn't sure if it was because she'd been my nurse that night, or because I was fucking terrified that something was going to happen to her and Reb because of me.

I'd put the Aces on some pussy college kids' radar when I'd started buying off them, and I'd pissed them off when I wouldn't agree to sell their shit. I'd had no idea that one of them had been trying to make friends with Dragon's daughter, Trix, in order to get in with us a different way, and had lost patience when she didn't want anything to do with him. There'd been no way for me to know that they'd go off the rails and shoot up our family barbeque.

It had been a snowball effect, sure, but all that shit had started with me. I'd made the first move and four of our people were dead because of it. My baby brother was dead because of it.

That's why I took the shit jobs, why I always offered to go on the long runs, why I took the risky meets. I was paying my penance, and fuck Dragon for saying that my head wasn't in it.

"I'm here," I said, lifting my hands palm up. "I do what needs to be done."

"You good for a run up to Montana, then?" Dragon asked, pulling a pack of cigarettes out of his shirt pocket. "Need to meet with some boys up there about the Russians. Looks like the idiots are trying to get permission to run their shit through to Canada. We need to make sure that's not a possibility."

I started nodding before he'd even finished speaking. "When?"

"Tuesday. Hulk and Samson are goin' to ride up with you. Sam knows some of the boys up there pretty well, hopefully that'll make shit run smooth."

My stomach sank, but I kept my face expressionless. Rebel's surgery was on Thursday and Molly was going to flip her shit when she realized I wasn't going to be there.

"Alright," I said, sliding off my bar stool. "That all you needed?"

"For now," Dragon said, watching me closely.

"Catch you later, then." I walked outside and cursed as I found my jumpsuit in a puddle. At least the rain fit my mood.

★ ★ ★

"Ma, you here?" I called the next day as I pulled my boots off at my parents' front door. I usually just left them on in the house, but I was soaked and I didn't want my mom following me with a towel to mop up my footprints.

"In here!"

I followed her voice into the living room and snorted when I found her sitting at the coffee table with about fifteen dolls spread out in front of her.

"Oh, shut it," Mom said with a smile, spraying one of the dolls with a little spray bottle.

"What the hell are you doing?" I asked, pulling off my coat and the beanie I was wearing. God, I hated the rain.

"I got this recipe off Pinterest, and I'm trying to detangle the hair on all of Rosie's dolls," she said seriously as she dropped the spray bottle and started painstakingly combing out the hair of a little blonde doll.

"Why?" I dropped to the couch and rubbed my face. I'd tried to clean up at the club, but I still felt like I had little pieces of dirt in my beard.

"Well, your sister doesn't play with these anymore, so I thought I'd pass them down to Rebel," she replied, shrugging her shoulders.

"Don't think she plays with dolls," I said seriously. I'd never seen Reb with any, only stuffed animals.

"That's okay," Mom said, shaking her head. "I'll give her a couple just in case she gets interested later."

"Mom," I mumbled, sighing. "Might wanna do that tonight before I get to Molly's."

"Why? What did you do, William?"

"Jesus, why's it always me? Maybe Molly fucked up."

"No, she didn't or you wouldn't be here. You came over because you're feeling bad about something, not because you're pissed."

"I come over here all the time," I argued, leaning forward to brace my elbows on my knees.

"Not when you know it's just me at home. Now tell me what's going on."

"Reb's getting those tubes put in her ears on Thursday," I said, lifting up a doll that had hair down to its feet.

"How's Molly doing with that? I was so nervous when the boys had them put in."

"She's freakin' the fuck out."

"Okay, so what did you do?"

"Nothin' yet." I lifted my head and found her staring right at me, her hands unmoving on the table. "Gotta go on a run Tuesday and there's no way in hell I'll make it back for the procedure."

"Oh, Will," Mom sighed.

"She's gonna be pissed," I mumbled, setting the doll back on the table.

"Couldn't you ask—"

"No." I cut her off with a shake of my head. "Club comes first."

"Bullshit," she snapped, climbing to her feet.

"Not havin' this fight with you," I said, following her as she stormed into the kitchen. "You wanna bitch at Dad, that's between the two of you."

"Maybe I will! Maybe I'll ask why his son is leaving town when his old lady's kid is having surgery!" She smacked the palm of her hand down on the countertop in emphasis.

"She's not my old lady," I argued, lifting her hand up to make sure she hadn't hurt it. "And I don't need you in my shit, causing problems."

"I'm your mother!"

"I'm twenty-one years old! I can handle my own shit."

"Then why did you come here?" she snapped, wrapping her arms across her chest as her eyes filled with tears.

"Christ, Mom," I groaned, pulling her rigid body forward until I could wrap my arms around her shoulders. She was so much shorter than me that her face lined up with my sternum. "Stopped by because I wanted to see you and I needed to get some advice. I didn't stop by so you could get into a big fight with Dad about shit that's none of your concern."

"You'll always be my concern," she said, her body relaxing as she put her arms around my waist and squeezed. "I like Molly. She's good for you. I just don't want to see you mess it up."

"I'm tryin' not to," I replied, kissing the top of her head before pulling away. "But I've got responsibilities—"

"When are you going to stop punishing yourself?" my mom asked quietly as I stepped back.

I froze. "Don't know what you're talkin' about," I said, refusing to meet her eyes.

"You know exactly what I'm talking about," she argued, her voice still quiet. "You think I don't know things, Will? You think your dad keeps me in the dark? Just because I don't say much about the club, doesn't mean I don't know most of what goes on there, especially when it has to do with my kids. I know about that supplier that you—"

"You're an old lady," I said stubbornly. My gut burned with shame, but I let a surge of anger overpower it as I made eye contact. "You keep your mouth shut."

Mom's eyes flared wide, then shuttered as she took a step toward me. "I love you, Will," she said, her voice hard. "But if that filth ever comes out of your mouth again, you won't be welcome in this house."

She didn't rush as she walked around me, and I didn't turn around as I heard her start up the creaky stairs to her bedroom. She was going up there because she knew I wouldn't follow. My parents' room had always been off-limits to us kids, for obvious reasons, and also so that my mom had a place that was all her own where she could get away from us for a few minutes. She'd gone up there because she wanted to get away from me, and I wasn't surprised.

If my dad had heard that conversation, he would have knocked me on my ass and I would have deserved it.

"Shit," I glanced around for something to hit, then dropped my hand. I couldn't leave a hole in one of my mother's walls.

Stomping out to my bike, I glanced up to see my mom standing in her bedroom window watching me leave. She didn't acknowledge me as I climbed on my bike, though, just stared like she was trying to figure out when her son had become such an asshole.

Molly was at work for another hour, so I stopped and grabbed a bottle of Jack then drove over there, letting myself into the quiet trailer. I sat down at the table and cracked the seal on my bottle of oblivion.

I didn't know what the fuck I was doing. I couldn't get out of the fucking run. No way. Dragon was looking for any reason to be up in my face. If I tried to get out of it, I'd only be proving his point about my head not being at the club, where it was supposed to be. I'd been standing on thin ice for so fucking long, I didn't even remember the last time I'd felt comfortable taking care of my own shit without worrying about the blowback from the club. The Aces were my brothers. The only family I'd ever known. I couldn't screw that up, especially for a woman who'd refused to even stop by my parents' house when I'd invited her to Thanksgiving dinner because my dad freaked her out. I was pretty sure she'd never step foot on the club grounds if she could help it, and where the fuck would that leave me? Choosing between the two?

I was taking a drink straight out of the bottle when Molly's door was shoved open and Reb came through, carrying a stuffed cat, her glasses crooked on her face.

"Hey," Molly called as Rebel came to me, lifting her arms for me to pick her up.

"Hey," I called back, pushing the bottle of Jack to the middle of the table where Reb couldn't reach it.

"Damn, you're not messing around," Molly said, eyeballing the liquor. "No chaser."

"Only bitches use chasers."

"Uh, language," she huffed, dropping Reb's bag on the floor. "And don't be an ass."

"You can say ass but I can't say bitches?" I mused as she slid off her coat and came to pull Reb's off, as well.

"What's going on?" she asked quietly as she tugged on Reb's sleeve.

"Nothin,'" I mumbled as Reb's hand smacked me in the mouth.

"You sure?" She looked at me in concern, and that burning guilt started roiling through my gut again. She was so gorgeous. Sweet as fuck. She didn't push or prod, didn't ask where I was when I had a late night, never turned me away from her bed, even when she was on the rag and I knew she was uncomfortable with the mess. She supported herself, didn't expect me to do it, even though I wanted to. Took care of her kid with no complaints, even when Reb was waking her up all night. Hell, she even knew when to keep her mouth shut. She hadn't even told her best friend that she'd seen me in the hospital.

She was fucking perfect, and I knew there was no way in hell it would ever work.

"Everything's fine, sugar," I said softly, reaching up to grip the back of her neck to pull her in for a kiss. Her lips met mine and I knew I was a fucking psychopath, because I was going to take that trust she gave me and break it, but before I did that, I was going to fuck her into oblivion over and over again so she'd never forget the way I felt inside her.

We were on a timeline that she had no idea was ticking down, and I wasn't going to tell her. I was going to savor it instead.

"You want some dinner? I brought home some steaks," she said, pulling away a little, but not far enough to stop the fingers she was running through my hair.

"Sounds good," I replied gruffly, sliding my hand down her back until I held her ass in my palm.

"You hungry, Rebel?" she asked, leaning down to kiss Reb's cheek when the baby ignored her.

I'd noticed Rebel did that a lot, ignoring the people around her. Sometimes she was right there with you, but other times it was like you weren't even in the room. She was just off in her own universe, completely unconcerned with what was happening around her.

"You're a pain in the ass, kid," I mumbled into her hair as Molly went to the other side of the kitchen and pulled out a pan. Rebel ran her fingers through the stuffed cat's fur over and over again, like I hadn't even spoken. "But I love you, anyway."

She glanced up at me briefly, then went back to the cat's fur.

★ ★ ★

"One more time," I said, trying to catch my breath as Molly panted beneath me.

"I can't," she argued, her sweaty hair sticking to the sides of her face. "Enough."

"Yeah, you can." I slid out of her, making her wince, and rolled her until the top half of her body was pressed face down on the bed and her hips were twisted to the side. I couldn't get enough of her. We'd been going at it for hours, and every time we caught our breath, I was dying to be inside her again. She'd sucked me off the last time, probably just so her pussy could get a break, but it had backfired when she'd gotten so worked up that she'd practically climbed me when she was done.

"Gentle," she yelped as I slid back inside her, bracing myself on one hand while I used the other to push her knee to her chest. "I'm so sore."

"Too sore?" I asked as I slowly pulled back out.

"No," she moaned, the word drawn out until I pressed inside again.

I paused as I caught her grimace, pulling back out even as she reached for me.

"Too sore," I said softly as I leaned down to kiss her thigh.

"It's okay."

"This'll be better." The cool air of the room against my sweaty skin made me shudder, but I didn't pause as I ran my tongue down her thigh, admiring the red spots I'd left earlier in the night. I couldn't remember the last time I'd given a chick a hickey, but when she'd been sitting on my face as she'd sucked me off, I hadn't been able to stop myself. I wanted to tattoo my name on her ass so any fucker that got close enough knew she belonged to me.

Mostly because she wouldn't belong to me for much longer.

"So gorgeous," I murmured against her skin when I finally reached the soft, dark pink skin of her pussy. The longer we messed around, the redder her skin got, especially if she came more than once. She'd come so many times that night, her clit was red, like a fucking bullseye hiding in her short blonde pubic hair.

"Will," she mumbled, her hands finding the back of my head as I gently nudged her clit with my tongue. We'd stopped using condoms since Molly was on the pill, and I loved that she tasted like both of us now. Smelled like both of us.

"Shh," I whispered as I slid one finger inside her, still smoothing my tongue over her clit in soft strokes. She was swollen around my finger, and I wasn't sure how I'd fit my dick in her just a few minutes before.

"More," she gasped, rolling her hips against my hand and mouth. "Please, Will."

I sucked her clit into my mouth, pinching my lips around it as I licked back and forth, and just like that, she was coming. So fucking wet.

I needed just one more time.

Even though I knew it was going to sting, I jerked up off the bed and wrapped her legs around me, shoving inside in one thrust.

"Fuck!" she hissed, her nails digging into my chest. "Yes."

Sweat dripped down my cheek as I thrust once, twice, and then like a virgin, I was coming so hard it hurt.

"Jesus," I groaned, falling forward until my face was pressed against the side of her neck.

"Feel better?" she asked, wrapping her arms tightly around my back. I huffed out a laugh and gently pulled out of her.

"Don't leave yet," she murmured drowsily as I moved to get up. "Cuddle me for a minute."

"Cuddle you?" I asked softly, my lips twitching as she grinned.

"Yeah."

"How 'bout I go clean up, then I'll come back and cuddle you?" I needed a minute to myself. The thought of being without her was starting to make me anxious and I had to get my shit together.

"Fine," she mumbled, sliding her hands across my sweaty back as she let go.

I climbed off the bed and walked into the bathroom. Shit, I needed a shower, but I was too tired to do more than piss. When I was finished, I shut off the light and walked back into the bedroom to find Molly completely passed out on her belly, one arm dangling off the side of the bed.

She'd asked me to hold her, and I'd left her to fall asleep alone. I was such an asshole.

I crawled in next to her and pulled her against my chest, swallowing hard when her arm automatically slid around my waist as she slept.

Chapter 11

Molly

"Time for bed," I sang to Rebel, trying to get her calmed down. She'd been racing around the house all night, barely able to sit still, and I knew it was my fault. I was strung so tight my shoulders had begun to ache from the tension, and there was no way that Rebel hadn't picked up on it.

"Do you want to go potty on the big toilet?" I asked, catching her as she tried to run past me. She clung like a monkey as I sat her on my hip and carried her into the bathroom.

She wouldn't be potty training until she was older, but she'd seemed so fascinated with the toilet that I'd been letting her sit on it before bed and when she woke up in the morning. Oddly enough, I used it as incentive both for her to wake up and let me get her ready, and so that she would calm down for bed. It seemed to be working so far, though we'd only started it a couple days before.

"What a big girl you are," I said, smiling as I sat her little bare butt on the seat.

I tried really hard not to cry as she grinned at me, completely clueless that anything was wrong. She felt the tension, of course, but she had no idea what was going on. In her world, everything was normal.

"Good job, Reb!" I told her as she dropped clean toilet paper into the toilet. "Now, we wash our hands."

I helped wash her hands and wrists, then brought her into her bedroom to get her dressed in her brand new puppy pajamas. I'd bought them in a lame attempt to commemorate her surgery, because the next morning I'd be driving her to the hospital so early that they'd told me to just bring her in her jammies. It worked better that way, since dressing was Rebel's cue for *time to eat*, and she couldn't have anything before the procedure.

"You're getting so big," I said softly as I zipped up the new pajamas. "I can't believe it."

"Mama."

"I know, you're talking now!"

She signed for water and I glanced at the clock to make sure I could give her some, even though I knew it wasn't after midnight. After carrying her into the kitchen for a drink, I brought her back into the bedroom, my hands trembling slightly as I sat down in the rocking chair. I wasn't ready to put her down yet, so instead, I wrapped her blanket around her and began to rock.

"You're going to do so good tomorrow," I whispered against her hair, even though she had no idea what I was talking about.

Reb laid her head on my shoulder and sighed, her little body relaxing against mine. After a few minutes, before I'd even sang the "Ten in the Bed" song, she was asleep. But I didn't put her in her crib until two hours later.

★ ★ ★

"Hey, Will," I said into the phone late that night, trying hard not to let my voice indicate how hard I'd been crying. "So, I haven't talked to you since yesterday morning and I'm getting kind of worried. I mean, I know you have other stuff going on, but—" I snapped my mouth shut and grit my teeth as tears dripped out of my eyes. I cleared my throat before speaking again. My nose was stuffed, and I knew I sounded awful, but I had to try one more time to reach him. "I just wanted to remind you that Reb's getting those tubes in her ears tomorrow, and I know you wanted to be there. I hope everything's alright . . . Okay, bye." I pressed end on my phone and tossed it on the couch beside me.

He was fine. Of course he was. He probably just broke his phone or something. We'd talked every day since we'd started seeing each other, but that didn't mean we *had* to. We'd been together less than two months. It wasn't like we were married.

And it wasn't like he *had* to be there for Reb's surgery. He wasn't her dad.

My mind processed all of that, but it didn't help the nervous nausea that had me bent in half as I tried not to get sick. Mel had asked if I wanted her to spend the night with us, but I'd told her to meet us at the hospital the next morning because I'd thought that Will would be with me.

But he wasn't.

He wasn't anywhere. He wasn't answering any of my texts, or any of my phone calls. He'd left right after breakfast the morning before, and I hadn't heard from him since. I was starting to panic.

He always called, even if it was just to see how my day was. He sent me texts asking for blowjobs, and memes he thought were funny, and random pictures of Rebel that he'd taken on his phone. He'd never been silent for so long, not since those three weeks after we'd slept together the first time when he'd been out of town.

"He's fine," I said out loud, my raspy voice breaking the silence of the house. "He'll show up in the morning with some excuse."

I wasn't a clingy girl. I wasn't needy. I liked being by myself, and I didn't mind when Will had to work long hours. I didn't call him constantly or expect him to be at my beck and call.

I was just so scared, a bone-deep fear that felt like it was seeping in more and more hour by hour. The closer it got to the time I had to wake Rebel up, the more debilitating the fear became. It wasn't adrenaline-inducing fear. No, instead it was the type that left you paralyzed, barely able to breathe.

I glanced at the clock and lifted my hand to my mouth, my chapped lips and torn cuticles stinging as I began to pull at the skin of my lower lip.

He might still call. God, I just needed him to call. It was too late to call Mel or my dad. They were already sleeping because they had to meet us at the hospital in four hours. I probably wouldn't even wake them up if I called.

I stood up and began to pace back and forth across the living room, my eyes so tired that they stung. Time was moving too fast, and also so slow I thought I was going to go crazy. When my steps became too frantic for the small space, I went all the way down the hall and back.

I kept moving, showering and getting dressed in between pacing the house. Finally, the alarm on my phone went off, indicating that my wait was up. It was time to wake Rebel.

★ ★ ★

"THIS STUFF'LL KNOCK her right out," the anesthesiologist, Doctor Grant, told me two hours later, handing me a little cup of liquid while I sat with Rebel on her hospital bed. "At the very least, she'll be so relaxed she won't care what's happening around her."

"But she'll be asleep before you do anything else, right?" I asked, moving Reb's hand away from the buttons on the side of the bed.

"Of course," he reassured me gently. "We've done this thousands of times."

"Not to my kid," I murmured, lifting the cup to Rebel's lips. She drank it greedily since she hadn't had anything to drink yet, even though she'd been asking for water since she'd woken up.

"You're right," he said, chuckling. "Not to Rebel. But she'll be fine. I'll be back in about thirty minutes to see how it's working."

He left the room as Rebel climbed onto my lap, the little gown she was wearing tangling in her legs. She'd been pissed when they had me strip her down to her diaper, but I'd calmed her with a new stuffed owl I'd packed to keep her occupied.

"Hey, girls," Mel called softly as she pushed back the curtain shielding the door. "Auntie Mel's here."

"Hey," I answered dully, smoothing down Reb's hair.

"How you doin', mama?"

"I'm ready for all of this to be over," I said softly, kissing the top of Rebel's head as she leaned heavily against me, her hand fisting in my ponytail.

"Almost done," Mel said kindly, sitting on the opposite side of the bed. "Where's your dad and Will?"

"Dad went to get coffee," I said, meeting her eyes.

"Will?"

"I haven't heard from him." The words came out weird, almost garbled.

Mel's eyes widened in sympathy. "That dick!"

I shrugged. I couldn't even think about Will anymore, not with Reb's surgery looming so close. God, I was being such a wuss. It was freaking tubes in her ears. Thousands of kids got the procedure every day, even kids with Down syndrome. The chances of something happening were higher for Rebel, but they were still small. I needed to suck it the fuck up, but I just . . . couldn't. She was my baby. She was everything.

I looked down. She was also asleep.

"It worked," I said in relief, tears hitting my eyes for the thousandth time in the last twenty-four hours.

"She's out," Mel said in amusement. "She's practically drooling."

"Thank God," I whispered, resting my hand on her chest for a moment before checking her pulse. I was a nurse. I couldn't stop myself.

I gently pulled Rebel's glasses off her face and handed them to Mel as my dad came back in the room.

"Is that medically induced?" he asked, nodding at Rebel.

"Yeah, they gave her something after you left," I whispered, laying Rebel down on the bed next to me.

"Good," he said as he handed me a mocha from the hospital cafeteria. He turned to Mel and handed her a cup, too.

"Ah, Mr. Duncan you're a saint," she said airily, making my dad roll his eyes behind his glasses.

She always flirted with him. It was disgusting, but my revulsion didn't bother her in the slightest. Ever since she'd seen my dad with his shirt off when we were seventeen, she'd had this weird thing for him. Thankfully, my dad ignored it. I was pretty sure I would have killed him if he'd even acknowledged it.

"How we doing?" Doctor Grant called as he came back through the door a few minutes later. "Ah, looks like everything's going as planned." He smiled at me, but I couldn't make my lips form one in return.

A nurse came in behind him, and I glowered as she pulled a tray in with her.

"You're not doing her IV," I said, startling her with the venom in my voice. I turned to the anesthesiologist. "Where's a fucking pediatric nurse?"

"Molly," he said chidingly. I both loved and hated that we were at the hospital where I worked. It was comforting to know how good the doctors and anesthesiologists were, but it also meant that I knew which nurses were fucking horrible at finding veins for IVs.

"She's not getting near my child with a needle," I growled, meeting the nurse's eyes, knowing I was making an enemy, but not caring in the slightest. "I've seen the shit job you do."

"She's not going to change her mind," Mel said into the tension-filled silence. "You should probably get another nurse."

"I can do it," I said decisively.

"You know it's against hospital policy," Doctor Grant said, waving the nurse out. "Who would you like to put the IV in?"

"Who's working?" I asked stubbornly.

He went down the list of nurses working and I immediately picked one. "Jan. She actually knows what the fuck she's doing."

"I'm sure she'll be glad for the endorsement," Doctor Grant said dryly. "I'll go get her."

"Jesus," Mel said with a laugh as soon as he was gone. "You're never going to be able to come back to work."

"Fuck her," I mumbled.

"Calm down, Molly," my dad said softly, reaching out to rub my back.

"That nurse leaves bruises the size of golf balls," I said in irritation, climbing off the bed and away from his hand.

It took less than ten minutes for nurse Jan to walk in the door, her hands above her head. "I come in peace!" she called out jokingly, making my dad chuckle. "Hey, girl. Sounds like you're making friends left and right this morning."

"Samantha does a shit job and everyone knows it," I replied stubbornly. "You're good."

"Well, thank you," she said, giving me a smile as she walked over to the bed. She swept a soft hand over Rebel's arm, then lifted it and looked it over. "Check out those pretty veins. Piece of cake."

I had to force myself not to get in Jan's space as she prepped the IV site, but I couldn't stop myself from rounding the bed. "Should it be in her foot?" I asked, immediately clamping my lips shut when my dad shot me a look.

"If I thought it would work better, I'd do it," Jan said softly. "But, no. Arm will work just fine, mama."

It was over quickly, and Reb barely flinched, relaxing back against the bed before Jan had even applied the tape to keep the IV in place.

"All set," Jan said, cleaning up the supplies.

"Thanks, Jan," I said quietly, leaning down to kiss Rebel's head.

"No problem, honey. I'm the same way when my kids go to the hospital. Celeste broke her arm last year and I wouldn't let Doctor Marv set it," she said softly, giving me a sympathetic smile. "We know what's best for our kids, probably more than most."

She left the room just as Rebel's primary care doctor came into the room.

"How's she doing?" Doctor Mendez asked, moving forward to get a good look at Rebel.

"She's good," I said, a feeling of relief rushing through me. I knew all of the people who'd come into the room since we'd been admitted that morning, but Doctor Mendez knew *Rebel*. None of the others had watched her grow. They didn't know her history. They hadn't checked for ear infections, or noticed that there was something wrong with her eyesight. They hadn't calculated her growth and cheered at every benchmark she'd reached since she was a newborn. To those people, my coworkers, she was just another patient. I understood it. But she wasn't just another patient to Doctor Mendez. Rebel was *her* patient.

"I won't be doing the procedure, but I'll be there the whole time," Doctor Mendez said, holding my gaze. "I won't leave her for a moment."

I nodded, swallowing hard. She didn't have to show up that morning, but when I'd taken Rebel in to get her ears checked the day before and she'd seen what a wreck I was, she'd promised she'd be there.

"Looks like I'm with you this morning," Jan announced to Doctor Mendez as she came back into the room.

"Great." Doctor Mendez glanced at me. "I heard you kicked one of the nurses out."

"She sucks. I've worked with her before," I said, holding my ground. They could bitch all they wanted. If Samantha went anywhere near Rebel, I was going to find her in the dark parking lot after a nightshift.

Doctor Mendez laughed lightly. "Okay, then." She nodded. "You ready?"

"Are you?" I asked seriously.

"Easy peasy," she replied with a reassuring smile.

I took a deep breath and leaned down to kiss Rebel again. "I'll be right here when you wake up, boo," I whispered. She didn't stir.

I leaned back up, nodded once, and before I could change my mind, Jan was kicking off the brakes on the bed and rolling Rebel out of the room.

"I'll come get you as soon as we're done. Quick in and out. We'll be back before you can finish your coffee."

"Not quite," I said tightly.

"Pretty damn close," she shot back. "And then no more ear infections."

She walked out of the room and as soon as she was gone, I staggered backward into Mel.

"You're good," she said, squeezing my shoulders. "Now, let's get out of this room for a few minutes. You're going to be in here for hours until Rebel's released. No use staring at these walls longer than you have to." She gave me a little shove and I started forward, pausing only slightly as my dad wrapped his arm around my shoulders and escorted me out of the room.

"Less bloodshed than I'd imagined," he said as we hit the hallway and turned toward the waiting room. "Nice work."

An hour later, when I was close to losing my shit, Doctor Mendez found us in the little surgical waiting room.

"Everything went well," she said before she'd even come to a stop. "No problems with the anesthesia and the tubes were placed easily."

"Is she off everything?" I asked, moving toward her. I'd already been on my feet. By that point, they were aching from all the pacing I'd been doing.

"Everything but the IV," she said with a nod. "But you knew they wouldn't take that out right away."

"Is she in her room?"

"Jan was taking her there, and I came to find you. By the time you get there, she'll be there—" The words were barely out of her mouth before I was calling *thank you* over my shoulder and racing down the hallway.

It had been the longest hour of my life. Longer than the hour I'd waited for news on Mason after someone had told me he'd collapsed on the football field. Longer than the last hour of labor.

I was shaking with relief when I got to Rebel's room and found Jan tucking her more securely into the bed she was in.

"Didn't want to leave her until you got here, since they didn't put her in a damn crib like they should have," she said, shaking her head.

"Thank you," I said tearfully as I rounded Rebel's bed and climbed up next to her.

"No problem," Jan said as she threw some trash away and moved for the door. "She'll be waking up soon I bet, but she'll be groggy—you probably already know that." She laughed and left the room.

"You did it," I whispered, curling my body around Rebel's. "Good job, baby."

I closed my eyes and shuddered, wrapping my arm around Reb's body, careful not to jostle her.

A few minutes later, I opened my eyes as Mel and my dad came quietly into the room. They'd been awesome during the surgery, talking to each other and to me, but not expecting me to answer. I'd been like a zombie, completely unable to function until I'd known that Rebel was okay. They were just . . . there. Exactly like I'd needed them to be.

Exactly the way I'd needed Will to be. I shook my head once. I was done worrying where the hell Will had disappeared to.

"Everything good?" my dad asked as he sat down in the chair by the bed.

"Yeah." I sighed. Everything was good. I let my eyes drift shut again. I was so fucking tired. I guessed that was what happened when you stayed up the entire night worrying.

The sound of a camera made my eyes shoot open, and I glanced at Mel, who was messing with her phone.

"Sorry, I forgot to turn the stupid sound off," she mumbled.

"What're you doing?" I asked groggily.

"Commemorating Rebel's first successful surgery," Mel said, smiling.

"Only surgery," I corrected.

"Of course."

"Look at me," my dad ordered. When I looked up, he took a photo, too. I groaned as the flash burned my eyes.

"Whoops," he said, messing with his phone.

"Jesus, Gramps," Mel teased. "I think it's bright enough in here without the flash."

"Oh, now I'm a grandpa?" my dad said drolly. "Not ten minutes ago you were—"

"Stop right there," I snapped, lifting my head off the bed. "I can't deal with any more bullshit today."

Mel snorted loudly and Reb jerked awake.

"Finally," I said, smiling down at my bleary-eyed baby. "Good morning, sunshine. Did you have a good nap?"

She looked at me for only a second before her eyes shot down to the IV in her arm, and before I could stop her, she'd ripped it out and was howling in pain.

"Shit!" I hissed, scrambling up to my knees.

"We need a nurse!" Mel yelled into the hallway as I gripped Reb's arm, my thumb putting light pressure on the IV site.

"I *am* a fucking nurse," I mumbled as Jan came running into the room. "I knew something like this was going to happen."

Chapter 12

Will

By the time we'd pulled onto club grounds Saturday morning, I was a fucking nervous wreck. Molly had called and texted when we were on the road to Montana, but I hadn't heard a word from her since. I had no idea how Reb's surgery had gone and it was driving me insane.

I wasn't going to call Molly. I'd already decided that when I left Tuesday morning. Nothing could come of it. She brought up too much old shit, made me feel like I was being pulled in too many different directions. With her apathy for the club, there was no way we could have worked long term. It was better that I'd made a clean break.

"Hey," Dragon's teenage son, Leo, called as we shut off our bikes. He was underneath one of the picnic tables out front messing with the joints.

"Whatcha doin'?" Cam called, doing a squat to stretch his knees. It had been a long day.

"Tightenin' up these tables," he called back. "Lil sat on one earlier and it was so fuckin' wobbly, she almost ended up on her ass."

"Good man," Samson said, kicking Leo's boot as we passed him.

"Your sister here?" Cam asked.

"Nah, she's at your house with the boys."

We filed into the clubhouse, and I immediately started rubbing my hands together, trying to get some warmth into them. It had been a cold and miserable ride back from Montana. Some places we rode though had fucking snow.

"Hey, son," my dad said, coming up behind me as I headed for the coffee maker. Since it was Saturday and the weather was shit, there were a ton of people crowded in around us. Men were bullshitting, playing pool, and it looked like someone had started up a poker game in the corner. They were going to wish they hadn't once Samson realized they were there and sat down with them.

"Hey, Dad," I said, giving him a nod as I grabbed a cup of coffee from some woman playing bartender. She must have been new because I'd never seen her before. Long, light brown hair brushed her tits as she moved, and my eyes got caught for a second before I turned away.

"Everything good?" Dad asked, leaning against the bar next to me.

"Yep, they thought we were nuts for ridin' up. They had no plans on working with the Russians to begin with," I scoffed. Dad probably already knew that since we'd been in constant contact with him since we'd left town. It still irritated the fuck out of me, though. It had been a completely useless trip. "How's Rock?"

"He's fine." Dad motioned with his head toward the corner, where Rock was hanging with Mel. Ah, Christ. "He's been giving names to Duncan as he remembers, but it's takin' longer than they thought."

"Why?"

"Because it was his damn wedding. He was plastered and eager to fuck his wife, so he's havin' a hard time rememberin' everyone who was there," Dad said with a grimace.

"You think he's draggin' his feet?"

"Nah, I think he just wants to make sure he doesn't leave anyone out, since his deal with them depends on the names he gives."

"Makes sense," I mumbled.

"How's your girl's baby doin'?" Dad asked, making me jerk in surprise.

"Don't know," I said, taking a long pull of my coffee and burning the shit out of my mouth.

"You don't know?"

"That's over." I froze when Dad grimaced and shook his head. "What?"

"Your ma took over a couple of Rosie's old dolls this mornin'," he said with a huff.

"Fucking fantastic," I hissed, running a hand over my face. "And?"

"Far as I know, Molly didn't say anything. She just thanked your ma, gave her some coffee and that was it."

My stomach clenched at the thought of Molly not hearing from me for days then having to deal with my mother. "Is Mom here?"

"Nah, she's at home with the girls," he answered, referring to Lily and Rose. If they weren't at our house, they were together at Casper and Farrah's place. They'd always been really close, but I wasn't sure if they'd spent a day apart since the day Lily had gone blind.

"Alright," I said, setting my mug on the bar. "I'll stop by later and let Mom know what's up."

"Probably a good idea, seeing as how she was planning on stopping by Molly's with dinner tomorrow," he said dryly.

"Christ." I walked away and without thought, found myself moving toward Mel and Rocky.

Mel was on Rock's lap and they were talking quietly when I sat down at their table. Before I could even open my mouth, Mel's head was turning toward me and her entire body had stiffened.

"All good?" Rock asked nonchalantly, his arm tightening around Mel's waist.

"Yep," I answered, wishing I hadn't put my coffee down so I'd have something to do with my hands. "Mel," I greeted.

She glared at me for a long moment before Rocky nudged her and she replied, "Will."

"How's Reb?" I didn't want to ask. I wanted to make a clean break.

But I couldn't stop worrying about the kid.

Mel pulled her phone out without answering, and I waited impatiently as she messed with it for a minute before setting it down on the table between us. "She's fine," Mel said emotionlessly.

I didn't reply. I couldn't make myself say anything at all. Right there on her phone was a photo of Molly and Rebel in a hospital bed. Reb was sleeping, her mouth barely hanging open and an IV in her arm. She looked okay. Really fucking small in that hospital bed, but fine otherwise.

It was Molly that caught my attention. She looked like she hadn't slept since the night I'd been with her. There were dark circles around her eyes, and her face was drawn with exhaustion. Her arm was lying over Reb's belly, and she was pretty much curled around the baby, her knees pulled up under Reb's feet and her head lying on the pillow, her lips pressed against Rebel's head.

"That was before Reb woke up and ripped her IV out of her arm and all hell broke loose," Mel said, laying her hand over the phone and pulling it back across the table.

"She alright?" I asked roughly, scratching at my beard. My heart was pounding and I could feel a headache starting at the base of my skull. Everything I felt showed on my face, and I knew it. I wanted to fucking run from that table, but I couldn't let Mel see that she'd gotten to me.

"She's fine now," Mel replied, stuffing her phone back in her purse.

"And Moll?"

"She's fine, too."

"Good."

"Yep."

I glanced up to see her staring. "Thought you'd be ripping my head off about now," I mumbled.

"I don't have to," she said quietly. "This is your place, so it's not like I could do much anyway, but I don't have to rip your head off."

"Oh, yeah? Why's that?"

"Because you're done. It doesn't matter what you do from here. You could go straight to Molly's, but it wouldn't make a difference. She won't see you." She wrapped her arms across her chest and sat up straighter. "You fucked yourself over far worse than anything I could do to you."

She couldn't have stunned me more if she'd reached across the table and punched me in the face. And the way her words came so easily, like she was talking about the weather, made it that much worse. She wasn't trying to convince me. She didn't need to. Because she was completely confident that Molly was done with me.

It was what I'd wanted, wasn't it?

I sat there silently, seeing nothing as Mel asked Rock to take her home. I didn't move when they got up from the table, and I didn't acknowledge Rock when he cuffed my shoulder as they walked away. I'd wanted to be done with Molly. It was for the best. We weren't working.

Except that we had been. We'd worked. Shit had been easy with us. No drama, no games.

As I sat there at the table, I realized that somewhere in the back of my mind, I'd convinced myself that if I could find a way to have the club and Molly, I'd get her back. She loved me. She hadn't said it, but I knew she did. I hadn't really let myself believe that what I was doing was final.

The chair across from me screeched across the floor and I glanced up to find Poet, the former vice-president of the club, sitting down across from me. The guy was grizzled as shit and had given up his seat when the old president, Slider, had died in the shooting at our barbeque. He'd said he just didn't want the title without his best friend at the helm. We'd all understood it. He stuck around, though, still part of the club. Hell, his daughter was married to the current president, so it wasn't as if he'd have gone far anyway.

"You okay, boyo?" he asked gruffly, leaning forward on his elbows.

"Probably not," I said derisively.

"Woman troubles, eh?"

"I fucked up."

"We all fuck up," he said with a laugh. His face lost all humor when I didn't crack a smile. "Well, it can't be as bad as all that."

I said nothing, just held his eyes across the table.

"I think we need a drink," he said confidently, lifting up his arm and waving it from side to side to get the bartender's attention. In just a few minutes, the brunette from the bar was setting two shot glasses on the table with a bottle of expensive whiskey that only Poet bothered with. "Thank you," Poet said politely.

At any other time, I would have laughed at his good manners, but I didn't then.

After he'd poured our first shots and we'd knocked them back, Poet began to speak. "You've probably heard my story, eh?" he said, pouring more whiskey into our glasses. "It's a bit of a tale now, getting passed on like a game of telephone since you were a babe."

"I've heard pieces," I said quietly, taking another shot.

"Ah, well, then. You probably haven't heard the best and worst parts." He took his shot, immediately filling the glasses again, and began to tell his story. Halfway through telling me about his life in Ireland before he'd come to the US, his wife, Amy, came and wrapped her arm around his shoulders. She didn't protest as he pulled her down onto his knee and continued speaking, and soon, both of them were telling me the story from their own points of view.

Because it wasn't just Poet's story. It was Amy's, too. Even though they'd been apart for thirty years of their marriage, the story very much belonged to both of them. I tried not to cringe as they described their flight from Ireland and all the things that had gone wrong, but I took two shots as Amy quietly glossed over her time in Ireland after Patrick had left. That's what she called Poet—Patrick. And the way she said it made her sound like the teenager she'd once been.

I didn't make it to the end of the story, even though I wanted to know what happened. Unfortunately, the whiskey and exhaustion worked against me, and I found myself passing out with my face pressed against the sticky table. There was probably a lesson in that long tale somewhere. Poet didn't tell stories without a reason, but I had no idea what wisdom he'd been trying to impart.

★ ★ ★

"Jesus," I groaned at some point the next day, lifting my head from the bed in my room at the clubhouse. I shivered and pulled at the blanket I was laying on until I could wrap it around my shoulders.

I still had my cut on, but someone had pulled my boots off my feet when they'd helped me into the room. I closed my eyes and tried to remember who'd moved me, but the night was a blank slate after I'd laid my head down on the table while listening to Poet discuss his first years at the club. A couple of the boys must have carried me in, I decided. If a woman had helped me, she would have at least covered me with a blanket. It was cold as fuck in my room.

I knew I needed a shower, but I really didn't want to let go of the little heat I'd found once I'd wrapped myself up like a burrito. I groaned as I threw the blanket back off and climbed to my feet, wiggling my arms like that would help warm me up. I made it halfway across the room to the old dresser I had pushed against the wall before I remembered what had started me drinking the night before.

"Fuck," I yelled, remembering Mel's confident words. I lifted my keys from the top of the dresser and threw them as hard as I could against the wall. The sound they made wasn't even close to satisfying. I searched the room for anything else I could throw, but there was nothing. I didn't have knickknacks.

My eyes caught on the top drawer of my dresser, and without thinking, I'd yanked it out and tossed it across the room. It hit the wall loudly, splintering into pieces as boxer briefs and socks fell all over the floor.

My hands hit the top of my dresser, and I braced myself as I got the anger under control. "Fuck!" I yelled again as the door to my room opened.

"You okay?" Woody asked, his wide eyes taking in the mess.

"Yeah, kid," I said gruffly. "I'm fine."

I strode past him and across the hall to the bathroom, slamming the door behind me. I needed a shower and a cup of coffee. Then I'd head over to Molly's and prove her best friend wrong.

★ ★ ★

Two hours later, I was pulling up in front of Molly's trailer. It actually took four cups of coffee and a big breakfast before I was ready to face her. I wasn't sure what I'd be walking into, but I was pretty confident that we could figure it all out.

I still wasn't positive that we could make it work, but I'd been stupid to break shit off. I'd made it all worse in my head than it actually was. I could keep Molly and the club separate. She just had to know that the club came first. That sometimes, I'd be out of town and she'd have to wait. That's just the way it was. She didn't have to go to club events and shit, but I did. So she'd also have to get on board with that.

I climbed off my bike and strode toward the door confidently. Before I could knock, it swung open, revealing Molly in a pair of yoga pants and a sweatshirt that hung off one shoulder.

"Hey, sugar," I said, leaning down to kiss her.

My stomach rolled when she jerked her head away and took a step backward.

"What's up, Will?" she asked. The words weren't unfriendly. In fact, they were almost pleasant.

"Just came to see you and Reb," I said, walking into the house, even though she sure as shit hadn't invited me in. There were open rubber tubs full of Christmas decorations covering the floor of the living room, and I glanced around to see that she'd moved the furniture so she had room for a Christmas tree. I wondered who was going to help her get one, and almost offered.

"Rebel's playing in her room," she said, reluctantly closing the door behind me. She couldn't stand there with it open because it was so cold outside, but I could tell that she also didn't want to give the impression that she was letting me stay.

"Look," I said, smiling at her. "I know I fucked up, alright?"

"It's fine, Will."

"Nah, I can tell you're pissed."

"I *was* pissed. I'm not anymore." She reached up and absently scratched her shoulder before relaxing against the wall.

"Thank fuck," I murmured, stepping toward her.

"Uh, no," she said, wrinkling her nose as she held up one hand to stop me.

"No, what?"

Molly laughed in disbelief and stood up straight. "No, I don't want you anywhere near me."

"You just said you weren't pissed anymore," I said roughly, ignoring her outstretched hand as I moved closer.

"I'm not," she said, shaking her head. "I'm not mad at you. I just don't want anything to do with you."

My head jerked back in surprise. "What?"

"Will, you disappeared for almost a week."

"I was out of town!"

"Oh, my God, shut up!" she yelled, her eyes widening in disbelief.

"I don't care if you were trapped in a lifeboat in the middle of the goddamn ocean, because here's the thing—Rebel had surgery on Thursday, so you shouldn't have even been in the *goddamn ocean!*"

"I'm supposed to plan my life around *your* kid?" I asked. The minute the words were out of my mouth, I knew how bad they were. I knew, but I still almost staggered at the change that came over Molly's face.

"Mama!" Rebel's voice called, rising as she came down the hallway. "Mama! Mama!"

She got to the end of the hallway and caught sight of me, and I thought my legs were going to give out when her eyes widened behind her glasses and her lips pulled up in a huge grin. "Wiya!" she said happily. "Wiya!"

Holy shit. She could say my name.

Rebel started toward me, but Molly scooped her up before she could get anywhere close.

"I think you need to leave," Molly said quietly as she tried to keep Rebel from squirming away. "Right now, Will."

"Molly—"

"Go."

I held her eyes, hoping that she'd change her mind, but after a moment, I knew she wouldn't. I turned and let myself out the door as Rebel said my name again.

I ignored her. I needed to get the fuck out of there before I lost it.

I'd gotten what I thought I wanted. We were done. It was over.

Chapter 13

MOLLY

18 months later

"I CAN'T BELIEVE you're still seeing him," I said to Mel, throwing my hair into a ponytail. "I did not see *that* coming."

"What're you talking about?" Mel asked, throwing some sodas and juice boxes into my cheap little foam cooler. "You love Rocky."

"He's a good guy," I replied with a nod. "But he was married when you got together."

"Yeah, what a shit show," she mumbled, snorting. "But he's not anymore!"

Her tone had me whipping my head toward her and staring intently. She was grinning, her hands resting on the cooler with one hip cocked out to the side. When my eyes went to her ring finger, she scoffed.

"He didn't ask me to marry him, doofus."

"Then what's with the face?" I asked, tossing her a bag of chips off the table.

"Nothing, I'm just happy." She shrugged her shoulders and stuffed the chips into a huge reusable grocery bag. "And I'm spending the day with my favorite girls and my favorite guy, at my favorite swimming hole."

"Hopefully your favorite girls won't be too tired after an hour," I said dryly, then called for Rebel.

"She's still having a hard time sleeping?"

"Not really," I said, shaking my head. "She's just waking up at the ass crack of dawn. It might be nine for you, but it's practically lunch time for us."

Little footsteps came barreling down the hall, and Rebel slid to a stop on the linoleum, her hair wild around her head. She was already dressed in her little swimsuit with built-in pockets for floaty things, but she'd refused to take her socks off so I could put sandals on her feet.

"You can't wear socks and sandals," Mel told Reb, crouching down to meet her eyes. "It's against the law."

"Socks," Reb answered, looking down at her feet with a decisive nod.

She was such a cool kid, but so goofy. I laughed at her annoyed expression. She wouldn't let me paint her toenails because she couldn't stand the feeling of the brush sliding over her nails, but it was a fight to get her to wear sandals because her feet weren't 'pretty' like mine.

"Hey, Reb," I called, walking toward the door where I'd hung my purse high on a hook. I'd started hanging it at eye level when Rebel had started getting into everything she could reach.

The knives were stored above the fridge. All medicines and vitamins were kept in a lockbox on the top shelf of a bookcase in my room. There were outlet covers on all of the electrical sockets, safety latches on all the cabinets and my dad had installed slide locks high on all doors leading outside *and* the bathrooms. I couldn't be too careful.

The older Rebel got, the more we were able to understand her and her quirks. We'd realized after she'd begun talking that she was definitely on the autism spectrum, though that wasn't uncommon in kids with Down syndrome. It was just another facet of Reb, nothing more, nothing less. She had sensory issues, but I'd already known that. And she didn't talk as much as other kids who were three and a half years old, but that wasn't really a surprise, either.

The tubes in her ears had helped with her verbal skills, though. It was like she'd finally been able to hear herself unmuffled for the first time, and the words had come pouring out. Doctor Mendez reminded me more than once that that wasn't how the tubes worked, but I still wasn't convinced. After the tubes had been placed, Rebel had started speaking like never before.

I hated that her second word was Will's name, but I chose not to think about it. She'd asked for him almost every day for a full year before she'd finally let it go, but there were still days when she'd look at me and say his name like she was wondering if he was real. I'd learned to change the subject.

She had the memory of an elephant. If I told her that we were going to my dad's and we weren't able to, she'd remind me every day for a month in a mixture of modified sign language and a spattering of spoken words.

There still weren't full sentences. I didn't expect them.

I pulled out a pair of water shoes from my purse and moved back toward Rebel. "Look what I got you. These are shoes for the river." She tried to take them out of my hand, but I lifted them above her head, making her huff in annoyance. "You can't wear them with socks."

"Socks," she ground out, throwing her arms up in her sign for *I'm sick of your shit*.

"No socks, Rebel," I said, still holding her water shoes out of her reach.

"Yes."

"No."

"Yes."

She threw her arms up again, and watched me closely for a reaction. When I didn't give her one, she plopped down on her bottom and slowly peeled the socks from her feet. Then she stuck her hand out for the shoes.

"You need help?" I asked as I handed them to her.

Reb's hand made a shooing motion and I heard Mel's choked laugh behind me.

"She told you."

"Can you imagine her as a teenager?" I asked in exasperation, standing up and grabbing a pair of scissors from the top of the fridge.

Yeah, scissors went up there, too. For a while, I'd tried to hide that I'd put everything sharp up there, but Rebel had figured it out and one morning, I'd caught her using a chair to climb onto the counter so she could reach them. My dad had helped me tie the chairs to the table legs after that.

I cut the little plastic tie between Rebel's new water shoes as soon as she had them on her feet then watched her walk gingerly around the room. After a few minutes, she glanced in my direction, but not directly at me, and nodded once.

I guessed they'd passed the test.

Within minutes, we were piled into my car and headed toward the river. It was still pretty early in the summer, so we probably wouldn't swim, but the sun felt nice after the gloomy winter and spring we'd had. A light on my dash flashed on, and I debated how far I could drive before I ran out of gas, deciding at the last minute to pull into a gas station.

"I'm only putting ten bucks in," I warned Mel as she took off her seatbelt. "Don't take forever."

"I won't!" she protested, even though we both knew that it would take her a solid ten minutes in the store. She had the hardest time deciding on what to buy, it didn't matter what she was shopping for. "You want something to drink?"

"We've got soda in the cooler," I reminded her.

"Yeah, but that's not gas station soda. That's grocery store soda." She climbed out of the car, then leaned back in the open window. "I'll get you fountain soda."

She blew me a kiss and sauntered into the gas station just as the attendant came to my window. He took my wrinkled ten dollar bill and started the pump as I tried to get more comfortable in my seat. My thighs were sticking to the fake leather, but my air conditioner was broken so it didn't matter how much I moved, they were still going to sweat and stick.

I'd just tugged my shorts a little lower on my hips when the sound of a Harley's pipes filtered in my window, making me freeze. They always made me freeze.

Over the past year and a half, I'd only seen Will four times, and only because I kept my eye out for him. Once at the grocery store, twice when I was driving to work, and once when Reb and I had been walking out of her speech therapist's office and he'd been going into the building across the street. I never talked to him. I practically hid.

The attendant was unhooking the pump from my car when the bike rolled to a stop just fifty feet from us in a parking spot. A man and a woman got off, and my stomach sunk in realization.

Will's hair was longer than it had been when we were together, and it was tied back in a super short ponytail at the base of his neck. A few strands fell forward as he pulled off his helmet, and he unconsciously brushed them behind his ears as he laughed at something the woman said. I glanced at her and my stomach rolled. She was pretty. Long brown hair that looked tangled from the ride, and light eyes, either blue or green. I couldn't tell the color when she moved her sunglasses to the top of her head.

I sat frozen as Will fiddled with something in his saddlebags, and I contemplated just leaving Mel in the store and taking off, but I was too afraid to turn my car on and bring attention to myself.

Will was turned away from us when Mel finally walked out of the glass doors carrying a couple of fountain drinks and a little bag, but her eyes widened in recognition when she glanced toward him. She practically sprinted across the parking lot.

My eyes were glued to Will as Mel jumped into the car, taking in the easy way he set his hand on the woman's hip as she messed with the front of her shirt, the way his head tilted toward her like maybe he couldn't hear her or he just wanted to be a little closer. My throat grew tight as I watched his fingers squeeze for a second and pull her toward him.

"Molly," Mel said quietly. "Let's go."

I jolted out of the weird space I'd been in, and turned the key, breathing a small huff of relief when Will's head didn't move in our direction.

But then I heard something in the back seat. A tentative word. Rebel said it again a little louder, like she was getting used to it, like she was making sure it sounded right. Then she was yelling it at the top of her lungs, and it was flying out her open window and across the parking lot.

"Will!" Reb yelled excitedly, kicking her legs and pulling at her seat buckle. "Will!"

I watched in horror as Will's eyes jerked to my car, his jaw dropping as he pulled the sunglasses off his face.

"Will!"

His smile was the widest I'd ever seen it in the entire seventeen years I'd known him.

He took a step forward and I frantically slammed the car into drive.

Our eyes met just as the woman he was with said something to him, laughing, and the smile dropped off his face.

"Holy shit," I mumbled as I jerked away from the pump, my hands shaking as I flipped on my blinker and sped back onto the road. "Holy shit. Holy shit."

"No!" Rebel yelled in the back seat. I looked in the rearview mirror to find her twisting toward the back window of the car. "No, Mama!"

"Calm down," Mel said, putting her hand on my thigh. "You're okay. It's over. You're fine."

I whipped into a parking lot less than a mile down the road and threw the car into park, covering my face with my hands.

"No!" Rebel was throwing a full-on tantrum in the back seat, ripping at her seat belt and arching her back against the restraints as I tried to get my breathing under control. "Will! No!"

"Jesus Christ!" I blurted, tears coming to my eyes as I frantically pushed myself out of the car. I wanted to go get her, hold her in my arms and tell her that everything was okay, but I couldn't.

Rebel couldn't stand for me to touch her when she was having a fit. It was too much stimulation. It had taken me a long time to get used to my baby not wanting me to comfort her, but I'd managed, even though it still killed me to leave her alone when she was having such a hard time. She was safe in her seat. She couldn't accidentally hurt herself. I needed to remember that.

"Goddammit!" I yelled, lifting my hands to my hair. "Motherfucking son of a bitch!"

"You're going to get us arrested," Mel commented as she followed me out of the car. "You about done?"

"Why does he still get to me? It's so fucking irritating!"

"Maybe because you haven't dated anyone else?"

"I don't want to date anyone. I like my life how it is!"

"Well, then, I don't know!" she yelled back. "Maybe it's because he did you dirty! Maybe it's because you have a kid that's reminded you of his existence every day for the past year and a half! Maybe it's because he was good in bed! How the fuck am I supposed to know why you can't forget him? Don't yell at me!"

"I'm sorry," I ground out. "I was yelling at the universe, not you."

"I don't think the universe is listening," she said simply, leaning against the hood of my car. "It's over. You saw him. He saw you. Reb saw him. It's over."

"Did you see her face?" I hissed, bursting into tears. "Jesus Christ, did you see Reb's face?"

"Yeah, girl. I did," she replied softly. "But listen, she's not yelling anymore."

We both looked in the front windshield to find Reb sitting silently, looking out her window.

"I probably freaked her out," I said in defeat, wiping at my face as I moved around the car.

"Nah, she's tough. She's heard me scream obscenities plenty of times," Mel said jokingly, turning to watch me.

I opened Reb's door and reached in, unbuckling her and pulling her into my arms. For a second, she held her body rigid against me then with a sigh, she relaxed, dropping her head onto my shoulder.

"Will?" she whispered.

"You ready to go to the river?" I asked, swaying slowly from side to side as I ignored her question. "Rocky's waiting for us there."

"Rock?" she asked, leaning back to glance at my face. She had tear tracks running down her cheeks, but I didn't wipe them away. She didn't like it when people touched her face, only letting me get near it if I was using a washcloth.

"You know it. You ready?"

She smacked the side of her suit and I nodded. "I know. We need to put the floaty things back in. We'll do that when we get there."

I got her back in the car and looked over the door at Mel. "Can you drive?"

"No problem," she murmured, rounding the car and sliding into the driver's seat.

"Goddammit," I whispered one more time before opening my door.

★ ★ ★

"Dad, I've been calling you for hours," I huffed into the phone as I opened my car door. "I have to work and you're supposed to be watching Reb. I'm on the way to your house right now, so you better be home." I pressed my finger hard against the screen of my phone, irritated that I couldn't slam it shut. Flip phones really had been satisfying when you were pissed at someone.

It was two weeks after I'd seen Will at the gas station, and shit had gone mostly back to normal. We'd had a good day with Rocky and Mel, and by the time we'd gotten home that afternoon, Reb had been too tired to pester me about Will. She'd pretty much just sat on the couch and watched *Sesame Street* for the few hours before bed.

The next morning, she'd been back with the questions, though. I guess it was just one question, really. All day, every day. "*Will?*"

There wasn't any answer she accepted. I could distract her for a while, but it always came back to Will.

I ground my teeth as I headed toward my dad's house. I was starting my first night shift at the hospital and I was already so tired, I wasn't sure how I was going to make it. Rebel woke up at four in the morning pretty much every day, so both of us were usually dragging ass by the afternoon. I hadn't asked for the shift change, but apparently, I didn't have a choice in the matter. Unfortunately, the daycare we loved that Rebel had attended for years wasn't open in the evenings. Thankfully, my dad had a room for Reb at his house, and he'd agreed that she could stay the night with him when I was working. I wasn't sure how other single parents did it.

We pulled slowly up my dad's driveway as I tried to avoid all of the holes that the winter rains had dug into the gravel. My dad lived on some property outside of town, and every year, he had to have his road re-graded because water had completely decimated it during the rainy season. It drove me nuts that he refused to pave it. It wasn't like he didn't have the money.

When we got to the house, there was a car in the driveway that I didn't recognize, and it irritated me because he knew he was supposed to be watching Rebel. I wasn't sure if it was a client or a woman, but I didn't really give a shit. I only had a half an hour to get to work on time, so they were just going to have to deal with a busy three year old running around the house.

"Come on, Reb," I said, climbing out of the car. She was busy on the Kindle she'd gotten last Christmas, and didn't even bother acknowledging me as I moved around to her side of the car and unbuckled her from her seat belt.

I carried her toward the front porch, practically dragging her overnight bag behind us. The thing was packed full of her pajamas, three pairs of clean socks, her blanket, four stuffed animals, a change of clothes for the next day, and the ratty old towel that Will had put her to bed with when she was little and she couldn't sleep without. My dad's door was closed, and he didn't answer when I kicked it repeatedly with my foot. I reached out and flung it open, glad it wasn't locked so I didn't have to go back to the car for my keys.

"Dad, you better be decent!" I yelled as I closed the door behind me. "You said you'd watch Reb tonight!"

I moved into the house, and only after I'd gotten like six feet from the front door did I notice how unnaturally quiet the place was. The hair on the back of my neck prickled, but before I could turn around, it was too late.

"Come in," an accented voice called from the kitchen, making my head snap up.

There were two men standing there, one older and fat, the other tall and bulky. The short one had his arms crossed and was relaxing against the countertop, and the big one was standing with his legs braced wide, his hands loose at his sides.

My dad was tied to a chair in the middle of the kitchen, and his face was almost unrecognizable.

I made a noise in the back of my throat, and for a split second, I wanted to run toward him. But then Rebel shifted a little in my arms and I immediately took a step backward as some character on her Kindle giggled.

"Uh uh," the short one murmured in amusement, making me break out in a cold sweat. "Come closer."

I contemplated running for less than a second, but I knew I wouldn't get far. Rebel was close to forty pounds. There was no way I could carry her out of the house with any sort of speed.

I didn't move closer like he'd asked. Instead, I planted my feet and dropped Reb's bag to the floor. I needed to make sure I had at least one arm free, though I wasn't really sure what I could do with it.

"You shouldn't have come," my dad mumbled through swollen lips, making the big guy punch him in the side of the head. I jerked, and pulled Reb closer.

"Your father and I were just discussing some business," the short one said calmly. "You're Molly, yes? When someone doesn't answer your calls, that usually means they are unavailable."

I shuddered as the man picked my dad's cell phone off the counter and dropped it to the floor so he could stomp on it.

"Cat got your tongue?"

"I'll just go," I said hoarsely, taking another step back.

"Now that you are here," the short guy said, shaking his head and lifting his hands up in a *what can you do?* gesture.

I took another step back, and hit something. When I glanced behind me, a scream got trapped in my throat. There was a third man.

"Mr. Duncan, this worked out not so well for you," the short one said jovially as the man behind me shoved me forward. I looked down at Reb to see her staring at her Kindle, and I was grateful for the first time ever that she'd checked out. She was in her own world at the moment.

"Let her go," my dad breathed, his voice barely audible.

"Come on," short man called, waving me forward. "Hold your granddaughter, Duncan."

The big guy cut the ropes from my dad's wrists, and his hands fell limply to his sides. I pulled Rebel even tighter against me as we got closer. My hands were shaking so badly that I wasn't even sure how I was still holding her.

Who were these men? What the hell had my dad gotten into? There was no way for me to call for help. My dad's cell phone was in pieces on the floor, and I'd left mine in the cup holder in my car. I briefly thought about the hospital noticing my absence, but knew instinctively that they'd just assume I'd been a flake. If I didn't show up by the end of my shift, they'd wonder why I wasn't there, but it's not like they'd file a missing person's report.

There was no one looking for us. No one to realize that we weren't where we were supposed to be.

"Give the child to Duncan, or I will," the short man ordered. He didn't raise his voice or do anything outwardly intimidating, but the calm way he'd spoken was almost worse.

I squeezed my eyes shut for a moment, and shook my head. I didn't know what the fuck they were going to do, but they wouldn't touch my kid as long as I was still breathing. I locked eyes with the short man, and his lips quirked up just a fraction.

"Hold her," he snapped at the man behind me.

I jerked when the man's fingers dug into my biceps, and Rebel's ear piercing scream rang through the house as the short man snatched her from my arms. I fought like hell, yanking as hard as I could against the hands that held me, but I couldn't get free. My scrub top ripped as I fought, and I bit my tongue as the guy shook me. As soon as the short man had Rebel, the man behind me pulled my hands behind my back.

Then, in less than ten seconds, it was over. Rebel stopped screaming as soon as the short man set her on my dad's lap. He held her awkwardly, like the weight of her was painful, but he didn't let go.

He met my eyes across the room, and I saw everything he was feeling. The fear, the apology, the determination. The love.

"Now that is done," short man said briskly, wiping his hands on a handkerchief. He nodded to the man behind me and I was shoved forward again, until I was just feet from my dad and Rebel.

"You have high pain tolerance, no?" short man asked my dad, tilting his head to the side. "Daughter have same pain tolerance?"

His words barely registered before his fist hit my belly, knocking the air out of me in a whoosh. I choked, panicking when I couldn't inhale.

"No!" my dad yelled, startling Reb. I glanced toward them as I sucked in a desperate gasp of air and met my dad's eyes again, just barely shaking my head.

He had Rebel. He couldn't draw attention to himself again. It wasn't worth it. The men were going to do anything they wanted. We couldn't stop them. I felt a sob climb up the back of my throat, but held it in.

They didn't seem interested in Rebel. When the short man had taken her, he hadn't hurt her. He'd been almost gentle. I had to focus on that.

"You make list, yes?" the short man asked my dad, looking at the big guy next to him and gesturing to me. "I would like that list. Simple trade, eh?"

My dad's swollen jaw twitched and he met my eyes, just as the big guy came forward, punching me in the face. My glasses flew off and an inarticulate sound ripped from my throat as my vision went black for a second, my legs turning to Jell-O beneath me.

"Mama?" Rebel's voice had my mouth snapping shut as I tried to stand back up. The man behind me was still holding me up, but I was having a really hard time bracing myself. My arms were already throbbing painfully.

"It's all good, Reb," I told her, my voice unnaturally high. "Sit with Grampy."

"You good mother," the short one said with a nod.

I stared at him uncomprehendingly as he nodded again and I took another fist to the face, the blow knocking my head backward so hard that it clipped the chin of the man behind me, making him grunt.

I didn't make a sound.

"You have list for me?"

My dad didn't say a word, and another blow caught me in the stomach, making me heave. I didn't vomit, but the dry heaves hurt like a motherfucker. I still didn't make a sound. I looked at Rebel, and the only thing I could see was the back of her head resting on my dad's chest. He'd turned her away. I was so grateful.

"Still, no answer," short man said to the man behind me with a shrug, like he couldn't believe we were being so stubborn.

I had no idea what he wanted. None. My dad seemed to know exactly what the man was talking about, but I didn't have a clue about the list he was asking for. What kind of list? Was it something my dad knew, or was it an actual list, like on a piece of paper? I knew where the safe was, but even if I showed it to them, I had no idea what the code to unlock it was. Even if I tried to help them, I didn't have anything they wanted.

As they hit me, I tried to think of any way I could get my dad to give them what they'd asked for, but the minute the blows stopped, I knew deep in my gut that if my dad refused to give it to them, there was a reason. I didn't understand what was happening, and I understood it even less as the kitchen around me grew hazy, but I knew that if my dad could stop them, he would.

They shuffled me around the kitchen, and I barely registered it as the man behind me let go of one of my wrists, his arm wrapping around my belly as we came to a stop. I could barely hold my head up, and my hair was hanging in my face.

I couldn't see my dad. I couldn't see anything but the tile on the floor of the kitchen. I wished I would have put my hair up in a ponytail.

My eyes flew wide as a loud thump filled the kitchen, and I couldn't stop the scream that burst out of my throat as fire flew up my arm.

"I'll tell you anything you want!" my dad yelled, his voice breaking. "Anything. Everything."

My body collapsed against the man behind me as I stared in horror at my broken forearm. It was bent down at a weird angle, and there was a large lump where it was already beginning to swell. I'd seen plenty of fractures as a nurse, but I'd never actually had one. Oddly enough, it was beginning to go numb until the short man gripped it in his hand, making me scream again.

"I'll tell you," Dad said again, as Rebel began to screech in short, staccato bursts. "Let them leave and I'll tell you."

"But how will I know that you keep your word?"

"I swear it," my dad promised. "I swear it."

Rebel stopped screaming and I peeked over to find that she was sitting at my dad's feet. He must have set her there when she'd started screaming. She hadn't wanted him to touch her. Even surrounded by those other big men, she hadn't wanted his comfort.

I felt a calloused hand grip my chin and my head was lifted until I was nose to nose with the short man.

"You go to police, you're dead," he said simply, shaking my head a little. "You go to police, father is dead."

"Okay," I rasped.

"You say nothing," he ordered.

"Okay." I was already imagining how fast I could dial my phone as soon as I got Rebel out of there.

He slapped my cheek. "You say nothing."

"Okay," I said again.

The man behind me let go and stepped away, and I stumbled, the kitchen tilting.

"Maybe, I keep you," the short man mused as I shuffled toward Rebel and my dad.

"I won't tell you a goddamn thing until they're gone," my dad rasped, glaring at the three men.

"Ah, not to worry. I have no use for child. Dirty business, making war with children."

I reached my dad, and laid my hand lightly on his arm as I called Rebel's name. The muscles beneath my hand flexed, but he didn't move as I rubbed my thumb across his skin. He didn't want to give the men any reason to change their mind.

I wasn't sure why he'd finally broken. I'd been beaten until everywhere above my hips throbbed with every beat of my heart, but suddenly my dad had been willing to talk. A small seed of resentment bloomed as I helped Rebel to her feet. I was bleeding, and I wasn't even sure where it was coming from, and after the last half an hour of getting the crap kicked out of me, my dad was going to tell them what they wanted to know anyway. It was all for nothing.

"Come on, Rebel," I whispered, my throat too sore to speak at a normal level. Had they hit me there? I couldn't remember.

As soon as I had Rebel's hand in mine, I looked at my dad. "I love you, Dad."

"You too, princess."

I stared into his eyes and I knew that was the last time I would. The grief was there, like someone tapping on my shoulder, but I didn't feel it then. I couldn't. I had to get my baby out of that house. It was the only thing I could focus on. Not the blood dripping down my neck, not the throbbing arm, not my dad's mangled face. No, the only thing I could think of was getting Rebel as far away as I possibly could. It was like I had tunnel vision. The only thing I could see was Rebel away from those monsters.

I walked her out of the house as quickly as I could, but it still wasn't very fast. She moved slow as a snail on a regular day, especially when I wasn't pulling her along behind me telling her to hurry up a little. We shuffled out the front door and I heard the short man's voice calling out, but I didn't stop. Not for one second.

I held Rebel back at the top of the stairs, then used my good arm to lift her when I reached the bottom. I realized somewhat vaguely that she'd dropped her Kindle as I stumbled to the car. Gripping the handle of her door, I moaned as I used the hand on my bad arm to pull it open. My stomach rolled.

"In," I said frantically, awkwardly shoving Reb into her seat. My hand wasn't working properly, so it took me three attempts to get her seatbelt buckled.

As I finally slammed her door shut, the big man that had held me came out onto the porch and I yelped as I threw my door open, falling into the seat even as I rushed to close it behind me. A wave of dizziness rolled over me as I turned the key in the ignition.

I shouldn't be driving. I could barely even see without my glasses, and I was bleary-eyed with pain.

I slammed the car into drive and braced my left arm against my chest as I spun the car around, spitting gravel at the man climbing into the car I hadn't recognized when I'd pulled up earlier. A quick glance in the mirror told me that he was following me, and I sobbed as I raced down the driveway, each pot hole jostling my small car so much that little whimpers left my mouth.

When I got to the road, I turned right. I didn't think it over or debate about it. I just hit the accelerator and tore down the road in the opposite direction of town. It would take me too long to get there and the man was right behind me. There was no one at my house. If I went to the police station, he'd kill me before I even got inside.

There was only one place that I knew people would greet me the minute I pulled up.

Less than five minutes later, I was at the Aces MC gates.

I didn't stop the car until my front bumper had hit the chain link.

"What the fuck?" one of the men standing on the other side of the fence yelled.

I looked in my rearview mirror to see the man race past my car, not even slowing.

"You lost, lady?" the other guy at the gate asked.

I shook my head, and reached across myself to open my door.

"Stay in your car," the kid called again. He seemed young.

Then I realized it was Tommy Hawthorne.

"Tommy," I rasped, practically falling out of my car. "Men—"

I couldn't catch my breath.

"Molly?" he asked dubiously, rushing for the center of the gate where a large chain held it closed.

"My dad's house. Russian men."

"Holy fuck!" he blurted as he got the gate open. "Go get help!"

The other guy went running as Tommy finally opened up the gate.

"Where's the baby?" he asked, lifting his arms like he wasn't sure where to touch me, or if he should.

"Backseat," I answered, just as I started sobbing in relief.

Chapter 14

WILL

My mother was a pain in my ass. She irritated the hell out of me, but I loved her so I could never tell her no. Even when she asked me to climb up on the makeshift stage at her birthday barbeque and jam with Leo and Trix like we were the fucking Partridge family.

Which was what I was doing at that moment.

It wasn't the first time she'd asked me to do it, and it probably wouldn't be the last time—but I wasn't in the mood. Trix and Leo were insanely good. The brother and sister came by their talent naturally. I'd seen their mom, Brenna, wail on the drums more than once and I'd heard that she could play a shit load of other instruments by ear. Her kids seemed to have followed in her footsteps. Both could play the drums, guitar and who knew what other instruments like they were born to do it, but I just barely got by on my bass, which made me feel like an even bigger asshole when I played with them.

We'd been playing at the barbeques on and off since we were kids, and for the past few years had started out our tried-and-true set with the same song. It was a tribute of sorts, and it didn't matter how many times we played it, all the women of the club stopped whatever they were doing and stood still, watching us. "I Will Follow You into the Dark" by Death Cab for Cutie wasn't really the older generation's style, but when Trix had sung it exactly a year after the shooting that had killed my little brother, great-grandmother, the Aces' president, Slider, and his wife, Vera, everyone had stopped and stared. A song about following your spouse when they died, even if heaven and hell wouldn't take them—well, that resonated with the rowdy bikers and their old ladies. It was also extremely fitting for our fallen president and his wife.

I glanced at my mom and met her eyes as Trix sang, and I couldn't help but nod when she mouthed 'thank you.' Yeah, I'd do anything for that woman and she knew it. Thank God. She hadn't talked to me for weeks after I'd gone off on her the year before, but she'd eventually forgiven me.

As soon as the first song was over, we fell into a familiar pattern of songs that rarely changed. Leo sang most of them and Trix had a couple, too, but I kept my mouth clenched shut. I wasn't singing, I didn't care what kind of puppy dog eyes my mother gave me. I was fucking twenty-three years old, goddamnit. I'd been to prison. I wore an Aces cut. I made my own damn decisions. Just for good measure, I didn't look her way again.

We knew the songs, knew that everyone liked them, and knew we could get our asses off the stage when we hit the end of our short list. So I was surprised as fuck when a few songs in, Leo completely stopped drumming and singing—well, yelling. We didn't have any mics or anything, so he had to sing pretty loud.

My hands went still as I glanced over my shoulder at him. He was staring emotionlessly off to the side of the clubhouse, and when I followed his line of sight, I cursed under my breath.

Fucking Cecilia.

She'd just shown up in a barely decent top that I sure as fuck didn't want to see on my little cousin, and was chatting with a prospect. She knew that shit would piss Leo off. I had no clue what was going on with them, but they'd been dancing around each other, fighting and making up for the past few years.

Trix stopped when she realized we were no longer playing, and she turned abruptly to her brother.

It only took seconds for both of us to stop playing, but that must have been what Leo was looking for, because as soon as we were silent, he started yelling/singing again.

"*La, La, Lalala,*" he sang, a nasty smile on his face as he started drumming.

Oh, shit. The familiar Offspring song made me groan and I immediately looked at Cam, who was standing near Trix's side of the stage with their sons playing in the grass at his feet.

He was livid at Leo's choice of music. It was a good song, but fuck, "Self Esteem" was about a chick that kept fucking around on her man and he just kept taking her back.

And Leo was staring right at Cecilia while he sang it.

Trix looked at her feet, then glanced my way, shrugging her shoulders as she started to play. She wasn't about to leave her brother hanging, even if he was making a complete jackass out of himself. My fingers hit the notes on my bass without thought and I shrugged back as I joined in.

I watched the crowd as a few of the guys started laughing, but my dad, Uncle Casper and Dragon were not amused.

They were even less amused when my little sister, Rose, led our cousin Lily onto the grass directly in front of the stage. The two had been practically inseparable since they were born just six months apart, so it wasn't surprising to see them together. What *was* surprising was the fact that they must not have felt the tension that filled the field we were standing in. As they came to a stop, Lily's head was nodding along with the beat, her thin, fourteen-year-old shoulders moving slightly while Rose stood still next to her.

Then my baby cousin surprised the fuck out of me when she started rocking. *Hard.*

I couldn't help but grin when Lily suddenly let go of Rose and threw up devil horns, her hair flying all over the place as she danced.

She was really fucking moving, jumping and whipping her hair around, and most of the crowd around us stopped to stare. They weren't being rude—most had smiles on their faces, but they were definitely staring.

My little sister looked around with a scowl, then got this determined look on her face. I knew that fucking look, and I felt my shoulders get tight as I watched her.

My shoulders relaxed again as Rose began to move. She was tentative at first, barely nodding her head. Then she closed her eyes, shook out her arms, and started jumping and jerking alongside Lily. Making sure that the crowd was watching *both* of them.

Christ, I loved that kid.

Leo screamed out the lyrics about his girl sleeping with his friends, then his voice abruptly cut off as he caught sight of the girls dancing in front of us.

Trix and I stopped, too, and it irritated the shit out of me. Couldn't we make it through one fucking song? I wanted to finish out the fucking set and get off that damn stage.

"Hey," Lily yelled, pulling my attention forward again.

She turned her face toward the stage, her unfocused eyes pointed in our direction. "I want more Offspring."

I smiled as Leo chuckled. "Nah," he called out quietly, knowing Lily would hear him. "Pretty girl deserves a pretty girl song."

Leo met Trix's eyes and I had no idea how she knew, but she immediately started playing. I laughed quietly, then joined in, looking back at Leo for a second.

His eyes were soft—that's the only way I knew how to explain it. They were tender, indulgent, and they were pointed right at Lily, who was smiling sweetly as her hips moved from side to side, her arms high above her head.

Leo sang the first verse of "Sweet Child O' Mine" in his gravelly voice.

Lily's mom—my Aunt Farrah—whooped loudly, then made her way to our little makeshift stage, shaking her hips and singing along. My mom and Brenna followed her, shaking their asses, too, and I started laughing.

They were all dancing like crazy and signing along, and Lily was smiling so huge, her cheeks must have been aching.

Leo didn't take his eyes off Lily as she spun around and around in a circle.

We went through a lot more songs after that, and I couldn't even let myself bitch about it. Brenna's pop, Poet, and his wife, Amy, were dancing, his hands on her ass to the side of the stage. From the look on my mom's face as she sat on my dad's lap, he was singing in her ear, and Dragon and Brenna had disappeared not long after he'd pulled her from the dance floor and threw her over his shoulder.

It was fucking awesome to see everyone so happy. There was a time only a few years before that I hadn't imagined any of us laughing or having a good time again.

When we were finally done for the night and the boys were setting up the sound system, I had sweat pooling at the base of my spine and I was pretty sure I stank. Did I remember to put on deodorant that day? I wasn't completely sure—but I decided I'd just keep my arms down until I could grab a quick shower inside the clubhouse.

I was setting my bass back in its case when a bunch of loud voices came from the edge of the clubhouse to my left, not far from where Cecilia had been standing earlier. My heart thumped hard in my chest at the commotion, and my head snapped up to analyze the threat. I'd been caught unprepared in the past, but I never would again.

Then my jaw dropped as Samson and a prospect—I could never remember his name—came around the back, half dragging and half carrying a girl between them.

What the fuck?

My stomach sank as I recognized the yellow and blue scrubs with purple fish the woman was wearing and I jumped down off the stage, my bass forgotten as I jogged toward them.

It couldn't be her. No way. She wouldn't come out to the clubhouse.

I took the woman in fully from head to toe. Fuck.

She was bloody. Her scrubs were ripped and her head was rolling on her shoulders as she tried really hard to keep her feet under her.

I told myself that lots of women probably wore those scrubs. Lots of women had that color hair and those same ugly as fuck tennis shoes. I'd almost convinced myself when her head rolled to the side and I caught a glimpse of her face. Her blue eyes met mine, and she let out a short sob.

No.

"Will," she whispered, her lips trembling.

"Aw, fuck, sweetheart," I groaned, lurching forward so I could pull her slight frame gingerly into my arms. "What the fuck happened?"

"Some Russian guys were at my dad's," Molly whimpered in confusion. "I don't—I don't know what they wanted."

I opened my mouth to curse when my name was called. I jerked my head up as I wrapped my arm around Molly's waist and found my little brother carrying Rebel across the grass. She was squirming hard trying to get down, but he held her fast as he hurried toward me.

"She's fine," he said, catching my eyes. "It's just Molly."

"*Bad business making war with children,*" Molly said quietly, her Russian accent spot-on.

"Oh, God," my mom said as she came hurrying across the yard. There were still people everywhere, but they'd quieted down and were staring as I lifted Molly into my arms. She moaned deeply as I moved her, and that's when I saw her arm. It was black and blue and swollen as hell.

"Someone get Dragon!" my dad yelled. "Samson, Hulk, Casper,

meet you out front."

I hadn't even realized that he'd come up behind me.

"What happened?" my dad barked as I carried Molly toward my room. My heart was beating so hard, I wondered if I was about to have a heart attack.

"I went to my dad's house," Molly slurred as her eyes found Rebel in Tommy's arms. He was keeping pace with us, just enough distance between us that he wasn't in my way, but close enough that Rebel could see her mom. After she'd called my name, she'd gone silent, but she watched Molly like a hawk.

"Who was there?" my dad asked patiently as my mom held open the back door to the clubhouse.

"Three guys. Two big, one little. No—fat. Short and fat." More blood came out of her mouth and I didn't know if it was from cuts in her mouth or something else. I barely breathed as my dad swung open the door to my room and I stepped inside.

"Russian?" my dad asked as Farrah came running into the room with Brenna and Dragon on her heels.

"I think so," Molly said, pushing against me as I tried to lay her down on the bed. I stepped back just in time for her to sit back up, holding that swollen arm against her belly. "They didn't introduce themselves, but they sounded like Russian accents."

"Lots of eastern Europeans have similar accents," Dragon said, leaning against the doorframe.

"I might be wrong," Molly admitted as Tommy carried Rebel into the room. "Come here, boo."

Tommy set Rebel on her feet, and she walked slowly to Molly, peeking up at all the strangers as she went. Without thought, I grabbed her under the armpits and hefted her onto the bed. She'd grown a lot since I'd seen her last.

"They're at your dad's place?" my dad asked.

"They were when we left," Molly answered, wincing as Reb leaned against her side. Her little face was hidden in Molly's arm pit.

"Why'd you come here?" Dragon barked, making Molly's eyes drop to the floor.

"I shouldn't have," she choked out, bracing one arm on the bed as she tried to stand back up.

I jerked toward her, sure she was going down, when Dragon spoke again.

"You're Duncan's kid—always welcome here. Sit your ass back down." He sighed. "We'll head on over to your pop's, see what's goin' on."

"You'll be too late," Molly said seriously, lifting her eyes from the floor. "They wanted a list and he said he'd give it if they let me go. He's already dead."

"Motherfuck!" Casper hissed from the doorway.

"Gotta go," my dad said, kissing my mom's lips as he left the room.

"Be back soon," Dragon said to Brenna, pulling her in for a kiss as he left.

"Don't kiss me, just go," Farrah ordered Casper, making him grin. "I'll see you in a bit."

"Love you."

"If you get yourself hurt, I'll cut your balls off," she snapped, moving toward Molly. "I love you, too."

Tommy followed them out of the room, and it was just me and the women. I had no idea what the fuck to do. Part of me was anxious to follow my brothers, but I couldn't make my feet move. It was the closest I'd been to Molly and Rebel in over a year and I couldn't make myself walk away. A few seconds later, I heard the roar of pipes and realized my decision had been made for me. They were leaving me behind.

"What hurts?" my mom asked gently as she crouched down in front of Molly.

"Everything," she mumbled through swollen lips. Her words grew more garbled by the minute, probably from the swelling. It would get worse before it was better.

"Are you okay?" Amy asked as she pushed in the door, closing it behind her. She took in Molly's appearance, then met her gaze straight on. "You want Will out of the room?" Something in her voice made me stiffen, looking down at Molly's scrub bottoms that were covered in blood.

"I don't care," Molly mumbled, her eyes quickly flickering toward me. Farrah handed Rebel her phone with some obnoxious game showing on the screen and sat next to her, speaking quietly until Rebel moved out from under Molly's arm.

"Gotta take off that top to see what we're workin' with," Amy said calmly, moving farther into the room as my mom got out of her way.

"You sound like a porn director at a casting call," Farrah mumbled, making Molly huff a laugh, a lopsided grin pulling at her lips.

"You didn't make the cut, get out," Amy said to Farrah in amusement. Then her face fell as she saw Molly's arm.

"It's broken," Molly explained. "I can tell."

"I broke mine in the same place, once," my mom murmured in commiseration, making Farrah stiffen. "Hurts like a bitch."

"It's pretty numb now, unless I move it," Molly replied.

"We'll need to cut that shirt off," Trix finally said from the corner. "Gimme your knife, Will."

"I'll do it," I barked. I didn't know why I said it.

"William," my mom started to say before Molly cut her off.

"It's okay," she murmured, her voice small. "Will can do it."

I turned to Molly and met her swollen eyes, my throat going tight. She didn't know these women. She'd only met Trix a couple times, and she hadn't been around my mom for any length of time since we were kids. She didn't know that Amy would know best how to help her. She didn't know that Farrah was all sharp edges but was the softest hearted of the bunch. She didn't know that my mom would baby her, and Trix wouldn't really know how to help but she'd be there, willing to pitch in however she could.

She only knew me.

"You got Reb?" I asked Farrah as I pulled my knife out of the pocket of my jeans.

"Yeah," she said, slowly moving Reb to her lap. When Rebel didn't protest, Farrah shot me a thumbs up.

"I'm sorry," Molly said as I flicked the blade open. "I'd hold her but my arm is—"

"Can't hold her when Will's takin' off that shirt," Amy said simply. "Let Farrah take care of her for a bit. She'll stay right there next to you."

I got to my knees in front of Molly and gingerly pulled the bottom of her scrub top away from her skin. I made the mistake of looking up at her face, and my hands began to shake.

It wasn't supposed to be like this. She wasn't supposed to look at me with mixture of fear and relief in her eyes. It was wrong. All of it was wrong.

"Should've just grabbed a pair of scissors," Trix pointed out as I sliced through the shirt.

"Too late now," I shot back, dropping my knife on the floor so I could rip the shirt open the rest of the way. I wasn't getting anywhere close to Molly's breasts with a knife, it didn't matter how good I was with it. Being good with a knife meant I was good at cutting people, not good at *not* cutting them.

I pulled slowly and steadily until the shirt came completely apart, then stopped breathing.

"That's not as bad as I thought it would be," my mom said in relief.

"Me, either," Amy said to Molly, stepping in beside me to help her pull the shirt down her arms. "But I'm sure it's still painful as hell."

"I'll live," Molly replied, her eyes swollen into slits by then. Her face was swelling quickly and she was swaying on the bed.

"Come on," Amy said tenderly. As I got to my feet, Trix stepped forward and she and Amy helped Molly lay down on the bed.

"Will?" Molly called frantically.

"I'm right here, sugar," I ground out, physically moving Trix out of my way so Molly could see me.

"Keep Reb, okay? Call Mel."

"No problem," I said easily, brushing her hair away from her face, being careful not to actually touch her skin. It looked like she'd been hit all over, and new spots seemed to be darkening into bruises the longer she was there.

I stepped back as Amy shouldered her way in front of me. She spoke softly, but I still heard her words loud and clear in the room.

"We need to take off those pants?"

"No," Molly answered firmly.

I couldn't see her face. I didn't know if she didn't want them to take the pants off because she didn't want them to see her, or if there was no reason for them to come off. I gripped the back of my head as the muscles in my neck grew so taut I thought I'd choke. My mom's hand landed softly on my back just as Amy breathed a sigh of relief.

"Good," she said, clearing her throat. "That's good."

My entire body shuddered in relief.

"I'll go get a washcloth and some towels," my mom announced, patting my back. "We need to get you cleaned up before you head to the hospital."

"The hospital?" I ground out as she moved around me.

"She's got a broken arm, Will," Farrah scoffed. "You know how to set a broken arm?"

"He's not setting my arm," Molly blurted from the bed. "No, baby.

Reb, Mama's arm has an owie, you can't climb—"

I stepped forward and plucked Rebel from the bed as she tried to crawl up her mom's legs.

"Hey, princess," I said softly as I sat her on my forearm. "Mama's busy. You want to hang out with me for a bit?"

Rebel stared at me through a little pair of black glasses. I guessed she'd outgrown the purple rubbery ones she'd worn before. I wondered vaguely if Molly had kept them.

"Will," she said simply, tilting her head to the side.

"Rebel," I murmured back.

She ran her hand down her neck, telling me she was thirsty. Yeah, even in the midst of all the bullshit, I was pretty damn proud I understood her still.

"Hey, Moll?" I called softly, watching Rebel as her gaze moved around the room. "Reb's thirsty, so I'm gonna take her to get something to drink."

"Okay," she mumbled, her voice faint. The women were helping her get cleaned up, their quiet voices soothing, but I just wanted all of them to leave so I could see Molly's face. I wanted to take care of her. I wanted everyone to leave so I could lock us in my room. Just us. Me, Molly and Rebel.

I jerked in surprise then went completely still as little fingers burrowed into my beard. Oh, God. I'd missed them.

Chapter 15

MOLLY

"I WAS WONDERING why you hadn't shown up toni—" Doctor Lewin's words cut off as he looked up from my chart.

I moved my head to the side and shrugged my sore shoulders. "Hey, Mike."

"What the hell happened?" he said, taking in my bruised face and hurt arm.

"Four wheeler accident," I said flatly, holding his gaze as his eyebrows lifted in disbelief.

Will shifted in his seat, and Mike's head jerked toward him in surprise. I guess he hadn't noticed Will and Amy when he'd walked into the room, which was believable. He tended to have a one-track mind when it came to his job, and if he wasn't working on someone, he didn't even acknowledge them.

"That's Will and Amy," I said, pulling Mike's gaze back to mine.

"I'd like to speak with Molly in private," Mike directed at my posse, making me snort.

"Ms. Duncan," Will said darkly.

"What?"

"She's your patient, she's Ms. Duncan."

"Will, knock it off," I interrupted. If my eyes hadn't felt like they were going to fall out of my head at any moment, I would have rolled them. "Let's just get this over with. Will isn't going to leave and my arm is killing me."

"It's definitely broken," Mike said as he moved closer to the bed. "I can see that from here."

"No shit, Sherlock," I mumbled, hissing as he gently lifted my arm.

"Ah, now that you're a patient, you can give me shit, huh?" Mike asked in amusement as Will got to his feet. I could practically see the wheels turning in his head as I met his eyes and glared. I didn't need him hovering, and he could shove any misplaced jealousy he had up his ass.

"I always give you shit," I shot back at Mike, not looking away from Will.

"And that's why you're my favorite nurse," Mike replied. He had no idea how close he was to having his ass handed to him. Amy put her hand on Will's side and said something quietly to him, making him sit back down.

"You say that to all the nurses," I replied as Mike laid my arm back in my lap.

He checked out the rest of my injuries briskly, but I could tell that he was worried. He was playing it cool, but he wasn't convinced that I was telling the truth, and I was pretty sure that having a biker and an old hippie in my room didn't help matters. They stood out like sore thumbs.

"Let's get you down to X-ray and see what we're working with," Mike said finally. "It looks like the rest of this stuff is superficial."

I'd already figured that much out myself. After Will and Trix had taken Rebel to get something to drink earlier, the women had helped me change and cleaned up all of my little cuts and bruises. There had been shockingly little damage done, even though it felt like I'd been hit by a truck. I'd felt almost embarrassed after they'd cleaned me up and we'd seen how bad the damage *wasn't*. The man who'd hit me had hands the size of baseball gloves, so he had to have been holding back, at least until he'd broken my arm.

When I'd apologized for the fuss, the women had looked at me like I'd lost my mind. Then Amy said something I'd never forget. *"A woman lives in fear every day of her life that a man will use his strength against her. It's an intrinsic truth. It's not even a conscious thought, that fear, just basic instinct. It's why we double-check locks and search dark parking lots as we walk to our cars at night. Your level of injury does not change the fact that what you feared has come to pass. You were hurt by someone bigger and stronger than you. Every woman in this room has been there. You're not alone."*

She was surprisingly well-spoken.

"Won't a nurse take me to X-ray?" I asked as Mike kicked the brake off the bed I was in.

"I'm already here, I can take you," he replied easily, making me cringe. He was going to grill me. Everyone in the room knew it.

"I'll go with you," Amy said softly, dropping her purse in Will's lap with a *thunk*.

We left Will sitting in the chair by the window, and I closed my eyes as I was wheeled down the hall. I was sitting up in the bed, but the fluorescent lights on the ceiling still made me dizzy as we worked our way down the corridor. I was putting up a good front, but my stomach churned with nerves the longer we were at the hospital. I needed to know if they'd found my dad. I had to know if he was okay. Since the moment I'd known that Rebel was safe, he'd been all I could think about.

"You have anything you want to tell me?" Mike asked as he pushed me into the X-ray room.

"I told you what happened," I replied tiredly as he moved briskly around the room. "I crashed the four wheeler I was riding."

"Since when did you start riding four wheelers?" His voice dropped in disbelief as he stopped in front of me.

"Today," I said with a smirk, my split lip protesting the movement.

"Why do you think I crashed?" He opened his mouth to argue, but whatever he was about to say was cut off by the tech coming in, asking Amy to leave if there was any chance of her being pregnant.

★ ★ ★

Two hours later, I was drowsily leaning my head against the back window of Amy's car as we headed back to the clubhouse. I hadn't heard any news from the guys who'd gone over to check on my dad. I was pretty sure Will had been in contact with them, but he hadn't said a word to me and I was too afraid to ask him. He'd really only given me updates on how Rebel was doing with his mom.

"Boys are back," Amy said as we pulled in the gates. "Looks like Patrick waited for me, too."

"Like he'd leave without ya," Will teased as we came to a stop behind a long line of motorcycles. "You two are connected at the hip."

"Zip it," Amy ordered, putting the car in park. "And help Molly inside."

"I don't need help!" I called to her as she climbed out, ignoring me. "I don't need your help," I said again when Will hopped out of the front seat and opened my door.

"That's how it is, then?" he asked, falling into step beside me as I made my way slowly toward the front door.

"How what is?" I snapped. I didn't know why I was so irritated. He'd been nothing but nice to me since I'd shown up at their party.

"Me and you."

"There is no me and you," I said, coming to a stop.

"There's always gonna be a me and you," he argued, stepping toward me.

"Is that why you threw us away?" I blurted incredulously. "You have a funny way of showing your devotion."

"You told me to leave!" he yelled, his brows pulled together in confusion.

"You left a week before that!" I hissed back. "You acted like a pussy and disappeared instead of telling me you were done!"

"I wasn't done!"

"Bullshit. You took off and didn't answer a text or a phone call. I was freaking out, Will! I wasn't sleeping, I could barely eat because I was so worried about that surgery."

"Everything okay out here?" Will's dad asked from the doorway.

I ignored him.

"Oh, wait. You didn't care about that, right? Because Rebel is *my* kid. It's not your responsibility to give a shit." I swayed on my feet and Will reached out to grab me. "Don't touch me," I ordered, turning to face Grease as his presence finally registered. "Did you find my dad?"

"We did," he said with a somber nod.

I didn't know what that meant. I couldn't read the man's expression. He didn't even have one. His face was completely blank. I tried to take a step forward, but my feet couldn't seem to move. I glanced down at them in confusion and that's when everything went black.

I woke up in Will's darkened bedroom, the sounds of the club faint through the walls. Barely opening my eyes, I caught sight of a darkened shape lounging across the foot of the bed and instantly knew who it was.

"Did I seriously faint?" I asked groggily, rolling gingerly toward Will. Someone had tucked me in, and the heavy blankets were surprisingly nice.

"Yep."

I waited for him to say something else, anything else. But like always, when I needed Will to speak, he was silent.

"My dad?" I asked hoarsely.

"I'm sorry, Moll," he murmured back.

No.

I tried frantically to respond. I knew he was watching me, waiting for a reaction, but I didn't have any words. I just lay there, my heart pounding as I tried to untangle the thoughts running through my head. Memories of my dad, his tattooed arms flexing as he lifted me up, carrying me after I was way too old to demand he did. The way he'd pull off his glasses and dig his fingers into his eye sockets as he laughed at some harebrained scheme I'd come up with. His face in the delivery room when I'd had Rebel, white as a ghost, but so damn proud.

The way he walked. The way he laughed. The way he clammed up whenever my mom was mentioned. The way he would always sheepishly put a shirt on when I had a friend over. The scar on his ribs where he'd been stabbed in a bar fight before I was born. My name tattooed over his heart. Rebel's name tattooed down the middle of his chest. The time he'd grown his hair out. The time he'd asked me to shave it off and I'd left bald patches and he'd had to wear a hat for a solid month. The laugh lines at the corners of his eyes. The frown lines between his brows. The way he called me princess.

The look in his eyes the last time I'd seen him.

The look in his eyes the last time I'd seen him.

The look in his eyes the *last time* I'd seen him.

"Molly," Will barked, flipping on the light.

I'd known it before he'd told me, known it before I'd ever left that house. But still, somewhere inside me, I'd held out hope that Grease and the other guys would get to him in time. I'd been delusional, and I'd known it, but I'd still had that hope.

And now that hope was gone, leaving a deep, dark hole in its place.

"Molly," Will said again, ripping the bedding down my body. "Answer me."

I stared at him blankly as he pulled me out of bed.

"I'm fine," I mumbled incoherently as he lifted me into his arms.

"Mom!" Will called as he carried me into a dimly lit hallway. He walked quickly through an archway that had chips in the paint and some sort of writing all over it, and then we were in a loud room with people everywhere.

"Will?" An old man with a long, red beard laced with silver stepped in front of us.

"I think she's in shock," Will told him in a tone I'd never heard before.

"She's earned it, poor lass."

"I need—she needs—"

"Probably just you," the man said softly, reaching out to pat my shoulder. "Take her back in your room and care for her."

"Will?" another voice asked from behind me. "I didn't realize you were here."

"Poor timing, girl," the old man said.

I turned my head to the side and found the woman I'd seen with Will at the gas station staring at us in confusion. Oddly, I didn't even care.

"Go on, now," the old man said to her, waving his hand. "Shoo."

I dropped my head to the side and rested it on Will's chest.

"You seen my parents?" Will asked, settling me more firmly in his arms.

"Over by the pool table with the kids," the old man answered.

Then we were moving again, shuffling around people as Will carried me across the room. He hadn't said anything to the woman, hadn't acknowledged her at all.

"Oh, Molly," Mrs. Hawthorne said sadly when we finally reached her. "It's going to be okay, sweetheart."

"I don't know what to do," Will said quietly.

"I do," Grease mumbled gruffly. "Hold her tight."

I turned my head just as he set a familiar weight on the curve of my body.

"Mama," Rebel said in relief, leaning forward to rest against my chest. "Mama. Reb."

I shuddered, a sob bursting out of my mouth. I pulled her in tight, ignoring the way her heavy weight put painful pressure on my arm. "Hello, princess," I blubbered, kissing her head. "I missed you."

"Take them back to your room," Mrs. Hawthorne ordered Will. "They need to get some rest."

"Are you sure?" I asked quietly, meeting Grease's eyes.

"Yeah," he said simply, not asking me to clarify. "He fought like hell, though. Took one of the fuckers with him."

"Which one?" I mumbled through numb lips.

"Tall. Dark hair."

"Okay." That was the guy who'd held me. The other big guy had light hair, almost blonde.

Will carried us back through the room while I held Reb snug against my chest. She was smoothing her fingers through my hair repeatedly, humming a song that only she knew. I wondered if the events of the day would mark her somehow, or if for once, her inattention would work in our benefit.

Oh, who was I kidding? Rebel was never truly inattentive. She saw *everything*. She just didn't respond the way other kids would. Rebel might not freak out in a way that any other parent would notice, but she'd be fighting her own demons somehow. I pressed my lips against the top of her head as Will carried us through the door to his room, thankful that she was letting me hold her at all.

"Trix bought some Pull-Ups earlier," Will said as he set us down on the bed. He stood there awkwardly as Rebel climbed off my lap and laid down against his pillow.

"He would've died either way," I said croakily, raising my eyes to meet Will's. Looking for absolution. "If I hadn't been there, they still would've killed him."

"Yes," he replied firmly, crouching down in front of me. His hand lifted up and wrapped around the side of my neck. "They would've killed him whether you were there or not. The minute they had him, it was over."

"But I shouldn't have been there," I said softly.

"I wish to God you hadn't been," he murmured tenderly. "I'd take it all away if I could, sugar. But you bein' there didn't make one damn bit of difference for your dad—except maybe gave him the chance to say goodbye."

"He knew before we left. He *knew*. I could tell."

Will nodded. "And he still got you outta there. Good man."

"He let them beat me, Will," I whispered, my gaze holding his. "Why would he do that?"

"Don't know, baby. Could be, he thought that nothin' he'd say would help, which is probably true. They weren't lettin' you out of there without scarin' the fuck outta you first."

I let that sink in. Maybe Will was right. Maybe my dad had known from the beginning that they were going to beat me, but he hadn't realized how bad until they'd broken my arm. That's when he'd agreed to talk. When it had gone beyond a punch, he'd used his trump card.

Would they have let me go if he'd started begging them to when I'd first shown up? No. I knew deep in my gut that if my dad hadn't held out, Reb and I would be dead. I closed my eyes and let out a shaky breath. If he would've started begging when I'd walked through the door, they would have taken the list and never let me and Rebel go. He would have looked weak.

"Do you think he told them? Did they get what they wanted?" I asked, opening my eyes again.

"Not sure, Moll. We'll know soon, though."

"Okay," I said, taking a deep breath. I looked over my shoulder at Reb to find her watching us intently, her hands pulled tight against her chest.

"She won't sleep without her stuff," I murmured, looking back at Will. "I've tried before and she was still wide-awake at four in the morning."

Going home didn't even cross my mind, not when those men were out there somewhere. Surrounded by people in the clubhouse, I felt safe, the exact opposite of what I'd thought I would feel back when Will used to invite me out there.

"Got her blankets," Will said, his lips tipping up in a smile. "Give me a sec."

He left the room and I let my mind wander. Had anyone gotten ahold of Mel? I was surprised that she wasn't there. If she knew what had happened, there's no way she would stay away. I shifted on the bed and hissed in discomfort. I was so sore. My head and torso throbbed, even with the painkillers the hospital had given me. I wondered how long until the swelling in my face went down. I couldn't work looking like I did, but Reb and I needed the money. I barely made enough as it was, working when I could. Nurses made bank usually, but with my schedule and the number of times a week I had to get off work early to take Reb to her occupational and speech therapy appointments, we didn't have a lot of extra left over. I couldn't afford to take time off.

"Look what I have," Will said softly as he came back in the room.

My eyes watered when I caught sight of the bag full of Rebel's overnight stuff that I'd dropped at my dad's.

"How did you get that?" I asked as Rebel scrambled to the edge of the bed for her things. My poor baby was exhausted and she wanted her blankie and animals.

"Couldn't leave anything of yours there," Will murmured in apology as he set the large bag on the bed and pulled my glasses out of his shirt pocket. "Cops can't know you were there, baby."

My eyes widened in horror. I knew they'd found my dad, but it hadn't occurred to me that they'd just leave him there. He was their friend.

"They just *left* him?" I asked tearfully, lifting my glasses to my face before realizing that my face was too swollen for them to fit me. My hands began to shake as I started pulling soft items out of the bag. I froze as the tips of my fingers met the cold screen of Rebel's Kindle. They really *had* grabbed everything. "He's just lying there—"

"Had someone call it in," Will said soothingly, taking his cut off. "Cops were there hours ago."

"Are they looking for me?" My stomach churned at the thought.

"Probably will tomorrow, just to let you know that he's gone," Will explained, stepping out of his boots.

"I can't talk to them like this."

"You can," he assured me, sitting down next to me on the bed. "You got into a four wheeler accident today, so you stayed the night with your boyfriend so he could help you with Rebel."

"My boyfriend?"

"Nothin' else is going to make a damn bit of sense."

"But wouldn't I have called my dad if this happened? I left voicemails on my dad's phone asking him to keep Reb. I—"

"Already taken care of," Will cut me off. Got a tech guy that's tits. He got into your dad's voicemail and erased all of it. Casper found your dad's phone and it's toast. They find out you called him? Fits in with the story that you got hurt and you were trying to let him know."

"I don't know if that will work," I murmured, watching Rebel as she pulled a stuffed animal to her chest and hugged it tightly.

"It'll work, sugar. You just tell them that you were over here for the party and we decided to take a couple of the four wheelers out. You wrecked, I took you to the hospital. Did you call your dad? Yep. He didn't answer. Did you text him? Same thing—no response."

"You thought of everything," I said faintly, staring at Rebel as she made herself a little nest of blankets in the middle of the bed.

"Molly, look at me," Will ordered. I turned my head to find him watching me intently. "These men aren't fuckin' around. They find out you talked and it's gonna be that much harder to protect you. You gotta do what I ask, sugar. There's no other option."

"Why did this happen?" I asked in confusion, my breath catching. "I don't understand why this happened."

"Your dad was workin' to take them down, baby. He knew what the risks were."

"But why? How did he even know those guys?"

"That's not somethin' I can tell you," he answered, his voice dropping.

I nodded. Did I really want to know more than I already did? No. I didn't want an even larger bullseye on my back. This wasn't my life. I was the single mom of a daughter with special needs and I worked as a nurse. I'd been raised by a successful single father because my mom had died of an overdose when I was still a baby. I'd had the same best friend since third grade.

"Where's Mel?" I asked, standing so I could walk around the foot of the bed and crawl into the spot between Rebel and the wall.

"Her and Rock left for the weekend," Will said as he unbuttoned his jeans and dropped them to the floor. He grabbed a pair of sweatpants from the dresser and slipped them on before striding back to the bed. "They were goin' up campin' and we haven't been able to reach either of them."

"Do you think they're okay?" I asked as he lay down on the other side of an already snoring Rebel.

"Sure they're fine," Will whispered back. "Service isn't good out where they were headed. We'll probably hear from them when they head back in a couple days."

"Okay."

"It's going to be okay, Moll," he said, reaching over Rebel to rest his hand on the curve of my waist. "I'll take care of you."

"I don't need you to take care of me," I said groggily, letting my eyes fall closed.

"You been handlin' your own shit for a long ass time," he replied as I relaxed completely against the bed. "But not anymore."

Chapter 16

WILL

"CHURCH," CASPER ANNOUNCED the next morning as I sat at the bar with Rebel on my lap. She'd woken up at five, but I'd been able to smuggle her out of the room before she could wake up Molly. I wasn't sure how Rebel had woken up after less than five hours of sleep, but I didn't mind getting up with her.

She'd changed so much. Her wispy brown hair hand grown past her shoulders and the baby curls were gone. She'd also thickened up, and seemed sturdier than she'd been before. Her brown eyes were still the same, though, and still magnified behind the lenses of her glasses like a little bug. She signed a lot more, which meant I had no clue what the fuck she was trying to tell me most of the time. She also talked. Not much, but some. She knew what she wanted, and she didn't let you ignore her.

"I've got Reb," I said, getting to my feet. She growled and bent in half to reach the rest of her donut sitting on a paper plate on the bar.

"Bring her," Casper mumbled, stuffing a donut into his mouth.

One of the old ladies had sent out a prospect to get breakfast, and the bar was covered in bakery boxes. There were a lot of us in the clubhouse. Dragon hadn't announced a lockdown, but most of the families were there anyway. We had no clue what we were dealing with yet.

I followed Casper to the room behind the bar, and stopped at the threshold.

"You comin' in or what?" Dragon grumbled, his eyes bloodshot. He reached up and drug his hands through his hair.

"Got the baby this mornin'," I said, staying where I was.

"Take her to your ma," my dad ordered, dropping down into his seat.

"No," I shot back. I scowled at the table of surprised faces turned my way. "She's stayin' with me until her mother wakes up."

"Then wake the bitch up," Samson said with a frown.

"She needs her sleep," I ground out.

"Jesus Christ," Dragon barked, waving his hand at me. "Bring the kid in with you. I don't wanna be here all goddamn day."

I nodded briskly, then stepped inside, closing the door behind me.

"First, we haven't talked to Rock yet, but I'm not worried. He was headed up to the national forest and we all know cell reception is shit up there."

"Rock!" Reb said seriously around a mouth full of donut. "Auntie. Rock."

"It's a fuckin' daycare in here," Samson grumbled.

"Second," Dragon continued, ignoring them both. "Poet's got feelers out for the Russians. ATF and DEA were workin' through the ranks this week. I'm guessin' the man Molly saw at Duncan's was Rock's father-in-law."

"Ex," Hulk reminded him as Rebel mumbled Rocky's name again.

I tried not to be jealous that she was responding to another guy's name the way she was.

"He's pissed," Dragon continued. "With good reason. Those names Rock gave pretty much made the DEA's case for them."

"Took 'em long enough," Samson mumbled.

I silently agreed with him. Rock had given the Feds the list they wanted over a year ago, and they'd sat on that shit forever. Bureaucratic bullshit, if you asked me. Hurry up and wait.

"Russians got no idea who's next on the list, and they're scramblin' to find out what the feds know," my dad butt in. "Probably why they went to Duncan."

"Molly said they were askin' for a list," I agreed as Reb's sticky fingers found my beard.

"Dunc would've held out as long as he could with that list," Dragon said quietly. "Givin' the feds some time."

"Should've told them what they wanted to know," I snapped, wiping Rebel's hair away from her maple frosting-covered mouth. "He held out when his daughter was gettin' beat."

"They would've beat the fuck outta her anyway," Casper replied, using the same logic I'd fed Molly earlier. "She showed up. They weren't just gonna let her bounce—had to put the fear a' God into her first."

"You think they're gonna come here?" Hulk asked Dragon.

"Doubt it," Dragon said. "They got what they wanted. Probably halfway outta the country by now. Musta knew we were comin' if they left their man behind. Even Russians don't leave their own dead for the cops to find."

"How do you know they got what they wanted?" I asked.

"Killed him," my dad said quietly. "If there was anything left to know, they woulda kept him alive. Took him with 'em."

Dragon nodded.

A knock on the door interrupted us and I opened it up to find Trix's face pressing into the opening.

"Cops called Molly. They're on their way here."

"Shit," I grumbled as the men stood up from the table.

"You get that shit straightened out?" Dragon asked as I moved out from in front of the door.

"She knows what she's supposed to say," I assured him.

"Let's hope she sticks to it."

I nodded and left the room, searching for Molly. If she'd talked to the cops, that meant she was awake, and I wanted to see how she was feeling.

I found her sitting at a table with Farrah and Charlie at the edge of the room. Lily and Rose were standing next to them, and I could tell by the way that my sister was standing that they were begging for something.

"He's here now, you monsters," Farrah said as I walked up to the table.

"What's up?" I asked as Rebel dived for Molly. I barely caught her in time, then set her gently in Molly's lap, being extra careful of her arm. They'd sent her home from the hospital in a soft cast because her arm was still too swollen to put in a hard cast, and she had to go back tomorrow so they could change it.

"We wanted to come get Rebel so she could play with Charlie, but Mom wouldn't let us," Lily said, her hands on her hips.

"You know that room is off-limits," Farrah said.

"I just wanted to get Rebel."

"It doesn't matter."

"Why did Rebel get to be in there?" Rosie demanded, making Farrah raise one eyebrow.

"None of your business."

"Rebel, you want to go play with Charlie?" Molly said, breaking up the argument. Reb didn't reply, but she must have done something that only Molly had seen, because a second later, Molly was sliding Reb off her lap to the floor. "Be good."

Rose grabbed Rebel's hand and marched her and Lily toward one of the couches near the far side of the room, where Trix and her boys were playing with some big Legos.

"How you feelin'?" I asked, leaning down to kiss the top of Molly's head. She hadn't been responding to my touches, but she hadn't asked me to stop, either, so I was going to keep doing what I wanted. There was no way I could be near her and not touch her.

"Sore," she said quietly. She lifted a cup to her mouth and gingerly took a sip of her coffee, wincing. "The inside of my mouth stings like a bitch."

"Got a lot of cuts in there," I reminded her as I pulled a chair over and straddled it backwards.

"Just don't mess with them," Farrah told her. "The more you fuck with them, the longer it'll take for them to heal."

"I know," Molly replied. "But easier said than done."

"Rinse with some sea salt, too. It'll keep 'em clean," Farrah said. "Think I've got some in Casper's room from the last time I got pierced."

I looked at her, not remembering the last time she'd had a new piercing. Then I shuddered and looked away. If I couldn't see a new piercing, I sure as hell didn't want to know about it.

"Cops are at the gate," Tommy called from the doorway.

"Let 'em in," Dragon ordered, meeting my eyes across the room.

Showtime.

"You ready for this?" I asked Molly. She looked scared. Super nervous.

"What if they don't believe me?" she whispered.

"Baby, I'll be right here. You tell them you want me present if they ask. It's all good. They just wanna tell you about your dad—you're not on trial, for fuck's sake."

"Okay," she said a little louder.

I reached over and grabbed her hand, lacing her fingers with mine.

"I'm gonna go keep the girls occupied," Farrah said, standing up from the table. "Don't stress, Molly. They're coming to give you bad news, they'll be nice as hell."

She ran her hand over the top of my hair, messing it up, then walked away, stretching her arms above her head like she didn't have a care in the world. She'd always given that impression. The whole *I don't care if you like me* vibe. It had been years before she'd actually believed it, though. My Uncle Casper had a lot to do with that.

My dad met the nervous cops at the door, shaking hands and patting one of them on the back like he knew them. They spoke for a few minutes at the other side of the room until my dad pointed toward Molly. Then they headed our way.

"Molly Duncan?" the younger cop asked as they reached us.

"Yes?" Molly stood up awkwardly, looking back and forth between the men.

"Are you okay, ma'am?" the older cop asked, taking her in from head to toe.

"I was in an accident yesterday," Molly said softly, clearing her throat when she was finished. Jesus, she looked like she was afraid they were about to arrest her.

"An accident?" the older cop asked. "Did you report it?"

"Yeah." Molly shrugged one shoulder, wincing. "I wrecked the four wheeler I was riding. You don't have to report that, do you?" She glanced down at me like she was asking if I knew.

"No, you don't," the younger cop assured her.

"She was driving?" the older cop asked me. I felt Molly bristle beside me. The guy was a douche.

"Yeah, man," I said, reaching out to put a hand on Molly's hip. "I was ridin' 'bout a hundred yards behind her. Took a year off my life."

"Did my work call you?" Molly butt in, looking back and forth between the cops. "When I went in yesterday to get my arm checked, they were pretty worried. I think they thought Will beat me up or something." She gave an incredulous laugh as the cops raised their eyebrows. My muscles tightened, but I didn't let my expression change. Great, Molly. Tell the cops that the hospital thought this was a domestic abuse issue. Good fucking call.

"Did he?" the younger cop asked, setting his hand on his gun. Christ, now she'd gone and tripped the idiot's protective instincts. I could see his chest puffing out.

"Of course not," Molly snapped in disgust. Hell, at least that sounded real—since it was. "I'd rip his balls off while he slept."

The older cop coughed uncomfortably as the younger cop turned bright red.

"That's not why we're here, anyhow," the older one said. He glanced at me, then back at Molly. "I'm sorry, but we found your father dead in his house last night."

Molly staggered toward me. That was real, too.

"What?" she whispered.

"It looks like he'd been beaten," the cop said, pausing as he looked over Molly's face. "But we think he died from a gunshot wound."

"Oh, my God," Molly murmured, lifting a hand to cover her face. Real.

"Ma'am, are you sure that—" The younger cop's words cut off as Rebel walked between him and Molly, coming to a stop with her hand wrapped around Molly's thigh.

I think they were both surprised by Reb. She didn't say a word as she stared at them, just watched somberly behind her black framed glasses as they shifted on their feet. Molly looked like hell, but there was no arguing that Reb looked like an angel. She was in clean clothes, her hair was pulled back from her face in a little ponytail and her specs were clearly not a discount brand. Her face was still covered in donut leftovers, but that seemed to make her look even sweeter.

"Did—did you need something from me?" Molly asked, letting her hand fall to rest on the top of Rebel's head.

"Do you know of anyone that would want to harm your father?" the younger cop asked, his chest still puffed up with importance.

"He was a lawyer," Molly said flatly. "I'm sure there were a lot of people, but no one that I know."

"Have you ever seen this man?" the young cop asked, setting a photograph down on the table.

Molly inhaled sharply and jerked away, shaking her head as she got a good look at the dead Russian's face and the steak knife stuck in the side of his neck.

"Jesus Christ," I snapped, looking back at the cops. "You serious right now?"

"Sorry," the young cop mumbled, picking the photo back up.

"Okay," the older cop said, shooting an irritated look at the younger one. "We'll keep in touch."

He turned to walk away, but before I could relax, Molly spoke.

"Wait!" she called, making the cop spin back around. "Should I—do I need to call a funeral parlor or something? I don't . . ." Her words drifted into nothing, and my stomach clenched at how young she sounded. Real.

"Since it's an ongoing investigation, it'll be bit before we can release the—your father's body," the older cop said kindly. "But we'll let you know as soon as we've got a timeline."

"Thank you," Molly said softly.

With a nod, the officer turned and walked away, the younger cop following in his wake like an overeager puppy.

Molly dropped down into the seat next to me and wrapped her arm around Reb's shoulder.

"Man," Rebel said, wrinkling her nose as she wiped her finger over her top lip.

"Yeah, that was a pretty epic mustache, huh?" Molly replied, laughing a little.

Rebel woofed and Molly laughed harder.

"Did she just say that cop looked like a dog?" I asked, unable to keep the laughter from my voice.

"Dog," Rebel copied, dropping to the floor. She started crawling around and I cringed at the thought of everything that had been spilled on that floor. I'd need to clean her hands as soon as she got up.

"One of the therapists she goes to has this little dog, and the hair on his muzzle looks exactly like a mustache," Molly explained, watching Reb crawling around like a puppy and shaking her little butt.

"Cops are pigs, baby girl," I told her in amusement, making Molly elbow me in the side. "Oink."

Rebel started snorting and I couldn't help the loud laugh that spilled from my mouth.

"Don't teach her that," Molly snapped, but I could see her swollen lips inching into a smile.

My dad crossed the room to us and stopped on the other side of the table, meeting Molly's eyes. "Did good," he told her.

"You hear her tell them that her co-workers thought I beat her?" I asked incredulously.

My dad's eyes lit up with amusement. "Good to see you sweat a little."

"Fuck off," I replied with a grin.

Molly sighed and leaned toward the table, bracing herself on her good arm. "None of this is funny," she whispered, reaching up to touch her eyes before dropping her hand to the table.

"Gotta find the humor when you can," my dad told her seriously. "'Specially in times like this." He rapped his knuckles twice on the table then strode off, stepping around Rebel, who'd plopped down on her bottom and was scratching at the side of her head.

"Do you think they'll come back?" Molly asked, leaning back to look at me. "The cops?"

"Nah, Dad's right. You did good."

"They believed me?"

"Yeah. Probably helped that we've got a busted up four wheeler sitting on a trailer out front."

"How the hell did you manage that?" she asked, looking at me in surprise.

"Tommy wrecked it two months ago." I leaned forward and brushed my lips across hers before she could move away. She was doing so good. Most other women would be losing their shit—but not Molly. She was the easiest woman I'd ever met. No drama. She was hurting, you could tell by every expression on her face and every movement of her body, but she wasn't complaining and she wasn't hysterical. I got to my feet and inched around her, sliding my hand across her shoulders as I went. "Come on, Reb," I called, picking the little girl up off the floor. "Let's go wash your hands before you get salmonella or some shit."

★ ★ ★

"They're holed up in Ontario," Poet announced, dropping down into a chair in church later that night. "Not bein' quiet about it, the stupid bastards."

"Why Ontario?" Samson asked.

"Probably because the fuckin' feds are scouring Idaho for them," Casper replied.

"So what are we going to do?" Hulk asked, popping his neck. I hated when he did that. Fucking disgusting.

"Rock should be back tomorrow morning," Dragon said, leaning back in his chair. "We could leave then."

"Goin' after them, then," Hulk murmured.

"Duncan was one of ours," my dad said quietly. "Might not'a been wearin' a patch, but he was a good friend to the club for a lotta years."

"Got his daughter here, too," Poet pointed out. "Moose's girl."

"And she's beat to shit," my dad agreed, meeting my eyes. "Can't let that stand."

I nodded in thanks.

"Casper, you and Samson'll stick back on this one," Dragon said.

"Don't mind goin'," Casper replied.

"Know you don't." Dragon nodded. "But Grease is comin' with me and I need you here."

"Alright."

"Once Rock gets here tomorrow, we'll fill him in and take off. Me, Grease, Hulk and Moose. Probably Homer and Shady, too. They're too good as lookouts to leave behind."

I inhaled deeply at the thought of getting ahold of the guy that had messed up my woman's face and broken her arm. I wanted to tear him apart. From what Molly had told Dragon and my dad, the guy was massive, as big as Cam. I was looking forward to teaching him how it felt to be at someone's mercy, then giving him none.

"Molly's got her appointment tomorrow, doesn't she?" my dad asked, breaking me out of my fantasies.

"Yeah, might have to knock her out to set the bone," I replied. "Probably not, though."

"Chance of it," Dad said.

"Yeah."

"You sure you don't wanna duck out of this one?"

"You kidding?" I asked, glancing around the table. "I'm there."

"Alright," Dad said with a nod.

We went over the route we'd take and the stops we'd make on the way to Ontario, running through different possibilities for the next half hour. We didn't always plan out every single move we made, but when we were dealing with the Russian mob, we had to make sure all of our shit was tight. Ontario was just this side of the Idaho-Oregon border and was an easy day trip. We'd have to spend the night somewhere on the way back, but we'd be gone less than two days, no problem.

By the time we left the room, I was jacked up at the thought of taking off the next day. I'd been going on runs for the past few years, but none of them had caused adrenaline like I was dealing with then. Those past runs had felt mandatory. Sometimes I'd felt satisfaction that I'd been chosen to go, sometimes I'd been annoyed, but I'd never been practically frothing at the mouth as I waited to leave. If I could have, I would have left the minute I walked out of church.

"Molly and Rebel went to bed," my mom told me with a sleepy smile. "I think we wore them out today."

"Molly needs to rest, Mom," I replied with a frown. I'd spent most of my day in the garage finishing up a car that I'd said would be done the next day. I'd known that shit was going to go down soon, and I wanted to make sure that the owner didn't have to wait because I hadn't finished my job.

"She spent the whole day on the couch," my mom assured me, leaning in to give me a quick hug. "But there've been people packing up and leaving all day, so it wasn't exactly relaxing for her."

"I need to get her home," I mumbled, scratching at my beard.

"Well, she can't go back yet," my mom said as my dad came up behind her, wrapping his arm around her shoulders. "Better safe than sorry."

"She can stay with your mother tomorrow night," my dad said, making my mom glare at him.

"Of course she can," she told me, "but you could've asked."

"You pickin' a fight?" my dad asked with a grin.

I'd heard that a million times growing up. Without a word, I turned and walked away before I had to start watching my dad playing grab ass.

I let myself into my dark room and shut the door behind me, moving around by memory. I almost landed on my face when I tripped over Reb's bag, but caught myself before I hit the floor.

"You can turn on the light," Molly's soft voice called out in the dark. "Rebel won't wake up."

I reached over and flipped on the lamp. Molly was laying on the outside of the bed facing my way, her hair pulled into a knot at the top of her head.

"Nice hair," I said quietly, sliding my cut down my shoulders.

"I asked Farrah to pull it out of my face, it was driving me nuts."

"You look like a skinny sumo wrestler."

"But it's out of my face," she said with a small shrug. I didn't know why she kept doing that. I could see the pain in her eyes every time she moved her shoulders.

"How's the arm?" I asked as I pulled my t-shirt off. I'd slept in one the night before and I'd kept waking up thinking someone was trying to strangle me.

"It's throbbing," she admitted. "I'll be glad to have it set and casted."

"Then you just gotta deal with it itching and not bein' able to reach it."

She watched me unashamedly as I kicked off my boots and dropped my jeans to the floor, so I took my time setting my wallet and my keys on the dresser before I grabbed a pair of sweats and slipped them on.

"You didn't wear sweats before," she said as I turned off the lamp and walked toward the bed.

"Reb's gettin' older," I murmured as I leaned down and moved her to the middle of the bed. She was going to be squished in between me and Rebel and I was hoping Reb would spread out like she'd done the night before so that Molly would have to stay curled up against me.

Molly let me pull her close to my side as I settled in, being extra careful not to put pressure her arm. "Can you keep her tomorrow while I have my arm set?" she asked. Shit.

I sighed and ran a fingertip over her shoulder. "Can't."

"Oh," she replied, her body stiffening just a little. "Amy's bringing me to the appointment, so I just thought . . ."

"Headin' out in the morning, sugar," I said against the top of her head. "Won't be here."

"Where are you going?"

"Not a question you get to ask."

She jerked and her body stiffened even more. "Fine."

"Don't do that," I murmured, running my hand down her back.

"Do you think your mom will keep Rebel for me?" she asked, ignoring my softly spoken order.

"Yeah, but I'm pretty sure Mel will be here in the morning."

"Thank God," Molly said, her body relaxing again. "She'll take care of everything."

She said it like it was a foregone conclusion. Like I hadn't been taking care of her since the minute I'd seen her all beaten and bloody. Like it was a relief that she finally had someone to lean on, even though I'd been trying to be that person for her. I'd obviously been failing at that.

"Go to sleep, sugar," I said quietly. I rolled to my back and Molly moved with me, resting her head on my chest.

It didn't matter if she never fell asleep that way again, I still knew that I'd never be done with her. After a year and a half of no contact, she still did it for me. I smiled as Rebel snorted in her sleep. I wasn't going to walk away again.

Chapter 17

MOLLY

"**W**HERE IS SHE?" my best friend's voice yelled frantically from outside. I pushed myself up off the couch and stepped around Rebel just as Melanie came barreling through the front door of the club. She searched the room and as soon as she saw me, burst into tears. "Oh, my God, Moll."

"I'm okay," I said as she came toward me. "It's just a broken arm."

"And your face! Holy hell."

"It looks worse than it is," I promised.

"Your dad . . ." she whispered, glancing at Rebel.

"I know."

She hugged me gently, not letting go for a long time.

"This is insane," she mumbled as she let go, leaning back to look at my face again.

"I have to go in to get my arm casted today," I said, ignoring the question in her eyes. "Can you keep Reb for me?"

"Of course," she replied immediately. "Are you sure you don't want me to go with you?"

"Will's leaving today—"

"*What?*" she interrupted incredulously.

"So I need you with Rebel."

"What a dick," Mel spat.

"That's Will," I replied with a small deprecating laugh. "He's got places to be and people to see."

"Are you two a thing again?"

"No. Nothing's changed," I replied sitting back down on the couch. She followed me, saying hello to Rebel as she sat down beside me.

"I can't believe he's going to just leave."

"It's fine, Mel," I said, glancing around to make sure no one was listening to us. "Just leave it."

"What happened?" she said quietly, turning to face me. "Grease said that some guys killed your dad?"

"I don't know," I hedged, not meeting her eyes.

"They already told me, dumbass," Mel said dryly. "I know that you were there and that's how you got all that." She waved her hand in a circle in front of my face. "Do you know why?"

"No." I shook my head, and looked down at Rebel just as she looked up at me, wiggling the stuffed dog she was holding and lifting her eyebrows up and down. Silly girl. "I don't know what happened. We showed up because my dad was supposed to watch Rebel so I could work, and there were three Russian guys in his house."

"Russian?" Mel asked, snapping up straight. "Are you sure?"

"They sounded Russian," I answered, watching her closely. "Why?"

"It's just weird. Why would some Russian guys be pissed at your dad?"

"No idea."

"There's my girls," Rocky called as he came through the front door.

"Rock!" Rebel yelled back. She nodded her head, but didn't get up from her spot on the floor as he moved toward us. She was practically vibrating with excitement, though.

"How you doin', little Rebel?" he asked, crouching down and raising his hand so Reb would give him a high-five. Rebel smiled as she smacked his hand, but she didn't answer him.

"Hey, Molly," Rock said, standing up again. "How you doin', girl?"

"I'm sore," I said dryly. "But okay."

"Sorry about your dad." He moved around the couch and sat on one of the arms next to Mel. "He was a good guy."

"Molly says the guys who did it were Russian," Melanie told Rocky, looking at him intently.

"You know why?" Rock asked me as he set his hand on the back of Mel's neck.

"No," I replied, shaking my head. That hand on the back of Mel's neck didn't look like comfort. It looked like a warning.

"Sucks," Rocky said. "You need anything, you let Mel and I know."

"I just want my dad back," I said darkly, brushing my hair away from my face. "I just want to go back to the way it was before."

I stood up and stepped over Rebel, meeting Melanie's eyes for a minute to make sure she'd stay with the baby. Then I walked back to Will's room. Tears blurred my eyes as I knelt in front of the bag of clothes. I wanted my dad. I needed him to tell me that everything was going to be okay.

I was stuck in that clubhouse like a prisoner, and even though I knew they were just trying to keep me safe, the walls seemed to be closing in around me. I needed my own bed. I wanted to cook dinner and take a shower with my own toiletries, and be able to poop without wondering who was going to use the bathroom after I did. I wanted to take Rebel home. She needed her toys and her clothes. She needed to sleep in her own bed and eat at her own spot at the table. Routines were important for her, and even though she hadn't completely freaked out yet, that didn't mean that it wasn't building behind her eyes.

I just wanted all of it to be over. No, that wasn't true. I wanted to take back the last three days as if they'd never happened. I wanted to go over to my dad's house and plop down on his couch and let him make me dinner. I wanted to watch *Jeopardy* and call out the answers a half second after my dad did. I wanted to scoot across the couch and under his armpit that always smelled like Old Spice deodorant.

I covered my mouth with my hand and let out a painful sob.

Why was this happening?

Nothing had prepared me for the Twilight Zone I was currently caught in.

I glanced over my shoulder, making sure the door to Will's room was closed, and let another sob tear from my throat. Squeezing my eyes shut, I bent over the duffle bag, curling around my broken arm like I could hide it. Like I could pretend it wasn't there.

My nose clogged and snot ran down my lip as I let the tears pour out of my eyes. I couldn't even be bothered to wipe it. I couldn't do anything but try to catch my breath as I wailed quietly. It was ugly. Terrible. My face contorted, making me cry harder as my swollen lip cracked and my cheekbone throbbed.

I just needed a minute. Just a minute to myself so I could let it all out. All of the barbed wire fear and the shark infested memories. I needed to purge it.

I choked and gagged as I raised my sleeve to my face, trying to wipe the snot away. I had to leave in less than an hour. I couldn't stay there on the floor. But every time I tried to stem my cries, my chest heaved in agony and I couldn't stop.

"Molly?" Amy's voice finally called as she opened the door. "Oh, sweetheart."

I ignored her as she closed the door behind her, flipping the lock. I should have done that.

"It's too much," I whispered, hiccupping and coughing.

"It's not," Amy said, dropping to her knees beside me. "Just feels like it is."

"I want to go home," I blubbered. "But I'm afraid to be there. I know they weren't looking for me, but I'm still scared they're going to come back."

"You don't have to explain yourself to me," Amy said seriously.

"I miss my dad. I want my dad." I sounded like a baby. I didn't care.

"Oh, Molly," Amy sighed, moving to her ass and wrapping her arm around my waist. "I remember that feeling. I lived with Patrick's mum for most of my adult life, did you know that?" I shook my head. "Yeah, well, I did. When she passed, it felt like a part of myself was suddenly missing. The comfort of a parent—especially when you're a single parent yourself—is indescribable."

"I don't know what I'm going to do without him," I whispered, leaning my head on her thin shoulder.

"You'll figure it out," she replied, reaching up to smooth my hair back from my face. "I promise."

"Molly?" Will called from the other side of the door, slamming his hand against it. "Why's this door locked?"

"We're havin' some girl talk!" Amy bellowed back, making me snort. "Go away!"

"Open the door, old woman," Will said, no disrespect in his voice. "I'm taking off and I wanna see my girl before I go."

My stomach sank. "I'm not his girl," I murmured to Amy.

"Pretty sure I felt like that at one point, too," she replied with a conspiratorial wink. Then she got to her feet and went to unlock the door.

"What's goin' on?" Will asked accusingly, inhaling sharply when he saw me on the floor.

"Keep your head down," Amy said quietly to Will.

"Nah. Want 'em to see me," he replied distractedly, kissing her cheek before she left us alone.

"I was having a pity party," I said once he'd closed the door behind him. "I'm okay now."

"You don't look okay, baby."

"Leftovers from the party," I said with a sniffle, my eyes tearing up again.

"Moll," he said softly, dropping to his knees in front of me. "What can I do?"

His fingers came up to softly cup the sides of my face, and that only made the tears come harder. I'd known this man for so long. I'd recognize his light brown eyes anywhere. Could draw his tattoos by memory and point out the exact spot he had a cowlick, even if he was shaved bald. It didn't matter how long we went without seeing each other, I knew him instinctively.

He'd been such a prick before. It was so hard to trust him, especially when he looked at me the way he was then. He'd looked at me that way before, and after he'd left, I'd convinced myself that it hadn't meant anything. I'd been wrong. It meant everything.

He didn't complete me. I was complete on my own. But he seemed to fit me like an interlocking best friend's necklace. Since I'd come to the clubhouse, his side had been the only place that I'd felt like myself. The only spot where I'd been able to relax my guard and rest. The only place I'd felt even close to okay.

I didn't want him to leave. I was afraid for him to go. I didn't care how codependent that made me.

"I'm okay," I lied, giving him a watery smile. "I have to get ready to go to my appointment."

"You're gonna be late," he said with a crooked smile.

"It's not like they can start without me," I choked out as he leaned forward and brushed his lips against mine.

"My nose is running," I pointed out softly. I was pretty sure if my face hadn't already been black and blue, my blush would have been out of control when he chuckled.

He pulled out a handkerchief from his pocket and lifted it, wiping my nose gently.

"I can do it," I protested, raising my hand for the piece of cloth.

"Done already," he said, his eyes crinkling as he smiled at me. "Now you gonna let me kiss you?"

"Careful," I warned as I leaned forward.

"Always careful with you, sugar," he murmured into my mouth. I inhaled sharply at the feel of his tongue barely touching mine. I hadn't needed to warn him. He was ridiculously careful as he kissed me, barely making any contact at all.

But I still lit up like a Christmas tree. Not turned on, really. It was more of a warm feeling. Comfort. Love.

"I'll help you get dressed," Will said after he'd pulled back too soon. "Come on."

He helped me to my feet, then helped me take my t-shirt off, barely ogling my boobs as he slid my bra up my arms and reached around me to hook it in the back.

"I hope you appreciated that," he said dryly as he helped me put a clean shirt on. "Because I'm hard as a rock."

"I'm not sure if I should be flattered or disgusted that you're into girls whose faces look like ground beef."

"Number one," he said as he crouched and jerked my pants down my hips, making me yelp out a small laugh, tears still leaking slowly out of my eyes. "I'm not into *girls*. I'm into you. Even if you look like you went a couple a rounds with George Foreman."

I curled my hand into a familiar rude gesture, then wiped beneath my eyes with my middle finger.

"Number two," he said, laughter in his voice. "I can't imagine a scenario when you wouldn't get me hard. Believe me, I've tried. You're even hot as a zombie."

"You're so weird," I replied, smiling as he pulled down my underwear and groaned. "I can do that, you know."

"I'll do it," he replied, taking a deep breath like he was bracing himself. I lifted each foot so he could pull the pajama pants and underwear away, then did it again when he held out a clean pair of panties. "Because I'm obviously a masochist."

As soon as I was dressed, Will got to his feet with an exaggerated sound of relief. "Number three," he said quietly, tipping my head up.

"What's number three?" I asked when he was silent for a long time.

"I don't remember," he replied, huffing out a laugh. He kissed me again, a little harder than the last time. "I have to go," he reminded me when he was done. "Walk me out?"

I nodded and let him lead me out into the main part of the clubhouse, where there was a crowd of couples saying their goodbyes. Dragon's lips were tipped up in a small grin at Brenna as she talked a mile a minute. Grease was kissing Mrs. Hawthorne in a way that made Will scoff in disgust. Cam was lifting Trix off the floor until her legs were wrapped around his waist, and I could hear him chuckle as Trix tipped her head down, her long hair shielding their faces.

Something about the tableau made my insides clench, but I couldn't pinpoint what bothered me about it.

"I'll be back tomorrow," Will told me as he pulled me forward. "Quick trip."

"I'll be here," I said, meeting his eyes.

"Yeah?"

"Yeah."

"Good news," he murmured with a grin. "Got a lot to talk about."

I didn't reply because he was suddenly hugging me, his lips at my throat. "Text me and let me know how the appointment goes," he said against my skin.

I nodded as I felt my bottom lip tremble. I was glad he couldn't see my face as I tried really hard not to cry. My hands shook as I rested the unhurt one on his waist, the cool leather of his cut smooth against my palm.

He stepped back and kissed my lips quickly.

As he pulled away, it was as if his entire body changed. The boy I'd known my entire life morphed into a stranger. I stared as he straightened his shoulders, tightened his upper body and let his face fall into a hard, emotionless mask. I knew in an instant that I was looking at the other side of Will. The side that my dad had warned me about and I'd never seen before. This was the Ace. The outlaw. The criminal.

He looked just like his dad and I finally understood why Grease made me nervous. There was the leashed violence just underneath the surface of both men.

Oddly, it didn't scare me anymore. I didn't fear Will at all.

With one last glance at my face, he turned and walked toward the group across the room. When he reached them, the couples broke apart and, as a unit, the men strode out the doorway.

I startled when Mel was suddenly at my side. "Did you see that?" I asked quietly as the women started bustling around.

"Yeah," Mel replied. "It's like they're going off to war."

My eyes widened. Oh, my God.

I didn't hesitate. I was practically running for the door before Mel had finished speaking. When I got outside, I was too late.

Seven bikes were rolling away, single file down the long driveway. The gates were swung open as the first bike reached them, and without slowing, the bikes pulled onto the main road, quickly disappearing from view.

"You ready to go?" Amy asked as she followed me outside.

I didn't answer her right away. I was too busy staring blankly at the last place I'd seen Will's bike. Fourth in line. Three men in front of him, three behind him.

"I need to say goodbye to Rebel first," I finally responded, turning slowly back toward the door.

"He'll be okay," Amy said as I reached the door. There was something in her voice. A surety. She knew exactly what was going on.

I nodded, but didn't say anything else as I went back inside.

"Hey, Mrs. Hawthorne," I called, interrupting her conversation with Farrah.

"Call me Callie," she said with an easy smile. It wasn't quite convincing. "You're an adult and we aren't at school."

"I'll try."

"What's up?" she asked. I glanced at Farrah, whose face was completely emotionless.

"Mel's going to stay with Rebel, so you don't have to keep her," I replied. "But thank you anyway."

"Sure. I didn't mind."

"Molly, we better hit it or they're gonna make you reschedule," Amy called.

"Thanks anyway," I said again with a smile before turning and moving toward Rebel. She was on Mel's lap, signing something quickly. I think she was talking about the donut Will had given her the day before. I usually didn't let her eat that crap. I was trying to teach her healthy eating habits, since obesity was something we'd always have to fight against. At some point, she was going to be an adult and I wouldn't be able to make all of her choices for her.

"Hey, Reb," I said, catching her attention as I reached them. "Mama's gotta go to the doctor. I'll be back in a little bit."

"No," Rebel said, her brow furrowing. "No."

"Yep," I answered cheerfully, leaning down to kiss her forehead.

"No!" she yelled, almost pulling me off balance when she suddenly wrapped her arms tightly around my neck.

"Rebel, stop," I said calmly, reaching up with my good hand to try and pry her arms away from my neck. I was bent in half and every time she jerked against me, she slammed into my bad arm, making my vision go spotty from the pain shooting up from the break. "Rebel, let go," I said again, almost panicking.

"Rebel," Mel said sternly. "Let go right now."

Reb shook her head against my neck and I sighed, pulling her against me instead of away. My arm felt like it was on fire, but I ignored it as she pressed up against me.

"I'll be back in just a little while," I said softly, sitting down next to Mel with a feeling of relief. For a moment, I'd thought I was going to hit the floor.

"Mama," Reb mumbled against my throat, exhaling loudly as her body relaxed against me.

I sniffed as I shifted her onto my lap. She was freaked out. I didn't blame her.

"You're going to stay with Auntie Mel," I said softly, slowly swaying from side to side. "And I bet she'll turn on Elmo for you."

"No," Rebel said again.

"I'm only going to be gone for a little bit," I tried again. Negotiating wasn't going to work, I knew that before I even tried. But I really didn't want to leave her when she was freaking out. If I was feeling scared and overwhelmed, it must have been a thousand times worse for Rebel. She didn't have the words to explain what she was feeling. She didn't have the same outlet I did. Everything just built and built inside her until she couldn't take it anymore.

I glanced at Mel, then closed my eyes. "How about Auntie Mel takes you for some ice cream?" I asked, playing the only trump card I had.

I wanted to stay there comforting her for as long as she needed, but I *had* to get to the hospital for my appointment. I couldn't leave my arm the way it was any longer.

"Ice," Rebel said, drawing the *s* sound out. She leaned back a little to look at the side of my face, but didn't let go of my neck. "Mama."

"Mama can't go today," I said softly, rubbing her back in light circles. Too much pressure would set her off again. "But Auntie Mel can."

One of Rebel's hands left the hold on my neck, and came forward slowly, her fingers running through my hair. My throat tightened as she twirled a piece around her finger. People often asked me how I did it. Other parents who showed up to therapy because their doctors suspected that their child was on the spectrum. They always looked so afraid, like their lives were going to change with that single diagnosis.

I never understood the question. Not really. How did I do what, exactly? How did I love my child? Easily. How did I deal with the occasional outbursts? Probably like every other parent who had a three year old. She was just Rebel. The baby I'd grown from an egg so small it was invisible to the human eye.

Sometimes she couldn't meet my eyes, and sometimes she completely refused to talk or sign, and sometimes I had to call her name fourteen times before I caught her attention.

She also had a husky laugh that came from deep in her gut, and was impossible to resist. She liked boy singers, every one of them, from Hunter Hayes to Shawn Mendes. There was something about their voices that she clicked with. I'd cried the first time I'd caught her humming along.

She liked to play with my hair, but didn't like me to brush hers unless I used a specific brush. She said *Mama* with reverence, as if she didn't know any word that she liked better. She wrinkled her nose when she stole a drink of soda, and it usually made her sneeze.

She was everything. She filled me to the brim with every emotion possible, then made them spill over with a giggle.

"Ice," she said finally, her eyes darting to mine before she let go of me.

"I'll see you soon, princess," I said in relief as Mel plucked Rebel off my lap.

I barely remembered to grab my keys and wallet as I rushed out of the room before she could change her mind. I stopped outside the door where Rebel couldn't see me, and waited for a minute, then started walking again when I didn't hear her start to fuss. Success.

"You're good with her," Amy said a few moments later as she led me to her car.

"I do my best," I replied ruefully, climbing in and buckling up. "Not sure how well I'm actually doing."

"We all think that," Amy mused, turning the car on.

"You have kids?" I asked in surprise as she whipped the car around and started down the driveway.

"Just a son," she said, smiling at the boys who opened the gate for us. "He lives up in Portland."

"He's not a biker, then?" I said dryly, relaxing back into my seat.

"Oh, he is." She smiled, pulling out onto the road. "He's just not an Ace."

"That must be a relief," I blurted without thinking, snapping my mouth shut when Amy raised an eyebrow.

"Not really," she said. "He was beaten in an alleyway once."

"Oh, no," I murmured.

"Patrick and the boys took care of it," she said softly, glancing at me before focusing back on the road. "But if he'd been wearing a cut, he probably wouldn't have been attacked in the first place."

"Maybe," I murmured, staring out my window.

"Bad things happen to everyone," Amy said a few minutes later as she pulled into the hospital parking lot. "But the protection of the Aces prevents them from happening far more often than it causes them. Remember that."

I nodded, thinking about the way the men had said goodbye to their wives less than an hour before. I wished I had asked Will to stay, but I was terrified that he would have said no. That would have been infinitely worse than facing this alone.

"Let's get you fixed up," Amy said as we got out of the car. "Once you get that hard cast on, you can show Will who's boss."

Chapter 18

WILL

I ONLY MADE it an hour before I signaled the guys to pull off the highway.

My chest had felt tight since the moment I'd caught a glimpse in my rearview of Molly racing out of the clubhouse to watch me leave, and the farther away we got, the worse it was. When we'd finally hit Oakridge I'd known, but it had taken me a bit more time to get my head straight.

I wanted to catch the fuckers that killed Duncan. The urge was almost painful in its intensity, and the thought of walking away made my fingers twitchy and my skin tingle. It went beyond a little payback. I had to know that they were no longer on this earth, not only because they'd killed Dunc and had beat the hell out of Molly, but because they'd seen her vulnerable and scared. They'd made her that way. They didn't get to live. It was as simple as that.

"What's goin' on?" Dragon asked as I shut my bike off. "You good?"

I shook my head and ripped my helmet off in frustration. "Can't do it," I croaked, scratching at my beard.

"What?" my dad asked, pulling off his shades. "Can't do what?"

"Can't go with you."

"You alright?" Hulk asked as I wiped the sweat from my forehead.

"Molly's havin' surgery today," I said, tapping my helmet against my knee. "I shouldn't have left her." It was the first time in years I'd backed out of a job. The words tasted like gravel in my mouth, but my chest felt instantly lighter once they were out.

The worried frown on my dad's face morphed into a look of relief.

"Fuckin' took you long enough," Hulk joked, shaking his head.

"What?" I asked in confusion, looking around the group.

"Man, you fucked it up last time," Dragon grumbled, leaning back on his bike. "Been takin' runs you didn't have to, leavin' your girl for some fucked up reason that you're not coppin' to."

"I was doin' my job," I ground out.

"Son," my dad said, taking a pack of smokes from his pocket and lighting one before he continued. "You been racin' toward some shit and *I* can't even see where you're headed. Takin' blame for shit that woulda happened one way or another."

He'd said it before, taken me aside and told me that the shit that happened a few years ago hadn't been my fault, but it hadn't been true then and it wasn't now. I wasn't going to argue with him, though. That wasn't what this was about.

"Molly's havin' a hard time," I said instead, changing the subject.

"It was Brenna or one of the kids?" Dragon said quietly as he held out a hand to bum a cigarette off my dad. "Wouldn't have left, either."

"Not just the surgery," Hulk said with a nod. "Molly's been through some shit. Needs her man with her, not ridin' across the state."

"They need to pay for this shit," I said, digging my fingers into my tired eyes. "Needed to make it happen."

"How's that workin' out for ya?" Rock asked from behind me.

"Fuck off, Rocky," I shot back. If it wasn't for his shit, we wouldn't even be on the Russians' radar.

"Head on back," my dad said, interrupting us with a jerk of his head. "We got this."

"You sure?"

"Boy, we been doin' this since before you were a twitch in Grease's pants," Dragon replied, scoffing. "Good to have ya, but pretty sure we can handle it without ya."

"I was givin' you another hour before I beat some sense into ya," Hulk said quietly. "You see your woman come runnin' out of the clubhouse when we left? Need to take care of your family, man."

"You'll let me know when you got 'em?" I asked. As I put my helmet back on, I was already regretting my decision. I was itching to get back to Molly and Rebel, but the urge to find those fuckers hadn't gone away.

"Send you a picture," my dad said with a wide grin. The rest of the guys chuckled.

I gave him a nod and fired up my bike, turning it toward home. I didn't watch them leave. I couldn't. They were going to take care of my business. Those men were mine. They'd fucked with my woman and kid. I should have been the one to teach them a lesson. Instead, I was riding away from them.

The closer I got to Eugene, the more anxious I was to get there. I knew Molly's appointment had already started, and I had no idea if they'd had to knock her out or not. The idea of her getting that bone set or waking up without me there made nausea rise in my gut.

"Will?" Amy asked, getting to her feet as I strode into the waiting room. "What happened?"

I gave her a small smile and leaned in to kiss her cheek when I reached her. She was a good woman. She'd come into the family when I was a kid and had stepped right into a grandmother role like she'd been there the whole time.

"Nothin' happened," I replied gruffly. "Molly in with the doc?"

"Yeah, we got here late, so they had to fit her into another slot," she said with a nod. "They just took her back."

"Thanks," I said. I was already walking toward the receptionist's desk.

After a full minute of arguing with the woman, I ignored her squawking and rounded the desk. They didn't keep the door locked to the back offices, so I just walked right in.

It only took me a couple seconds to find her.

"Hey, baby," I called as I pushed the door to her room open. She was sitting on the hospital bed, her arm completely unwrapped and looking like shit, and she was sweating like she'd just run a mile.

"Will?" she said in surprise, her voice shaking. "What're you doing here?"

"You're here," I said simply. As soon as I reached her, she leaned against me heavily, breathing a sigh of relief. The nausea in my gut disappeared.

"I'm freaking out a little," she said, tipping her head back to look at me.

"Why?" I murmured, leaning down a little to kiss her. She tasted good, like always, but I didn't like the way her swollen lips felt. They didn't feel like hers. I'd never say that out loud, though.

"I've got a low tolerance for pain," she replied ruefully, her lips pulling up into a crooked grin.

"You had a baby," I reminded her with a laugh. "You can handle gettin' your arm set. Piece a'cake. They numb it and it's over in a minute."

"You broke your arm when we were eleven, right?" she asked. Her legs were practically bouncing against the side of her bed, and her good hand was jittery where it wrapped around my back.

"Yep," I answered. "Took off on my dirt bike, even though I was told not to—" Molly laughed. "—and wiped out in less than ten minutes. Pretty sure if I hadn't walked back to the clubhouse with my arm danglin' at an angle, my dad woulda beat the hell outta me."

"Why weren't you supposed to be riding?" she asked distractedly. I was pretty sure she just wanted me to talk so she didn't have to think about getting her arm fixed. Poor baby.

"Dad had been workin' on it and the handlebars weren't tight," I confessed.

"Oh, no."

"*Oh, no* is right. Fuckin' stupid kid mistake." I rubbed my hand against her back, trying to get her to relax a little. She was stiff as a board. "Funny thing about the whole thing was my mom gave my dad hell about it. Askin' why he hadn't finished the project and shit before I got ahold of it."

"Your dad must've been pissed."

"Pretty sure he was just glad I didn't kill myself," I mumbled as the doctor came into the room.

"Okay," she said cheerfully. "Let's get that arm fixed up."

I thought Molly was going to hyperventilate.

★ ★ ★

"You think everythin's okay now," Molly mumbled an hour and a half later as I lifted her out of Amy's car and carried her into the clubhouse. She was slurring pretty good after the drugs the doctor had given to calm her down. Jesus, she'd almost given herself a heart attack over a procedure that was easy as shit. I didn't know what she would have done if I hadn't been there. "Everythin's not okay now, Will. Is not okay."

"Alright, sugar," I said calmly, trying not to laugh.

"You did me dirty. So dirty."

"Let's talk when you wake up, yeah?" I asked as we passed Farrah and Casper sitting on one of the couches.

"Dirty," Molly said even louder, making Farrah smirk.

"Where's Reb?" I called over my shoulder. I wasn't stopping. Who knew what the fuck would come out of Molly's mouth?

"Melanie took her to your mom's to play with the girls," Farrah answered. "They'll be back in a few hours."

Good. Hopefully Molly could sleep that anxiety shit off. Between the pain meds and whatever other shit they'd given her, she was out of it.

"Just left!" Molly was mumbling as I used my shoulder to open the door to my room. "Ghosted me. Thas what thas called. *Ghosted*."

"You're lit," I said, the truth of her words making me sweat.

"Shouldn't forgave you." She held on tight as I tried to set her on the bed, and I ended up half on top of her, trying hard as hell not to crush her. "Where's Reb?" She looked frantically around the room.

"She's with Mel," I said soothingly, moving so I wasn't on top of her anymore. "Hangin' out with my mom."

"Oh, good," she sighed, moving her bleary gaze to me. "She didn't want me to leave her today."

"Understandable," I said softly as she rolled toward me, dropping her heavy cast on my chest.

"She doesn't show it, ya know," she said insistently, her eyes tearing up. "She doesn't say it when she's hurt, but I can tell. I can tell. I'm her mother. I can tell."

"I know you can, baby." God, she was killing me.

"I know when she's sad." She nodded her head sloppily. "I know when she's scared and happy and mad."

"That's 'cause you're a good mama," I replied, pulling her closer.

"I can't die," she told me seriously, her face suddenly lucid. "No one else can tell when she's sad."

"You're not gonna die."

"Almost died," she mumbled, pressing her face against my chest.

"That ain't ever gonna happen again," I told her, my voice breaking. I grabbed her hair and gently pulled her face from my chest. "You believe me?"

"Those guys—"

"Those Russians are dead men. You don't ever have to worry about them again."

"Okay," she said tiredly, her eyes drooping.

"You ready to sleep for a bit?" I asked, letting her face burrow back against the side of my chest.

"Yeah," she said blearily.

"Alright, Moll. Sleep, sugar."

I dropped my head back against the pillow and stared at the ceiling. Fuck.

"Good job, nephew," Farrah's soft voice called from the doorway.

I shifted my head to the side and realized I hadn't closed the door and my aunt had been standing there watching us.

"I'm glad you got your shit together and came back."

"Why does everyone keep sayin' I didn't have my shit together?" I asked, looking back at the ceiling.

"Baby, you've been ridin' hell bent for leather for years. And I get it. When I was around your age, I went off the fuckin' rails. But at some point, you gotta lean on the club and let them carry the weight for a while."

"Is that what you did?" I asked, glancing at her.

"I let Cody carry it. Your great-gram, too."

"Just wanted to take care of those fucks," I admitted. "Kills me that I'm not."

"I get that, too," she said softly. "But you're needed here at home. Sometimes you gotta let your brothers have your back, Wilfred. That's the only way this works."

"It's not Wilfred, it's William," I corrected quietly, a familiar sentence that I'd said to her a million times before.

"Oh, right. Well, that's boring," she replied with a soft smile. The little joke was her *I love you* to me. It always had been. She left the room, pulling the door closed behind her.

I closed my eyes, but I couldn't relax. I wondered where the boys were. If they were getting close. If those Russians were still holed up in the hotel or if they'd moved on. I really hoped that they hadn't. It made me sick to think of the boys getting there and not being able to find them.

Molly shifted, and I reached down to pull off the sling she had wrapped around her. It didn't seem to bother her, but the way she was laying meant that it pulled pretty tight on the back of her neck. Her cast ran all the way up and over her elbow and she was going to have a hell of a time doing anything.

I was looking forward to helping her in the shower, assuming she even let me help her. I hadn't been deluded enough to think that she was going to let me skate by without bringing up shit from the past, but for some reason, I'd thought she'd forgiven me already. She'd been letting me take care of her for the past few days and hadn't said shit about it, and I'd assumed that we were going to let that shit go for now.

Apparently, I was a stupid asshole, because from the crap she'd been saying as I carried her inside, we were far from forgiveness. Not that I blamed her. I'd fucked up big time when I'd taken off without a word.

"Wanna get down?" Molly mumbled against my cut, startling me.

"What?"

"Wanna get down?" she asked again.

I couldn't help the rumble of laughter that came from my mouth. "Nah, sugar, I'm tired. Let's sleep for a bit."

"Fine," she groused. Two seconds later she was asleep again.

★ ★ ★

"You find 'em?" I asked, answering my phone that night. Molly had woken up groggy but lucid, and she'd been laying on my bed watching Rebel play on the floor for the past hour. I'd tried sitting with her for a bit, but eventually I'd had to find something to do. Currently, I was reorganizing shit behind the bar.

"Found 'em," Hulk said, his voice low. "But we're gonna be here a bit longer."

"Why?" I asked, something in his voice making my gut churn.

"Kozlov's got lots to say, man. Fuckin' tons of shit to say." There was a message in there somewhere, but I had no fucking clue what it was.

"You need me up there?" I asked, glancing toward the hallway leading to my room.

"No. Stay where you are." Someone said something in the background that I couldn't hear, and the phone was covered up, because there was silence for a few seconds before Hulk came back on. "I'll call you back, man. Stay there—it's all good."

I stood there staring at my phone like it was going to bite me. What the fuck was that? Something was happening in Ontario and I had no fucking clue what it was.

"Hey," Molly called, coming from the hallway holding Rebel's hand. "We're hungry."

"That right?" I asked, a smile pulling at my lips, the phone call pushed to the back of my mind. They looked so damn sweet together. Moll's hair was messy as hell and she was in nothing but yoga pants and one of my t-shirts since she couldn't get the cast through the arm of any of hers, and Rebel was already dressed for bed since she'd come back to the clubhouse covered in makeup. Lily and Rose hadn't been watching her too close when she was in Rose's room with them. "Whatcha hungry for?"

"Pizza?" Molly asked, looking down at Rebel. "Sound good to you, princess?"

"Pizza," Reb answered, lifting her eyebrows up and down.

"I love it when she does that," Molly confessed, laughing. "And now she's figured it out, so she does it whenever she wants something."

"You know what's up, huh, Reb?" I asked, hopping over the counter. "Got Mama wrapped around your finger."

Reb did the eyebrow thing again, followed by a goofy smile.

"You're cute," I told her, lifting her into my arms. "You want pizza?"

"Yes," she said seriously, all silliness gone.

"What kind do you guys like?" I asked, glancing at Molly.

"Cheese."

"Boring," I sang, making a face at Reb. "Don't you want anchovies?"

"No."

"Pineapple?"

"No."

"Pepperoni?"

"No."

"Fine," I sighed, poking her little belly and making her double over in exaggerated annoyance. "I'll get you cheese pizza."

I pulled my phone out of my pocket and was about to dial the local pizza place when my mom, Tommy and Rose came in the front door. There were a few guys around, a couple in their bedrooms and one in the garage, but no one else was, so it was weird that my family just showed up.

"What's goin' on?" I asked as Rose ran toward me.

"We're staying here tonight," my mom said, frustration clear in her voice.

"Why?"

"No idea."

"Can I play with Rebel?" Rose asked, lightly grabbing Reb's foot.

Molly opened her mouth to answer, but before she could, Reb was shaking her head *no*, her hand going straight for my beard as she laid her head on my chest. I grinned superiorly at my little sister, making her roll her eyes.

"I think she's too tired, hun," Molly said in apology.

"That's okay," Rose replied, pulling her phone out of her pocket as she turned to walk away.

"You guys have dinner?" I asked my mom as she reached me.

"No, I hadn't even started it yet," she mumbled, reaching out to set a soft hand on Reb's back. "She played hard today, no surprise she's tired."

"Thanks for having her over," Molly said.

"She's always welcome," my mom replied.

"You guys want pizza?"

"Sounds good," she nodded then turned her head in surprise when Trix came in, carrying one of her boys on her hip and leading the other one by the hand.

"This is such a pain in the ass," she grumbled.

"The fuck is going on?" I said under my breath. I didn't want to freak Molly out, but if all the old ladies were coming to the club, something was happening. It pissed me right the fuck off that I had no idea what it was.

"You need help?" Molly asked hurrying forward.

"Nah, I'm okay. I left all our stuff in the car. My little brother can get it when he heads over from my parents' house."

Within an hour, all of my family had shown up. Any old lady who had a man in Ontario was staying the night in the clubhouse, and both Poet and Casper had brought their families, too.

"What're you not telling me?" I asked my uncle after I'd finally ordered like twenty pizzas.

"Know as much as you do, Will," he said quietly. "Grease called and said get your ass to the club, here I am."

"Jesus Christ, what a clusterfuck," I snapped, wrapping my hands around the back of my skull. "None of 'em are answering their damn phones."

"Take it down a notch, bud," my uncle said quietly, making me bristle. "They need to talk to us, they'll call."

"I should be there."

"Shut the fuck up," he growled, looking at me like I was an idiot. "You're here with your woman and kid. That's where you need to be."

"You're seriously not pissed that you're not out there with 'em?"

"Will," Casper sighed. "Nah, man. I'm not. Me and you got the most important job, makin' sure these nutcases are safe." He gestured to where Farrah and Cecilia were trying to get my mom to dance with them. I scowled at the way Cecilia was shaking her ass, and glanced over to see Leo staring at my little cousin from across the room while holding one of his nephews.

"It's been a long ass day," I said finally.

Casper nodded his head. "Fuck yeah, it has. For you, especially. How's Molly feelin'?"

"Sore."

"She was high as hell when you brought her home," he said with a chuckle.

"Yeah."

"You know, the truth is usually easier to spew when you're not in your right mind," he said, thumping me on the back. "Don't ignore that shit she was sayin'."

"I won't." I looked over and found Molly lying on the couch, her head pillowed on one arm and Rebel tucked into the curve of her body. They were both sleeping in the middle of the loud, crowded clubhouse. I fucking loved that.

Chapter 19

MOLLY

"Pizza's here, sugar," Will's voice said quietly into my ear. "Wake up and get some." His lips hit my neck as I slowly opened my eyes.

"Oh, shit," I grumbled, looking around the room. "I can't believe I fell asleep. I just slept all day."

"I can," Will said, lifting Rebel from the couch as she woke up. "Your body's healing, baby. You need the rest."

"Why's everyone here?" I asked as I pushed myself to my feet. "This isn't normal, is it?"

Will looked at me for a minute, then shook his head. "No," he replied. "It's not normal."

"Is this everyone?" I asked as he pressed his hand against the small of my back, leading me over to the pizza-covered bar top.

"Nah, about half," Will answered. "Just the families of the guys that went out of town."

My eyes widened as I looked around. There were a ton of people in the room, mostly ones I recognized, but a couple of women I'd never seen before were sitting in the corner with a little boy around Rebel's age.

"Cheese?" Will asked as he let go of me to grab a couple of plates.

"I can get them," I answered absently, taking the plates out of his hand. "You want some?"

"Nah, I'll grab a plate later."

I nodded silently and moved over to the pizza. I didn't understand why everyone was in the clubhouse. The atmosphere was subdued. Not worried, exactly, but not cheerful, either. I knew the guys were up to something, had known it since they'd left that morning, but I think it all really began to sink in then.

As soon as Rebel and I sat down at a table, another thought occurred to me. "Where's Mel?" I asked Will in confusion.

Will's head snapped up and he searched the room hurriedly. "Fuck!" he blurted. He got to his feet and yelled for Brenna.

"What?" she asked, spinning toward Will.

"You call Melanie?"

"No," she said slowly. "Thought Molly told her."

"What?" I asked. "Why would I tell her?"

"You wouldn't," Will said, shaking his head. "Not your responsibility."

He dug his phone out of his pocket and pounded his finger against the screen before raising it to his ear.

"Mel? Get to the clubhouse." He scratched at his face in frustration. "Rock wants you here," he said deeply. "Don't care. Bring her." He paused. "Yep. See ya in a few. Straight here, Mel."

He ended the call shaking his head. "Fuckin' ridiculous," he murmured.

"What's ridiculous?" I asked, still watching him.

"Your best friend."

"And you're just realizing this?"

"Nah," he huffed, dropping down into his seat. "Still surprises me a bit, though."

"She's coming here?" I asked, oddly anxious.

"Yeah, she was at a movie with her sister. Who answers a phone in the fucking theater?"

"Mel," I said dryly. "She wouldn't want to miss something."

"Sounds about right," he said absently.

"How do you have her phone number?" I asked quietly, looking down at Rebel, who had already eaten half of her pizza slice. Thank God she'd grown out of the eczema or that cheese would be wreaking havoc on her later.

"I got all of the old ladies' numbers," Will answered. "All of us do."

"Even yours?"

"What?" he asked in confusion. "Yeah, I got your number."

"No, that woman you were with before," I said, looking up to meet his eyes. I'd been thinking about her before Rebel and I had fallen asleep on the couch. I hadn't seen her since the day before, but that didn't really mean anything. Maybe she was working or something.

"Woman I was with before?" His words faded to nothing. "Casey? She's not my old lady."

"She's something," I replied, watching him squirm.

"She's a friend."

"Bullshit."

"I'm not with her."

"You've fucked her," I said flatly, immediately regretting it when Rebel shifted on my lap.

"Yeah," he said slowly. "I have."

I nodded, looking away.

"Casey and I were never together," Will said, reaching across the table. I moved my hand to my lap before he could touch me. "Molly, it was never a relationship."

"It doesn't matter," I said, shaking my head.

It mattered. It totally mattered.

"Sugar, look at me."

"We weren't together," I mumbled, reaching up to mess with the pizza I hadn't even touched yet.

"Molly," Will persisted. "Look at me."

When I met his eyes, there was apology there. I looked away. I shouldn't have asked. It was none of my business. It wasn't like I could deal with any of it then anyway. I was still reeling, my life completely upended in a matter of a few hours. Rebel and I hadn't even been home in days and it still felt like my dad was going to call me at any minute asking where the hell I was.

"She's not someone you gotta worry about," Will said, making me tense.

"I'm not worried," I said flatly.

"Baby, she's just—"

His words were cut off as my best friend pushed through the front door. "What's going on?" she asked, never slowing as she stomped toward us. A few seconds later, Heather followed her in at a much slower pace.

"Slumber party," Will said dryly as he watched them move closer.

"I was watching a very well-done sex scene when you interrupted," Mel said dramatically. "Hi, monster," she greeted Rebel, giving her a kiss that Rebel tried to dodge.

"Leave her alone," I griped as Rebel almost wiggled off my lap.

"How's the arm?"

"Still attached," I answered.

"Is that medical humor? Because it wasn't very funny."

"Damn, recreational vehicles are obviously not your thing," Heather said, her gaze darting over my face as she reached the table. "You should probably stick to walking."

"Hey, sisterbeast," I greeted with a smile. I loved Heather. She was a freshman at University of Oregon, but she still offered to babysit Rebel and stopped by my house at least once a week to check on us.

"Hey, yourself," she said, kissing Rebel just like Mel had, but with better results.

"Hawk!" Rebel said, grinning.

"Hey, Sparrow," Heather said, catching Rebel as she lurched off my lap.

"Hawk?" Will asked, raising his eyebrow.

I glanced at Heather, taking in her bleached, chin-length hair. "Rebel couldn't say Heather for a long time," I said with a smile.

"I had a mohawk," Heather explained, tickling Reb's belly. "And you could say Hawk, couldn't you?" She looked at Will. "So I'm Hawk and she's Sparrow. Because we're badass."

"Totally badass," Will agreed, his lips twitching.

"Can I grab some of that pizza? My sister wouldn't even buy popcorn."

"Have at it," Will said, waving his arm toward the bar.

"Sweet." She turned and carried Rebel off.

"She's such a pain in the ass," Mel said, sitting down at one of the open chairs.

"You're just pissed that Reb likes her more."

"Yeah, I am!" Mel bitched with a smile. "I get that kid all sorts of cool shit."

"Maybe you need a mohawk," Will said, standing up from the table. He walked away without another word.

"What's going on with you two?" Mel asked as soon as he was far enough away that she didn't think he could hear her. "Looked like that conversation was bordering on serious when I came in."

"Nothing," I replied, shaking my head. "I don't know."

"Well, he wants you back. Clearly."

"Yeah."

"So what're you going to do?"

"I don't know."

"Is there anything you *do* know?" she asked in exasperation.

"I know that my dad is in the morgue of the hospital where I work, and my arm hurts like a motherfucker right now," I snapped, losing patience.

"*Well,*" she said, drawing out the word as she watched me take a bite of my pizza. "None of that has anything to do with banging Will."

She smiled as I glared and stuffed even more pizza in my mouth.

★ ★ ★

"Are you sure?" I asked Heather later that night as I changed Rebel's Pull-Up.

"Yeah, she's slept with me tons of times," Heather replied. "Sleepover status: achieved."

"I know, but you guys aren't at our house," I said worriedly as Rebel reached behind her on the bed and pulled a stuffed animal against her face.

"You're right down the hall, Molly. I'm pretty sure we can hack it."

"Okay," I said, sighing. "Just bring her back if it doesn't work."

"I'm not coming anywhere near this room after lights out," Heather joked, raising her hands out in front of her. "That guy Will has a serious thing for you."

"We have history," I replied darkly.

"Don't we all," she said, nodding her head. "But sometimes that's all it is, just history."

"Do you have any idea what you're talking about?" I asked dubiously as I lifted Rebel into my arms.

"None whatsoever," Heather admitted. "Now gimme that baby."

"Good night, princess," I said softly, kissing Rebel's hair. "You wanna go with Hawk?"

She didn't answer me, but turned toward Heather and sleepily reached for her.

"Boom," Heather joked. "Told ya."

"Yeah, yeah," I grumbled, pulling all of Rebel's sleeping supplies off the bed and stuffing them into Heather's arms.

I dropped to the bed with a huff after they were gone. It was late, and I should have been tired, but I'd slept all day. I was wide-awake and had absolutely nothing to do. I wondered if there were any snacks to be had in the little kitchen off the side of the bar. I'd never been in there, but I'd seen people come out of there with all sorts of food.

I got to my feet and shuffled quietly out of the room, hearing different voices coming from random bedrooms down the hallway. It was close quarters, especially for the moms that had more than one kid with them. I could hear people making beds and arguing about phones—I was pretty sure that one was Farrah—and a deeper voice was talking to Trix. Probably her brother, Leo. He'd introduced himself earlier. He wasn't a super friendly guy, but that was probably because when he'd stopped to talk to me, I'd jerked in surprise at the scars on his face. I'd felt like shit afterward, especially since I knew what it felt like when people stared, but he'd seemed even more uncomfortable with my apology.

"—they're spillin' all sorts of shit," Casper was saying as I reached the main room. "Kozlov's soft. Dragon says he's singin'."

"Kozlov's Rocky's ex's pop, right?" Will asked, making my eyes widen.

"Yep. The man's—" Casper's words cut off as I cleared my throat.

"Hey, sugar," Will said, pushing off the bar. "Thought you were goin' to bed."

I glanced at the other men, smiling nervously when Amy's husband, Poet, shot me a little wave.

"I was," I said quietly when Will got to me. "But I was kind of hungry."

"Figures," Will said, grabbing my hand. "You barely ate today."

"Get what you want," Casper said with a nod. "Food's there for everyone."

"Thank you," I mumbled as Will pulled me past them.

"Finish this in a bit," Will said, lifting his chin.

"Eh, that's fine, boyo," Poet said. "Take care of your woman."

My eyes went wide when we got into the kitchen. The appliances were all restaurant sized and stainless steel, and the pantry took up two full walls. They had everything, from Froot Loops to big cans of baked beans.

"Holy crap," I muttered.

"Whatcha hungry for?" Will asked, moving toward one of the walls. "Salty or sweet?"

"Sweet," I said, searching the shelves. "Oh, a Twinkie," I ordered, pointing to a huge box of them near the ceiling.

"You want a Twinkie?" he asked, walking to where I'd pointed. "Classy."

"Twinkies are good," I argued as he shook the box, then stuffed his hand in the side and pulled two out. "I hope both of those are for me."

He shot me a look and tossed me the snacks before reaching back in the box and grabbing one for himself. "You want something to drink?"

"No, I've got some water back in the room," I answered around the pastry thing in my mouth. Was it a pastry? It was a kind of cake. Sort of.

"Come on," Will said, herding me back down the hallway while I stuffed my face. God, those things were good.

When we got to his room, I expected him to leave me there, but he didn't. Instead, he closed the door behind us and leaned against the dresser to eat his Twinkie.

"Good, right?" I asked, opening my second one.

"It's a Twinkie," he answered blandly, stuffing it into his mouth.

"You're going to choke," I pointed out, biting mine in half.

"So are you," he said, the words garbled.

"Nope." I chewed and swallowed. "You've got some crumbs in your beard."

"You wanna get 'em for me?" he asked, taking a step forward.

That girl with dark hair flashed through my mind. Did she do that? Make sure he didn't have food on his face? Did they laugh about it?

"No, thank you," I answered after I'd swallowed the last of my food. "I've played that game before. It didn't end well for me."

His head jerked back like I'd slapped him. "We're doin' this now, then? Alright," he said, tilting his head to the side.

"I think it's better if we're just friends or something," I replied, reaching for the water bottle I'd left on the floor near the bed.

"We've never been friends," Will pointed out.

"Ouch," I mumbled, lifting the water bottle to my lips. "Fair enough."

"You wanna have this out?" he asked softly, coming closer. "Let's have this out."

"There's nothing to have out," I said, meeting his eyes.

"Baby, don't play that game."

"No game." I shrugged my shoulders and winced. "You moved on."

"I didn't fuckin' move on," he argued. "Told you that."

"You were sleeping with someone else."

"That doesn't mean shit," he growled, throwing his arms out to the side. "Just sex once in a while."

"You sound like a cliché."

"It's the truth! She knows the score. We hung out a few times around the club, fucked when we felt like it."

"And outside the club," I countered. "I saw you, remember?"

"Fuck yeah, I remember." He leaned forward at the waist, pointing toward the door. "I haven't been with her since."

"Should I be happy about that?" I asked incredulously.

"You shouldn't feel anything about it!" he snapped. "It's not even relevant."

"You dumped me and started sleeping with her," I shot back. "Pretty fucking relevant!"

"Jesus Christ," he mumbled, rubbing his hands over his face.

"Getting frustrated?" I asked in mock pity. "Poor thing."

"The fuck is wrong with your mouth?" he asked, looking at me in surprise. "When did you become a goddamn harpy?"

"I never had a reason before!" I yelled back, pushing to my feet. "Because stupid me, I never even thought we were fighting before you disappeared!"

"So this is the shit I have to look forward to?"

"You don't have anything to look forward to!" I screamed back, my mouth snapping shut when I realized how loud we were being.

"Bullshit!" he roared back, making me startle in surprise. "You wanna bitch at me? Hate me? Fuckin' hit me? Fine! But don't pretend that we won't be together."

"*You* made that decision!"

"'Cause I'm a fuckin' idiot!" he yelled toward the ceiling. He dropped his head back down. "You know I'm a fuck up."

"You're not a fuck up," I snapped back.

"Baby, my head was all over the place back then," he said softly, apology written all over his face. "Didn't know what to do, so I dropped the only thing that made sense."

"Me," I said flatly. "And how did that work out for you?"

"Knew I was an idiot the minute I walked out the door," he replied softly. "The instant I said that shit to you and your face fell like I'd slapped you."

I looked away from him. I had no idea what to say. Part of me was glad that he'd realized his mistake that fast, but the other part of me hated him for never trying again. He'd walked away like I was nothing, like Rebel and I were nothing.

"You never came back," I murmured softly, my eyes watering.

"Knew you wouldn't see me," he said, his voice as soft as mine.

"Didn't blame you."

"So you would've just never seen us again?" I asked, pushing him away as he tried to pull me closer.

"No way in hell," he said, dropping his hands to his sides. "Was already plannin' on callin' you when you showed up at the clubhouse."

"Easy to say," I murmured.

"Swear to Christ, Molly," he insisted. "I missed you like hell."

"You just left," I whispered, meeting his eyes. "*Who does that?*"

"I'm so sorry," he replied, his voice cracking. He cleared his throat and shook his head slowly. "I'm so sorry."

"Rebel asked for you, Will." I sucked in a harsh breath as I shook my head. "She asked for you every day for a *year*. Do you know what that was like? She didn't understand why you were gone. *I* didn't understand why you were gone."

"I'm sorry," he said roughly. "I was so fucking wrong about everything. I love Rebel. You know I do. I'd never hurt her on purpose."

"It doesn't matter if you did it on purpose. You still did it."

Will's lips trembled and his eyes grew glassy, then he cleared his throat like he had something caught in it.

"You—" I choked, swallowing hard. "You made me feel like *nothing*."

"Moll," he whispered, his face falling. "Never, baby. You were never nothing. Not for a second."

"The night before you left, you wouldn't even let me sleep! We had sex over and over again. I thought everything was great. I . . . I thought, this is it. This is *forever*. And then . . . then I realized, it wasn't forever, it was a fucking *goodbye*."

A sob ripped through me and I dropped my face into my hand. God, it had been so horrible after he'd left. I'd spent weeks wondering what I'd done wrong. I'd woken up in the middle of the night, wondering what the hell had happened. It had been months before I felt like myself again.

"Don't," he rasped. "Don't cry."

Will's chest pressed against my front, and then his hands were there. One wrapped around my back, and the other held my head against his chest.

"I won't ever make you cry again," he promised against the top of my head. "I swear to God, Moll. I'll piss you off, but I won't ever make you cry."

He lifted me up and carried me to the bed, keeping me in his lap as he sat down.

"I don't know," I finally said, lifting my head.

"I'll prove it."

"How?"

"By stickin' around," he said, his lips tipping up just a little.

He leaned toward me, and I didn't move as his lips hit mine. They were soft at first as he carefully brushed them over mine, but within seconds, I was opening my mouth and letting him press his tongue inside. I'd let him kiss me since I'd come to the club, but that time it felt different. Like a prelude. A promise.

"Thank you," he groaned, his fingers tangling into my hair.

"You're welcome?" I said automatically, making him laugh into my mouth.

"I love you, Molly," he said, pulling his face away from mine to gauge my reaction.

"I love you, too," I replied without hesitation. That was something that had never been in question. It was the trusting part that still needed work.

His mouth hit mine more frantically then. Pressing harder and kissing me deeper, but he was still really careful. He stood me up and dropped his head to my collarbone for a long moment, kissing me there before reaching for my sling and tenderly pulling it off.

"You feelin' okay?" he asked as I helped him push his cut down his shoulders.

"Yeah," I breathed as he tore his shirt over his head. "You got more ink."

"Just a couple," he said as he reached for my shirt. "Had some time on my hands."

"You got bigger, too."

"More time for workin' out."

"You missed me?" I asked, hating the vulnerability it exposed.

"I was wonderin' what you were doin' every hour I was awake," he replied, pushing my shirt over my good arm and off my head, then slowly pulling it over my cast. "Goddamn, I really missed you," he said reverently.

"You got harder, I got softer," I mumbled, looking down at my curves.

"Perfect," he said with a grin as he dropped my shirt to the floor.

I giggled as he pressed his face between my boobs and sighed.

"Are you going to help me with my pants?" I asked after a couple minutes of him resting against my chest.

"Yeah," he said, leaning back as his hands found the waistband of my yoga pants. "Just wanted a minute with my friends first."

"Your friends?"

"Hadn't seen 'em in a while."

I shook my head as Will peeled my pants down my legs.

"Your arm gettin' heavy?" he asked after he'd helped me step out of the fabric.

"Will, I get that you're being sweet," I replied, reaching out to run my fingers through his hair. "But I haven't had sex in eighteen months."

"No one since me?"

"Does my vibrator count?" I asked, jolting in surprise when he pulled me onto the bed.

"Scoot back," he ordered, as he started unbuttoning his jeans. "Middle of the bed."

It took me a second, since I couldn't use one of my arms, but I was glad that he didn't try to help me. Instead, he watched me hungrily, stripping off the rest of his clothes.

"Condom," I reminded him as Will set one knee on the bed.

I saw him cringe, and for a split second I felt bad, but it was gone quickly. He'd had sex with someone else. It wasn't something I could ignore. Even if he'd been careful with her—my stomach burned at the thought of it—he still needed to suit up.

"I'll get tested," he said after he'd rolled the condom on.

"Okay," I breathed as he knelt on the bed, leaning forward to grip my hips. He jerked me toward him and bent at the waist, bracing himself on one arm until our faces were just inches apart.

"You want my mouth on you?" he asked, his eyes crinkling at the corners.

"Yes," I replied, then instantly changed my mind. "No."

"Which is it?" he teased, his hand sliding up my side to grip my breast. His touch was soft, even though he was trembling with restless energy.

"Just fuck me," I said seriously, making him bark out a laugh.

"It's never *just* anything with you," he murmured, rubbing his nose across my jaw.

His hips shifted and then he was there, sliding inside me slow and steady. He'd barely touched me, and I hadn't needed anything but his strong body above mine to get wet. It was ridiculous, and if I remembered correctly, really convenient for quickies.

"Tell me if anything hurts," Will instructed, sliding back out. "We'll be careful."

"Careful sucks," I griped, reaching for him. My cast hit his shoulder with a *thunk*. "Oh, shit!"

"Okay," he said in amusement, moving my arm to rest by my head. "Maybe you're the one that needs to be careful."

"I'm sorry!" I blurted, my eyes wide.

"Make it up to me," he ordered, his eyes falling almost closed as he thrust again. "Goddamn."

"More," I breathed as he pulled back and thrust again. "Too slow."

"Always too slow for you," he answered, running his tongue across my breast. "Gotta be careful."

"I'm fine," I gasped as his tongue found my nipple. "I can't come like this."

"Bullshit, you can't," Will argued, biting down.

He ended up proving me wrong.

★ ★ ★

"Is she still going to be around?" I asked later, hating that I'd asked, but anxious for an answer. I'd taken another pain pill and it was making me slightly loopy. It took away the throbbing in my arm, though, so I could deal with loopy.

"That gonna bug you?" Will asked, running his finger along the skin on my arm where the cast ended.

"I'd like to say that I'm too mature for it to bug me," I hedged, pinching Will when he chuckled. "But yes. It would drive me insane."

"Alright, she's gone, then."

"But . . . are all her friends here?" I asked worriedly.

"Moll, you can't have it both ways."

"Right. Yes, I don't want to see her. Ever."

"Then, you won't. End of."

I nodded my head and closed my eyes. I loved the way Will smelled, and it was always strongest after we'd had sex. Not a sex smell, really, just his natural smell.

"Hey, Will?" I called. "Did you say that the guy who killed my dad was Rocky's father-in-law?"

Will's body turned to stone beneath me. "You eavesdroppin' earlier?"

"No, as soon as I realized you guys were talking, I let you know I was there. It's not like I was being quiet."

"Sugar," he sighed. "Better for you—the less you know. Alright? I'll tell you that, yes. Same man. But don't go askin' about it."

I thought it over for a minute. I wanted to know everything. Why he'd targeted my dad. What he'd been looking for. But I knew with certainty that the answers to those questions wouldn't really change anything. The *why* of it all would never make any sense, no matter what I knew, and I didn't ever want to have to try and lie to the police again.

"Okay," I said finally.

"Better get some rest," Will said in obvious relief, squeezing me tighter against him.

"Are you getting up?"

"Might in a while, see if Casper's heard from my dad. Won't be gone long, though."

"Okay," I said again, relaxing against his chest. "Night."

I was out in seconds.

Chapter 20

WILL

"Wнат're you doin' up?" I asked in surprise as I dragged my tired ass into the main room. My mom, Aunt Farrah, Brenna and Trix were seated around a table with a half-empty bottle of tequila resting in the center.

"Tradition," my mom said with a smile. "When the men are out of town, the mice will play."

"Cats," Brenna corrected, smacking my mom's arm. "Perfect time for us to visit."

"You see each other daily," I pointed out, making my mom roll her eyes.

"Ash already passed out," my mom said, chuckling. Samson's old lady was a notorious light weight when it came to tequila.

"Homer's old lady is knocked up, so she crashed before the kids, and Shady's old lady has their son with her," Trix said. "We were gonna wake Mel up, but we didn't want to wake Rebel, too."

"Good call." I looked around the room. "Where's Casper?"

"Your *Uncle* Casper is outside," Farrah mumbled.

"You're really givin' me shit when you're about to fall face-first into the table?" I joked.

"Be nice to me, Wilfred," she ordered, smiling.

"Always." I moved past them and headed toward the front just as my phone rang in my pocket.

"Hello?" I answered as I pushed through the front door.

"William," my dad's voice rasped. "You need to call everyone in."

"What?" I stopped in my tracks and caught sight of Casper jogging toward me, Tommy on his heels.

"Everyone in," my dad repeated. "Don't forget a single fuckin' person, you hear me?"

"I hear you," I replied, stunned. What the fuck?

I glanced in confusion at my phone when it went dead.

"What's goin' on?" I asked, falling into step with Casper as he slowed.

"Dragon called," he said, coming to a stop at the closed door. "Told me to pull the prospects off the gate and put Leo and Samson up there." He shook his head. "Sent the other prospects to the back entrance. It's all closed up, but who the fuck knows."

"Dad just called and told me to bring everyone in," I replied, lifting my phone up.

"Dragon told me the same. Lock everything down."

"What the fuck is going on?"

"No idea, but they're on their way back. We should know more in the morning."

"I'll call half and you call half?" I asked as he opened the door.

"Why can't the women—oh. Shit," he said, laughing a little.

Brenna was on the floor, flat on her back and snoring. Trix was laughing hysterically at the table, while Farrah debated the merits of drunk sex, gesturing with the tequila bottle. And my mom was hanging over Tommy's shoulder.

"Bringin' her to bed," Tommy said with a huff, shaking his head. "Hopefully, she doesn't puke all over my back."

"Ah, hell," Casper mumbled, moving toward the table. "I'll get Trix and you get your aunt."

"Why can't you get your own wife?" I asked, eyeballing Farrah.

"Because Hulk won't kill *me* for carryin' his wife to bed," Casper said in amusement.

I scoffed, but still headed straight for my aunt.

"Wilfred!" she sang as I pulled her up from the table.

"It's not Wilfred."

"Wilhelmina?"

"No." I bent at the waist and threw her over my shoulder.

"Will-you-take-me-to-dinner?"

"Nope."

"Well, then, what is it?" She asked, slapping my ass. Jesus.

"William Butler Hawthorne," I answered, walking quickly down the hallway to Casper's room.

"Well, that's boring."

"So you've said," I mumbled, jerking to try and keep her on my shoulder as she reached out to both sides and tried to touch the walls.

I carried her into the room and dropped her on the bed as she laughed.

"I liked you better when you thought your middle name was *butter*," she joked as I pulled her shoes off.

"No, you didn't."

"True. I had to wipe your ass back then."

"Can we never talk about you wipin' my ass again?"

"No promises," she murmured as she rolled onto her side. "Never know when I'll have to drop it into the conversation."

I laughed and shook my head, shutting off the light as I left the room. By the time I'd made it back to the main room of the club, Brenna wasn't on the floor anymore and Casper was sitting at the bar.

"You got the list?" I asked, sitting down beside him.

"Yup. I'll take the names from the top to here," he pointed. "You take the rest."

"I can help, too," Tommy said, coming out of the hallway.

"You start movin' tables," Casper ordered with a nod. "Gonna need the room for sleepin' bags and shit."

"What a fuckin' headache," I mumbled, scratching at my beard as I found my first name on the list.

"Better than the alternative," Casper replied darkly.

★ ★ ★

I WOKE UP the next morning to a little hand petting my beard.

"Good morning," Molly said huskily as I opened my eyes. Rebel was sitting between us with a stuffed duck in her lap.

"We need to get her a dog or something," I replied, trying not to move my mouth as Rebel's fingers found my mustache.

"I don't have much of a yard," Molly mused, scooting in closer to me. At some point, she must have pulled on a t-shirt while I was sleeping, because she'd been naked when I'd come to bed. Hell of a way to fall asleep.

"We'll get a place," I said, turning my head toward her when Rebel got bored with my beard.

"You want to move in together?" Molly asked, raising her eyebrows.

"Marry me first?"

"Eventually," she said with a secretive little smile.

"Wanna have more kids before Reb's old enough to be their mother," I told her, surprised when her head jerked back.

"Will," she replied, her face pained.

"What?"

"I just—" she shook her head. "I'm not sure that I want more kids."

"Oh." My mind went completely blank for a minute. It wasn't even something that had crossed my mind. Hell, there were four kids in my family. Everyone I was close to had at least two.

"The chances of having another child with Down syndrome is higher for me," Molly said quietly. "And I'm not saying no, I'm just saying that's something we'd have to discuss, you know? It's not a fly by the seat of your pants type of decision."

"No, I get it," I mumbled, looking at Rebel. She was licking her lips as she poked at the duck's eye, rubbing the pad of her finger over the smooth plastic. I imagined her as she grew. Going to school. Learning how to play a sport, maybe. Teaching her how to drive on the back of the club's property, the same way my dad had taught me. I let myself worry about the people who would try and take advantage of her, of the inevitable discussion Molly would have to have about men and being careful. I tried to imagine her as an adult. Wondered if she'd be able to live on her own, and decided that I didn't care if she ever moved out.

"I'm all in, sugar," I said thickly, meeting Molly's eyes. "You take as much time as you want to decide, but I'm good with whatever we get. Maybe we'll stop at one more, you know? If we think that's all we can handle." I looked back at Rebel. "But Reb needs a brother."

"Okay," Molly choked out, kissing my shoulder. "I'll think about it."

I lifted my arm and Molly moved in to lie against my chest.

"But you'll marry me?" I asked as Rebel got bored with the duck and tossed it behind her.

"That wasn't a proposal," Molly said dryly, sniffling. "A proposal comes with a ring."

I laughed, and it made the bed move so much that Rebel startled and gripped my thigh through the blankets . . . which only made me laugh harder.

"So I gotta get you a ring, huh?" I asked, still laughing.

"A big one," Molly confirmed.

"I can do that."

"Maybe by the time you find the perfect one, I'll give you an answer."

I shook my head and opened my mouth to reply, but a knocking at my door interrupted.

"Brother," Tommy called. "They're back."

Adrenaline hit me hard, and I sat straight up in bed. "Take Reb," I told Molly, making sure she had a good hold on her before I climbed off the bed.

Shit, I was naked. My hands went straight to cover my junk as I crossed the room to where I'd dropped my jeans the night before.

"Butt!" Rebel yelled gleefully, making Molly laugh loudly.

"She doesn't get in our bed when I'm naked," I ordered, going to the far side of the dresser to get my pants on.

"I didn't think you were going to go flying out of bed!" Molly argued. "She was on top of the blankets!"

"I'm serious, Molly. Not cool."

"Okay, okay. I'll be more careful," she promised, raising her hands in surrender. "I really didn't think that you'd get up before we did. You didn't come to bed until six this morning."

"Yeah, had some calls to make," I explained, buttoning my jeans. I didn't even bother with boxers.

"I noticed the clubhouse filled up while I was asleep," Molly said calmly, sitting up.

I'd noticed that she was still pretty quiet around everyone, but she hadn't had that deer in the headlights look that she'd gotten when I'd introduced her to my family for the first time. I wasn't sure if it was because of painkillers the doctor had prescribed, or the relief of friendly faces after the shit she'd just been through, but she'd handled meeting all the new people like a champ. She didn't even look nervous about the crowded clubhouse.

I nodded. "Yeah, baby. Went on lockdown after you went to bed. Just a precaution."

"Is there anything I should know?" she asked, scooting to the edge of the bed.

"Not at the moment," I answered, throwing on a t-shirt and my cut. "But when there is, I'll tell you."

"Okay." She tilted her head up when I walked over to the bed, and gave me a closemouthed kiss.

"Your morning breath doesn't bother me," I murmured against her lips.

"Yours does," she countered, wrinkling her nose.

"Funny." I pulled back and headed for the door, stopping as I opened it. "Lotta people to feed today if ya wanna help. Nobody'd blame ya if ya didn't."

"I'll help," she said with a nod, throwing her feet over the edge of the bed.

"Will!" Rebel yelled, catching my attention. She pursed her little lips and tilted her head back.

I felt about ten feet tall as I strode back across the room and gave her a kiss. "Be good for your mama." My beard must have tickled her cheeks because she let out this husky belly laugh and fell backward onto the bed.

Yeah, I thought as I walked away, *I'd happily have another one of her.*

The sounds of the packed club hit my ears as soon as I'd left the room and I practically ran to the front of the clubhouse. There were people every fucking where. Little kids eating at the tables, old ladies cleaning shit up and making food, teenagers watching the babies. It was a madhouse.

I made eye contact with Poet right away and he tilted his head toward the chapel, making me hurry toward the little room. When I got to the door, I pushed right in, not bothering to knock. One of the seats was mine, so I no longer had to knock on that door.

"Moose," Dragon said from the head of the table. "Nice of you to make it."

"Had to get my girls up," I answered, rounding the table. "Sorry about that."

"Everything good with that?" my dad asked.

"Solid," I replied with a small grin, making him nod in approval.

"We caught up with Kozlov in the hotel, no problem," Dragon said, tapping his fingers on the table. "Picked him and his lackey up and used Kozlov's car to bring 'em out to an old warehouse."

"Put up a good fight, though," Hulk murmured. He was sporting a gnarly black eye.

"Didn't take them long to start talkin'," Dragon continued. "We were right about the list Rock gave to the DEA. They wanted that shit, needed to know who Rock had outed." He paused for a long moment. "Made sure they hurt for a bit," he said to me. "And knew why they were hurtin'."

I nodded my head in thanks.

"That's the good news," Dragon said tiredly, pulling the ponytail out of his long hair and scraping it back up again almost in the same movement.

"What's the fuckin' bad news?" Casper grunted.

"Kozlov's low level," my dad said quietly.

"What? Fucker's been runnin' shit for years," Samson argued.

"All a front," Dragon murmured, slamming his fist down on the table. "Real head is named Pajari. Fucker was at the weddin' and Rock had no fuckin' clue who he was."

"But now the DEA does," my dad butt in.

"Right."

"That's the bad news?" I asked. That fucking sucked, but it just meant we hadn't cut the head off the snake yet. We would. Eventually.

"No," Dragon answered. "Bad news is, on top of everythin' else, they've been dealin' 'roids for the past five years."

Everything inside me froze.

"Had some boys out here, checkin' out the competition. Rattlin' some cages."

My vision went cloudy for a second.

"Sent some up to Montana for a while, too."

No. Fuck, no.

"William," my dad growled in warning as my hands tightened into fists at the end of the table.

"Wasn't you, wasn't Trix," Dragon said quietly, making Samson curse. "Those kids were sent for one purpose. Disposable soldiers."

"Calm, William," my dad warned again, pushing his seat back from the table. They were all watching me closely and it took everything I had not to fly out of my chair.

"That was just the beginning," Dragon continued. "Kozlov and his boys were round two."

"That was over three fuckin' years ago," I ground out.

"Long game," he replied. "Had to see where we were at. Try and assess weaknesses."

"What about Rocky?" I asked. I had to know. He'd come from there, had ties to the Russians that we'd known about when we let him prospect.

"He didn't know," my dad said, raising his voice so everyone could hear his answer. "He was with the club long before that shit started up."

"So what now?" Casper asked quietly.

The silence in the room was like static crackling in the air. No one moved. No one even breathed.

"We go to war," Dragon finally replied.

I stumbled to my feet and braced myself against the edge of the table as I struggled to breathe. Everything I'd believed for the past few years had been wrong.

In flashes, I saw the day that our world had been upended. The way Mick had wrapped his arms around Tommy's chest and tackled him to the ground as bullets sprayed across the yard. My mom, her eyes wide and afraid as we'd tried to stop her from bleeding out. Slider's lifeless body resting less than three feet from Vera's.

I gasped, but I couldn't seem to get enough air.

"Everybody out!" Dragon ordered.

People moved around, but I didn't see them. I stared at the table, my neck straining as I tried to inhale.

"Breathe, son," my dad said firmly, thumping my back. "Come on, take a breath."

I shook my head and closed my eyes tight, trying to snap myself out of whatever the fuck was happening. I opened my eyes as I started to feel dizzy, only to find that my vision was going hazy at the edges.

Oh, hell no.

I gasped again, finally bringing a little air into my lungs.

"Motherfuck," I wheezed as my dad's hand gripped my shoulder. "Jesus."

"Thought I was gonna puke when I heard that shit," my dad said quietly. "If we woulda questioned that kid longer . . ."

I remembered the night we'd killed him. The little psycho had been tied to a chair, beat to shit, and he'd still been running his mouth. I wasn't sure if Dad or I had fired the first shot, but in the end, we'd filled his body with bullets. I'd never regretted it before that moment.

"I walked right into that shit," I said, still trying to catch my breath.

"Hell, boy," Dad said, leaning against the table. "None of us had any fuckin' clue."

"What now?" I asked, repeating Casper's earlier question. "How the fuck do I keep my family safe?"

My dad sighed, staring at the door between us and the rest of the clubhouse. "Lockdown for now," he said. "We'll know more in the next few weeks and we'll make plans. This ain't our first rodeo, son. We'll get it handled."

"Yeah," I said quietly, pushing off the table.

He squeezed my shoulder again as I moved toward the door. My head was still reeling. All that time, we'd thought that we'd finished those kids off. Thought we were relatively safe. And all that time, there had been a bigger threat waiting.

The last three years of my life, I'd been killing myself thinking that I'd brought that mess into our club. That I'd gotten my baby brother killed.

I swallowed hard as I walked into the main room. It was so fucking loud I couldn't distinguish anyone's specific voice, but my eyes caught on Molly instantly. She was standing at the bar, holding Reb on her hip as she talked to Poet. He laughed at something she said, and then Rebel's little hand was reaching out to run down his long beard.

I reached them in seconds.

"Will?" Molly asked worriedly as she caught the look on my face.

"You're movin' in with me," I replied roughly, cupping her swollen cheeks in my hands. "Okay? No argument, baby."

"Okay," she breathed. "What's wrong?"

I took Rebel from her hip and pulled her against my chest, my heart thudding hard as she relaxed into me.

"I need you," I said quietly, meeting Molly's eyes. "Let's go in my room and get away from all this shit for a while."

She nodded and grabbed my hand, letting me lead her back into my room. As soon as I'd closed the door, she took Rebel from me and set her on the floor then wrapped her arm around my waist.

"What's going on, Will?" she asked softly, kissing my chest.

My throat grew tight as I put my arms around her, pulling her even closer. "Can't talk about it now, alright?" I asked hoarsely.

I wanted to tell her everything, and eventually I would. But looking down into her bruised face, the fear still present in the back of her eyes, I knew then wasn't the time. Instead, I pulled her to the bed and laid down with her, curving the front of my body into the back of hers as we watched Rebel walk around the room gathering stuffed animals.

I took in the smell of Molly's hair, the soft skin of her belly against my fingertips, and the sound of Rebel humming on the floor, and I stayed.

For the first time since Mick died, I stayed right where I was.

"Love you," I murmured against the back of Molly's head.

"Love you, too." Her fingers found and linked with mine.

Yeah. I wasn't going anywhere.

Chapter 21

MOLLY

I CLIMBED OUT of bed when Will fell asleep an hour later. He was obviously tired and I didn't want Rebel to wake him up. As I carried her out of the room, I wondered what the hell had happened to make Will so upset.

There were things he couldn't tell me. I was beginning to understand at least that much about the dynamics of the club. But, honestly, I was completely on board with that. After lying to the police, I didn't ever want to have to do it again. The more I knew, the more I'd have to lie about.

These guys were clearly not just mechanics. I'd always known that. I was finding that they weren't just criminals, either, though. They were family men. Some of them loved their wives to distraction, especially the ones in Will's family. I'd noticed others that morning that weren't super affectionate with their wives, but showed them blatant respect anyway. They played with their kids, helped them tie their shoes and changed their diapers.

I was finding that the one-dimensional picture my dad had painted about life inside the Aces wasn't even close to accurate. I wondered if he'd known that they had been my safe haven after I'd left him. I wondered if his attitude about my relationship with Will would have changed if he'd known how good they had been to me.

"Hey, girl," Trix said as I passed her in the hallway. "Will okay?"

"Yeah, he's sleeping," I said quietly, hitching Reb farther up on my hip. Holding her with just one arm was harder than I'd ever realized before I broke my arm.

"How about you?" Trix asked, leaning against the wall. "You okay?"

"Um," my face scrunched up in confusion. "Yeah."

She laughed. "I just meant with all of this." She waved a hand around. "I grew up here, so none of this bothers me. It's a pain in the ass, but I'm sort of used to it. But you're new to all of it."

"It's a little overwhelming," I confessed. "Everyone's been nice, but being on lockdown? That's crazy."

"Yeah," Trix said softly. "This type of shit doesn't happen very often, but this life isn't for the faint of heart, especially for us women. We have to deal with our men being out of town, getting locked up—" She reached over and knocked on a wood door. "—putting themselves in danger."

"I didn't realize what I was getting into," I murmured. "I get it now, but at the beginning?" I shook my head.

"And now you're stuck, am I right?" she asked with a rueful smile. "You're not the first woman to fall in love with an Ace and get sucked into a life that you hadn't imagined for yourself. My mom grew up here and still took off pregnant with me the minute she could, but like five years later, she came back to my pop. Hell, Will's mom was just a teenager when she met Grease. Try dealing with all this shit as a tadpole. Crazy."

"I didn't know that," I said in surprise.

"Oh, yeah. It was a big clusterfuck from what I've heard. Grease stepped in and protected her from some gang, and they've been together ever since. Us kids don't usually get the entire stories, but we hear the bones of most of them."

"Ya tellin' tales?" Grease asked from somewhere behind me, making me jump.

"Of course not," Trix said, smiling sunnily.

"You're trouble, kid," he told her indulgently.

"I'm the best kind of trouble," Trix said with a sly smile.

"I didn't need to hear that," he murmured in disgust, making Trix laugh.

She turned back to me and smiled. "You'll figure it out. Just takes a little time."

Trix walked away, leaving Grease and me alone in the hallway. Jesus, the club was full of people, and not one of them chose that moment to join us?

"Whatcha gotta figure out?" Grease asked as I turned slowly to face him.

"I . . ." my words trailed off as I met his eyes and I immediately shifted my gaze to his throat. "Nothing. All of this is just a little overwhelming."

"Ya gonna leave my son as soon as you're safe?"

"What?" I met his eyes again in surprise. "No."

"Good." He nodded, leaning against the wall and pulling a cigarette out of his pocket. I stiffened, but he didn't light it.

Rebel chose that moment to wiggle like crazy and I almost dropped to my knees in an effort to try and keep her steady.

"Here," Grease said gruffly as he stuck the unlit cigarette between his lips and plucked Reb out of my arms. My jaw dropped as he turned and opened the door behind him and set Rebel on her feet so she could walk inside the room. "Callie's in there," he explained as he closed the door behind her.

My mouth snapped shut as he leaned back against the wall.

"Know ya don't like me much—"

"I like you," I lied quickly, making him chuckle.

He pulled the cigarette out of his mouth and started rolling it over his fingers. "Nah, girl. Ya don't. I scare ya?"

I lifted my chin, refusing to answer.

"Just means you've got a sense of self-preservation," he said with a grin. "Nothin' wrong with that."

"I'm not scared of you," I mumbled, glaring at him.

"Good," his voice dropped. "Cause I'd never hurt ya. Ya know that? Don't hurt women on principle, but you? You're family. You're my son's old lady."

"I'm—" I started to argue but he sliced his hand through the air, cutting me off.

"Will's been outta control for a long time. Runnin' himself ragged lookin' for somethin'. Looks like he found it."

I swallowed hard as he stared at me.

"I'm gonna protect that. Doesn't matter if ya like me or not."

"I don't dislike you, you just scare me," I blurted.

He grinned like he'd won. "Truth will set ya free," he murmured.

"Oh, shut it," I said in frustration, then snapped my mouth closed as my eyes went wide.

"See? Free already."

I snorted in annoyance.

"You're a good girl. You're good for Will. Won't take his shit, but you'll give him a little growin' room. He's gonna fuck up, just stick with it, alright?"

"He's already had his fuck up," I retorted. "He doesn't get any more."

Grease choked and then laughed hard. It changed his entire face.

"Girl, life's a series of fuck ups and clean ups. You just gotta decide that you're in it, and then stick." He pointed toward the closed door. "Ya think I've never fucked up with Callie? Shit. That woman has dealt with shit ya can't even imagine. But once she was in, she wasn't goin' anywhere. Same with me. Made the decision and we stood by it."

My throat grew tight. Was that really all I had to do? Life with Will seemed like a roller coaster. I was so afraid to trust him. Afraid that he'd leave again. He pissed me off and worried me . . . and still, I couldn't imagine being without him anymore. I didn't want to be without him ever again.

"I'll try," I said finally, clearing my throat.

"Don't try," Grease said seriously. "Do it. Stick. Ain't nothin' better than knowin' someone's got your back, no matter what. You give that to my boy, he'll give it back."

I nodded as Grease stuck the cigarette back between his lips.

"Been dyin' for a smoke for two hours," he mumbled with a grin. He reached out and awkwardly patted my shoulder, obviously done with his little lecture.

When he moved around me, I turned with him, watching him go. I thought about Will sleeping in his room, and the tension between his eyes that hadn't relaxed and the way his shoulders were bunched tight around his ears.

"Hey Grease?" I called out right before he hit the archway that led into the main part of the clubhouse. "I'm worried about Will. Something's wrong."

Grease turned to look at me, his eyes sad. "I'll take care of it," he said softly around his cigarette. "Stick, Molly, yeah?"

"Okay." I wrung my hands. How would he take care of it? What the hell was going on? Did I even really want to know?

"Hey," Grease called, grabbing my attention again. "You're family. Call me Asa."

When he left, I knocked on Callie's door and opened it. Rebel was sitting on the floor and Rose was doing something to her toenails.

"Hey," Callie said from the bed, an E-reader in her hands. "We're having a spa day."

"Lockdown is so freaking boring," Rose mumbled.

"What're you doing?" I asked curiously, kneeling down beside Reb.

"She doesn't like the nail polish brush," Rose informed me.

"Yeah," I replied dryly. "I know."

"So Mom and I got some of those nail wrap things," Rose said easily. "They're little stickers, and then you put some heat on them and they stay on for like, weeks."

My breath caught as I watched Rebel sit patiently while Rose set a little sock filled with something on the top of her big toe.

"You can use a hair dryer for this part, but Mom and I thought maybe that would bug her. So we put some rice in one of my old socks and heated it up in the microwave." She glanced at me. "Looks like it works."

"Rebel," I said softly. "Are you getting pretty toes?"

Reb didn't look at me, but she nodded as she continued to stare at her feet. When Rose pulled the little sock away, Rebel's big toenail was covered in pink and white stripes.

My baby squealed in excitement, and leaned closer to her foot so she could check it out.

"That's awesome," I breathed, smiling at Rose. "Good idea."

"Lily likes these 'cause she can do them by touch. I just tell her what the pattern is."

"Seriously?" I asked, glancing up at Callie to find her watching us. "That's incredible."

"It took a lot of messed up nails for her to figure it out," Callie said with a laugh.

"Yeah, and these things are expensive," Rose grumbled. "We almost had to start panhandling to buy new ones."

I laughed and leaned back as Rose started on Rebel's second toe. I wanted to watch her put them on, but I was anxious that Will was going to wake up and not know where we were.

"We can watch her for a bit," Callie said nonchalantly, looking back at her tablet screen.

"Thanks," I replied quickly, kissing Rebel's head before getting to my feet.

I walked quickly back to Will's room, my head spinning.

The Aces were . . . shit, they were a *family*. And from what I'd seen so far, they were a *good* one. They took care of each other. It was clear in the way Grease had talked to me about Will. The way Trix had stopped to make sure I was settling in. The way Callie and Rose had figured out a way for Rebel to decorate her toenails.

Beyond the whole outlaw thing, they weren't anything like I'd expected.

"Hey, sugar," Will called groggily as I walked quietly into his room. "Where ya been?"

"Just took Rebel to see your mom," I said softly, kicking off my shoes.

Will lifted the blankets so I could slide in next to him then tucked them in around me once I was settled.

"Are you okay?" I asked, reaching up to run my fingers through the hair at the side of his head.

"Yeah, baby. I'm good."

"You didn't sleep very long."

"Missed ya when you got outta bed," he said simply, making my heart flutter.

"I didn't want Rebel to wake you up."

"She's fine in here with us," he argued. "Rather have both of ya with me, even if I'm tryin' to sleep."

"Okay." I relaxed into his body and tucked my head under his chin. We were quiet for a few minutes, but I knew he wasn't asleep. "So, I ran into your dad in the hallway," I said with a small grin.

"Oh, yeah? How'd that go?"

"He told me to call him Asa," I murmured, my smile growing wider.

"Ah, high praise comin' from him," he said with a laugh. "Mean's you're part of the family. Don't even think my Aunt Farrah has ever called him Asa."

"Really?" I tipped my head back so I could meet Will's sleepy eyes.

"Yeah, really. Only my mom and my great-gram called him Asa. Everybody else calls him Grease." He gave me a small smile, but he still had that stark look in his eyes, like . . . well, like I was sure my eyes had.

He looked like someone he'd loved just died.

"Take a nap with me?" he asked wearily, dropping his forehead against mine. "I'm fuckin' exhausted."

"Sure," I mumbled back, reaching to wrap my arm up and over his head like I could cocoon him in with me.

He fall asleep with his breath brushing my face, but I didn't move. Not for a long time.

I made a decision, and I stuck with it, just like Asa had asked me to.

Two weeks later, after the lockdown had ended and the families had been warned to keep their guards up, we buried my dad in a cemetery near his old house.

Without the ability to work, I had nothing to occupy my mind. I got bitchy, and weepy, and I lost myself in grief and frustration. Then it was Will's turn to stick with it, and he did.

I think Asa was right about all of it. Maybe the commitment was the key. Not the marriage certificate that we eventually got, or the house near his parents that we bought together, or the adoption papers that Will signed when Rebel was six. It was the not giving up that mattered.

I nagged Will about the money he spent, and bitched when he rode his murdercycle without a helmet. In the years after my dad was murdered, while the club was fighting a battle that I hoped to God I'd never see, I became resentful of the time he spent away from us and the fear that seemed like my constant companion, and I begged him to stop, even though I knew he was trying to make us safe. I got into an argument with Trix and refused to go to the clubhouse for two months and once screamed at him in front of the entire club because some skank at a party had sat on his lap for two seconds before he pushed her off.

Will was no angel, either. The life I'd envisioned with him when we'd started dating didn't exist. The man I'd seen through rose-colored glasses had been a figment of my imagination. He left me for days at a time to do business for the club. He occasionally got too drunk to drive home, and he'd pass out in his room at the club while I lay in our bed alone, wishing he were with me. He got arrested and couldn't attend Rebel's preschool graduation. He got into pissy moods and barely spoke to me for days, and sometimes, I looked at him, and just wanted to scream for no reason at all.

But, beyond all the bullshit and the hurt feelings and the fear and the frustration, I loved him so much that I ached with it, and Will proved every day that it was the same for him.

So, I didn't give up and he didn't either.

We argued and nagged and gave each other the silent treatment, but neither of us ever walked away again.

Acknowledgements

These acknowledgements usually end up being a chapter long. I can't seem to help myself. So I'm going to do this a bit different this time. Quicker. Hopefully.

Readers and bloggers: You're the reason I get to do what I do. I won't ever forget that. Thank you.

Mom and Dad: You rock. Thanks for all your help!

Girlies: I love you. Keep dreaming big. Also, good job on your report cards!

Sister: Thanks for listening to my venting and cheering me on.

Nikki: We did it again. You're the wind beneath my wings and the snarky comments on my manuscript.

Donna: I'll tell you thank you a million more times before I'm done.

Lola: You knocked it out of the park again. I wasn't surprised.

Franggy: Thank you for my photo of Molly. You're incredibly talented and I can't wait to see what you do next.

Ellie: Hi. Let's not make this weird.

Toni: Oh, hey. How you doin'? Peas and Carrots.

Rebecca, Tracy and Tiffany: Thanks for beta reading in a hurry! I owe you one.

Amber: Thank you for pointing out the next character I had to write. I hope I did Rebel justice. I would have never found the courage to publish this story without your input and it means the world to me.

www.ingramcontent.com/pod-product-compliance
Ingram Content Group UK Ltd.
Pitfield, Milton Keynes, MK11 3LW, UK
UKHW031430161224
3699UKWH00056B/2184